NAKED GAMES

Books by Anne Rainey

Naked Games

Pleasure Bound

So Sensitive

Body Rush

"Cherry on Top" in *Some Like It Rough*

NAKED
GAMES

ANNE RAINEY

APHRODISIA

KENSINGTON PUBLISHING CORP.
www.kensingtonbooks.com

KENSINGTON BOOKS are published by

Kensington Publishing Corp.
119 West 40th Street
New York, NY 10018

All Kensington titles, imprints, and distributed lines are available at special quantity discounts for bulk purchases for sales promotion, premiums, fund-raising, and educational or institutional use.

Special book excerpts or customized printings can also be created to fit specific needs. For details, write or phone the office of the Kensington Special Sales Manager: Kensington Publishing Corp., 119 West 40th Street, New York, NY 10018. Attn. Special Sales Department. Phone: 1-800-221-2647.

Aphrodisia and the A logo Reg. U.S. Pat. & TM Off.

ISBN-13: 978-0-7582-6903-4
ISBN-10: 0-7582-6903-X

First Kensington Trade Paperback Printing: August 2012
10 9 8 7 6 5 4 3 2 1

Printed in the United States of America

NAKED
GAMES

Prologue

Three years earlier . . .

Dean walked into the small apartment he shared with Linda, his girlfriend for the past year and a half, with a sense of excitement turning his stomach into knots. His hands shook a little when he thought of what he was about to do. As he looked down at the box in the palm of his right hand, he grinned. This was it. He was about to ask the woman of his heart to marry him. They'd dated long enough, damn it; it was time to put a ring on the woman's finger. To show everyone that she was taken. That she was loved. He wanted to hear her call him husband. Hell, he even wanted her to have his children. How crazy was that?

Sounds coming from the bedroom caught Dean's attention, and he frowned. He looked at the clock on the wall next to the bookcase. At three o'clock in the afternoon, Linda was supposed to be at work still. The waitressing job sucked and he wanted her to quit, but she'd refused, saying they needed the money. His construction business wasn't doing too badly though. Soon, she'd be able to ditch the crappy job and be a stay-at-home mom, the way she'd always talked about.

When another sound caught his attention, Dean tucked the ring in his coat pocket and headed down the short hallway. She was home and in bed; it wasn't the way he'd wanted to propose, but he could make it work. The closer he got to the closed bedroom door the more the hairs on the back of his neck stood up. Laughter spilled out from the small space between the door and the threshold. Not all of it feminine laughter, he realized. Dean's gut clenched as he took hold of the handle and turned. The sight on the bed had him frozen in place. Linda, the woman he was seconds away from asking to marry him, had her mouth wrapped another man's cock. Dean couldn't speak, could barely breathe. He shifted on his feet, and the movement was all it took to get the attention of the pair of lovers. Legs and arms flailed about as Linda and her nooner attempted to move apart and cover themselves. As Linda tried and tried to get the blanket wrapped around her nude body, Dean looked over at the blond-haired man sitting on the side of the bed—the same bed Dean had slept in not too many hours earlier—and frowned as he recognized him as the cook at the restaurant Linda worked at. Ah, so that's why she didn't want to quit. Christ, he'd been such a fool. A stupid, lovesick chump.

"Apparently you don't just serve greasy burgers and bad coffee at that shitty restaurant, huh, babe?"

Jimmy stood, his face bleached of color. "Uh, I—"

Dean held up a hand. "Save it. Just take your trash and go."

Linda's startled cry caught his attention. He pointed to her. "You might want to wipe the come off your chin before you leave," Dean bit out. "Could prove embarrassing."

"This was a mistake," Linda said as her eyes filled with tears. "A one-time thing, I swear, babe. I've never cheated on you before. Never!"

The look of disbelief that Jimmy shot her way said it all. One-time thing, my ass. Dean knew he'd been a blind fool, but his eyes were wide open now. He strode across the room and took hold of her chin in a firm grip. "Do us both a favor and don't speak. Just get the fuck out of my sight."

Dean released her and went to the door. "You have two hours to get your shit and go. You really don't want to be here when I return, trust me."

She shouted his name as he left. Dean could hear her all the way out the front door. When he reached the elevator and pushed the DOWN button his hand was as steady as a rock. Every bit of emotion seemed to have dried up. He felt completely numb clear to his bones. He'd loved her. She'd been sweet and loving. They'd been perfect for each other, everyone had said. Now the only thing Dean could see was her mouth giving another man a blow job. It would be forever branded into his brain.

As the elevator doors opened, Dean stepped forward. Once he was sure he was alone, he reached into his coat pocket and found the box with the pretty diamond ring nestled safely inside. "Never again," he said as he stared at it. Yeah, he'd been a fool, but he was a quick learner. Hell, he couldn't even claim it was the first time a woman had burned him. It'd happened twice before. The only difference this time around was the fact that Dean had been ready to marry Linda. To hell with it. It'd be a cold day before he let a woman get so close again.

When the elevator stopped and the doors slid open, Dean saw an older woman waiting to enter. They traded places, but before the doors could close again, he handed her the box. At the confused look she sent him, he explained, "As it turns out, I don't need it."

She opened the box and gasped. "It's a diamond ring!"

"Yep. Keep it. Sell it. Makes no difference."

The doors slid shut on her next words. Dean pulled out his cell phone and dialed his brother. Wade answered on the first ring. "What's up, bro?"

"Linda and I . . . broke up." He couldn't bring himself to

say how that came about. Seeing it was enough. He sure as shit didn't want to talk about it.

"Damn, that sucks. I thought for sure you two were going to be heading down the aisle soon."

"Yeah," he choked out. "Got any beer?"

"Better, I have whiskey."

"My hero. See you in a few."

"Hey, you okay?"

Dean rolled his eyes. "I'm not going to wrap myself around a tree, if that's what you mean."

"That's not quite what I meant."

"I know," he said, realizing Wade was worried about him. Wade was the oldest and as such he always worried. "Look, man, I'll be fine. This is nothing a good drunken stupor can't fix."

"Fine, but drive careful," Wade warned.

"Seat belt and all, *Dad,*" he tossed back.

They hung up and Dean was once again alone with his thoughts as he headed out of the apartment building to his car. The image of Linda, naked and loving another man, sprang right back into his mind.

He wondered how many years it would take before he stopped seeing it.

1

Present day . . .

Catherine sat in stunned silence for several seconds, absorbing all her mother's doctor had just revealed. He'd called early in the morning and asked if he could come over for a visit. He'd said he had something private to discuss with her. Something to do with her parents, he'd explained. Since her parents had died in a horrible car accident only two months before, Catherine couldn't guess what the doctor could possibly want to talk about. Curiosity had won out in the end and she'd found herself asking him over for coffee.

Doctor Cabel had been more than her mother's doctor, of course. He was their family physician as well as a dear friend to her parents for as long as Catherine could remember. The kind, older man with gentle brown eyes had given her her first shots. Still, listening to his rushed revelation, Catherine was beginning to think she'd fallen down the rabbit hole. Surely this was nothing more than a strange dream. Had to be. If that were the case, though, she wished like hell she'd wake up.

"Are you serious?" she asked, emotion causing her voice to shake. "This has to be a bad joke. It's simply not possible."

"I'm sorry, Catherine," Doctor Cabel said, sympathy in his gaze as he looked at her from across the perfectly polished cherrywood coffee table. "I'm very serious. You were adopted."

"How? Why?" She shook her head in an attempt to clear away the fog. It seemed to be descending at a rapid rate with each word the doctor uttered. "How could my mother not tell me?" She thought of her father, the way he used to give her whisker kisses, and her stomach knotted. "How could *they* not tell me?"

The doctor sat back in the chair and pushed his glasses up higher on his nose. He scrunched up his brows as if he was as confused as she. "I don't know the answer to that. Although, I truly wish I did. All I can tell you is that your mother is not your biological mother, Catherine."

Catherine had been devastated when she'd received the news that she'd lost both her beloved parents in one cruel twist of fate. They were both fifty-five years old, too young to be taken away from her. A drunk driver, the police had said. Catherine had worked herself to the bone to keep from being swallowed up by the grief she'd felt from losing them so unexpectedly. And now this.

"Are you telling me that Mama told you I was adopted but not me?" The betrayal had tears burning her eyes. "Why?"

The doctor shook his head. "No, no." He slumped in despair. All at once Catherine felt sorry for the man. He was only the messenger, after all. "I'm making a mess of this, and I'm sorry. The thing is, Jean never came out and admitted the truth to me. But, Catherine, I was your mother's physician and I examined her on several occasions. What I know for certain is that she never gave birth to a child. Any child."

Catherine wanted to lash out at someone, and who better than the man who'd unwittingly helped keep her mother's secret? Maybe it hadn't been his secret to reveal, but he'd known all these years and he'd never said a word. "Fine. She didn't actually confide in you, but you knew the truth, Doctor Cabel. Why didn't you ever ask my parents about me?" She threw her hands in the air. "I mean, didn't you think I had a right to know the truth?"

Her harsh words caused the doctor's cheeks to turn scarlet. "I didn't know all the facts. At first, I wasn't even sure she was keeping you in the dark. In fact, I could've easily brought it up to you on one of the many occasions you visited my office. Without even realizing it, I could've exposed your parents so easily." He shook his head and frowned. "They got lucky there."

Catherine's anger took on momentum at the doctor's statement. "Lucky? She kept this from me my entire life and you call that lucky?"

He held up a hand as if to stop the runaway train of her fury from running him over. "That's not what I meant. Look, I'm sorry to be the one to tell you this. All I can think is that she hadn't figured out the right way to tell you."

Catherine shot to her feet and strode toward the fireplace. She stared at the family portrait that hung above it, feeling the stab of betrayal clear through to her heart. Her smiling mama with the pretty green eyes and fair complexion seemed to mock her. Her father, so strong and trustworthy, stood behind them, every inch the proud husband and father. Catherine let out a breath she hadn't even been aware she was holding.

"I could think of any number of ways," Catherine gritted out as she clenched her eyes tight, as if by doing so she could lock out the pain. "Like, 'Hey, you're adopted, pass the peas.' "

Catherine turned and saw the misery on the doctor's face. She really did feel bad for him. It wasn't his fault her mother had lied, Catherine reminded herself. As she stared at him, however, something else struck her. "You're only telling me now because the doctor–patient confidentiality clause ended with her death, aren't you?"

He stood and crossed the room. As he placed a hand on her shoulder, Catherine felt a little better. "That's part of it, yes," he said gently. "But I also felt you should know the truth. I'm not just your doctor, Catherine." He awkwardly patted her. "I wish I could've said something sooner, but I simply couldn't. Please understand, dear, if I could've spared you this pain, I would've."

Catherine tried to smile, but it hurt too damn much so she gave up the effort. "The only person, or persons rather, to blame are gone." She waved a hand through the air. "They're buried, along with all the answers to the many questions running through my head."

The doctor dropped his hands in his trouser pockets and said, "Maybe there is something among your mother's belongings," he offered. "Have you gone through everything already?"

Catherine thought of her parents' bedroom and hope began to take seed. "No, actually. There is still quite a bit I have yet to deal with. I was going to spend today going through some of the stuff in the basement, but maybe I'll tackle their bedroom instead." She'd always thought of that room as their private domain. Catherine had been putting off going in there to sort through their things. Unfortunately, she no longer had the luxury of time. She wanted answers, because clearly there was a lot about herself she didn't know. For starters, Catherine wanted to know who she was and where she'd come from.

He nodded and smiled. "There you go. Maybe you'll find something that will help you understand why your mother chose to wait the way she did."

Catherine shrugged. "Wait? You talk as if she intended to tell me someday when that might not be the case at all."

"You and I both know that your mother wasn't a cruel woman," he gently chastised. "She loved you very much. I know she intended to tell you. I'm sure of it."

"Maybe, but it won't change the fact that she lied to me all these years. Nothing will fix that, Doctor."

"True, but just try and keep in mind that she didn't set out to hurt you."

Catherine was fresh out of things to say. Her heart felt bruised and her mind was in chaos. "Thanks for coming," she said, wrapping her arms around the man, bolstered when she felt him hug her in return. When they parted, Catherine pasted a smile on her face. "I know this had to be difficult. I'm sorry my parents put you in such a position."

"I cared for Jean and Russ. They were good people. My friends. I only hope you find something among their things that might shed some light on all this." He started out of the room, but when he reached the entryway, he turned to her and said, "Remember that I'm your friend as well. Call me if you want to talk. Anytime, Catherine."

"Thank you, I will."

It wasn't until the doctor left that Catherine lost her battle with the tears. She simply dropped into the nearest chair and cried herself dry. It was nearing dinnertime before Catherine was able to pull herself together enough to pick up the phone. Mary, Catherine thought, she would know what to do. She always did.

When her friend's cheery voice came over the line, Catherine nearly lost it all over again. "Mary, it's Cat," she explained, using the nickname her friend had given her when they'd first met back in high school. "Are you busy tonight?"

Mary laughed. "Jesus, no. I'm sitting her matching up socks and watching reruns of *Friends*. Please tell me you changed your mind about pizza and beer tonight."

Mary had called the night before and offered to come over and hang out. She'd done a lot of that since the news of Catherine's parents. No doubt about it, Catherine would've been lost without Mary these last two months. "I, uh, I'm not sure where to begin."

"What's wrong, sweetie?" Mary asked, suddenly sounding more alert.

Unwilling to get into it all over the phone, Catherine simply said. "Pizza and beer. We're going to need a lot of both."

"I've got it covered," Mary said. "I'll be there in a jiff. Just hang tight."

"Thanks," Catherine said. Her voice shook with emotion, but she was beyond caring.

After hanging up, Catherine sat back and waited. Mary would come and they would tackle this together, the way they'd done so many things over the years. "I'm not alone," Catherine reminded herself. But when she looked up at the family portrait she felt very much alone.

Or was she?

If she was adopted, then who were her biological mother and father? And did she have siblings? Questions swirled around inside Catherine's head until she thought she might be sick. Lies had a way of finding their way into the light, her mama had once said. Catherine shook her head when she thought of her mother imparting that bit of wisdom. She glanced up once more at the portrait of her grinning parents. "If only you practiced what you preached," Catherine bit out.

2

"Wow," Mary said. "Just . . . wow."

Despite the craziness of the situation, Catherine found herself smiling. "Yeah. I was pretty speechless too."

Mary frowned down at the half-empty bottle of beer in her hand. "This calls for something stronger than a Bud Light." Her blue gaze landed on Catherine. "Do you have any red wine handy?"

Catherine curled her legs underneath her as she polished off the last slice of pepperoni pizza. "There are a few bottles on the wine rack next to the microwave." She shrugged. "I don't want any, but help yourself."

Mary stood and brushed at her jeans. "Be right back."

Catherine watched her friend leave the room and shook her head. Once more she wondered how she could possibly survive without the tall, dark-haired whirlwind. From the time they'd met, Mary and Catherine had stood by each other. Mary had been a newbie to Catherine's high school, a transplant from a school up north. She'd been trying to find the physics classroom and Catherine had helped her out. They'd been friends

since. Her mother had once described them as twin opposites—
as close as sisters but as different as night and day.

When Mary came back into the room she held two full wine-
glasses. Catherine rolled her eyes as she took one. "I thought I
said none for me?"

"After a day like today? You need it, believe me." Mary
took a hearty swallow of her own wine, then said, "Okay, let's
take this party upstairs. We've put it off long enough."

Catherine stood. "I'm afraid of what I'll find." She winced
and admitted, "Or not find."

Mary waved a hand in the air. "Catherine, your parents were
awesome people. I don't know what the hell they were thinking by keeping this from you, but they did love you." In a
softer voice she asked, "You do know that, right?"

Catherine nodded. "I know, it's just difficult not being able
to face them and ask that one all-important question."

"Why didn't they tell you," Mary said, knowing exactly
what was on her mind.

"Yeah." Catherine shrugged. "I can deal with being adopted.
I can even deal with them wanting to wait for the right moment
to tell me. But this feels like a secret. Like they didn't want *anyone* knowing, not just me." Unable to look at her friend,
Catherine instead stared at the ruby liquid in her glass as she
asked, "Were they ashamed?"

"Of you?" Mary snorted. "Never in a million years. Your
parents were so stinking proud of everything you did. Even
when you screwed up they usually found a way to make it out
to be a good thing." Mary patted her on the back and said,
"No, this isn't about shame. And we won't know anything by
standing in the middle of the living room chatting about it either. So, what's our plan? I know you, you have a plan."

Catherine laughed and glanced up at the ceiling and knew
she was going to have to go up the stairs and dig through her
parents' belongings. "No big plan, not really. I want to go

through my parents' bedroom. There might be something there that can help me figure this mess out."

She nodded. "What about a safety deposit box? Could they have records locked away at the bank maybe?"

Catherine took another sip of her wine before saying, "No. Mama never trusted the bank. She was old school." Her fingers tightened around the stem of the expensive crystal. "Heck, I wouldn't be surprised if we found cash under her mattress."

Mary wagged her eyebrows. "So, it's sort of like a treasure hunt."

"You're incorrigible," Catherine said, swatting her on the forearm.

"I'm adorable and we both know it," Mary replied before taking her by the shoulders and turning her to face the stairway. "Now, scoot. We have secrets to uncover."

The nudge was all it took to get Catherine out of the room and up the stairs. As she reached her parents' closed bedroom door, she looked over her shoulder and stuck her nose in the air. "Who knows, maybe I'll discover I'm royalty or some-thing."

"Or, like, a long-lost Mafia princess," Mary whispered, as if imparting some deep, dark secret. "That'd be cool. I have a few people I'd like to take a contract hit out on. My boss for starters." She cursed. "The little weasel."

Catherine rolled her eyes as she turned the knob and pushed the door open. "I highly doubt I have Mafia blood in me. I can't even kill a spider without feeling queasy."

Mary reached over and flipped the light switch. "But it'd be pretty sweet if you were, right?"

Glancing around the large room with the king-size bed, Catherine felt the now-familiar pangs in her gut. Loss. Grief. It was all there. She could never get used to how empty the room seemed. She spotted her mama's blue robe hanging on the bed-post and had to swallow back the pain. If she picked it up it would smell like her. Gardenias. Her mother's favorite scent. "I'd rather be royalty," she said, trying to keep to the conversation and ignore the sadness welling up inside her.

"Well, let's hope we'll find out sooner rather than later."

Catherine heard the worry in Mary's voice and turned toward her. "You don't think Mama and Daddy kept any records here?"

Mary took one last sip of her wine, then placed the glass on the dresser. "There's only one way to find out. Where do you want me to start?"

Catherine placed her half-empty glass next to Mary's and looked around. When her gaze came to the closet, she pointed to it. "Start there. On the top shelf there's a big white box. Mama warned me away from it once when I asked what was in it. Maybe there's something that might help."

"She warned you not to mess with it and you listened." Mary shook her head. "That sounds just like you."

Catherine laughed. "You would've gone right for it the first chance you got."

Mary laughed. "Damn straight."

"I'll start with the desk," Catherine said. For the next hour they searched the room. Mary had found the big white box, but it turned out to be a dead end. The only thing it contained was some of her father's old nudie magazines. Just when Catherine was about to call it a night, Mary yelled her name.

Catherine crossed the room to where Mary knelt over the bottom drawer in her mother's nightstand. "What'd you find?"

Mary stood and moved back a few feet before pointing to the drawer. "Uh, I think you need to see for yourself."

Catherine's nerves were shot and she'd had way too much wine, but the serious tone had her alert and sober in an instant. She knelt down and peered inside, afraid to get too close. As if the contents would reach out and bite her. Catherine frowned when she spotted a stack of letters addressed to her mother and a slip of folded paper sitting next to it. Catherine picked up the letters and the paper, then glanced at Mary. "It's just sitting out in the open. It can't be anything significant."

"Not out in the open exactly." She dropped down beside her and tugged on the bottom of the drawer. To Catherine's surprise it came loose. "See? A false bottom. I found the letters under it, hidden. Pretty sneaky, really. You wouldn't know it was there unless you were looking for it."

Catherine stared down at the letters and felt her stomach pitch. "My mother had a secret hiding place. How is it possible that I never stumbled across this? I've lived in the house my entire life."

"Well, besides the fact that you'd never snoop through your mama's things, it would've been pretty hard to notice. The only reason I did was because I was looking for it."

She held up the letters and noticed no return address. "I'm afraid to read these," she admitted aloud.

"It's the only way you'll know, hon," Mary said, placing a soothing hand on her back.

"I know."

The slip of paper fell from her hand, and Mary picked it up and handed it to her. "Here."

It was folded in half. With shaking fingers Catherine placed the letters on the floor beside her and began to unfold the paper. She read the faded words and slumped. "It's just my birth certificate. It lists Jean and Russell as my parents. Nothing surprising there."

Mary picked up one of the letters and held it out to her. "Open one of the letters, then."

She frowned. "What if they're from Daddy? Like love letters or something. I don't want to read something so private."

Mary shrugged. "You only have to read enough to find out for sure."

Catherine was stalling and she knew it. She was afraid of

what she might find—or not find. *Time to face the music,* she thought as she dropped the birth certificate into the drawer and took the letter from Mary. As she started to read, her heartbeat sped up. "Oh, my God."

"What?" Mary asked as she tried to read over Catherine's shoulder. "Who is it from?"

"My birth mother." Catherine read the entire letter, then shook her head as if that would help clear away the shock coursing through her. "She talks about being glad that I have such kind people to raise me."

"Damn," Mary said in a low voice.

"Yeah." Catherine picked up another letter. She didn't stop until she'd read them all. After tucking the last one back into the envelope, Catherine sat back and looked over at Mary propped up against the bed, quietly waiting.

"It was a private adoption."

"And?"

"I have a sister. An older sister named Gracie Baron."

"Get out! Seriously?"

"Yep. According to Bridget—that's my mother's name—Gracie lives in Zanesville, Ohio, with her father."

"*Her* father and not your father?"

Catherine frowned. "According to my mother, Gracie's father isn't my father. In fact, she was never sure who my father was, actually."

"Yikes."

Catherine ran a hand through her hair. She was suddenly exhausted. "The letters read like a confession, Mary. It turns out that Bridget was dying from liver disease. Too many years of drinking, she said. But she wanted me to know that I had a sister."

"I wonder what this Gracie person is like," Mary said, staring at the letters. "Liver disease?" she asked, her gaze meeting

Catherine's once more. "Does this mean your birth mother died?"

"I think it does. In the last letter she said she wouldn't be able to continue to correspond." Catherine picked up the envelope and took the old, worn paper back out. The handwriting had gotten progressively worse with each letter. To the point that the last one was nearly impossible to read.

"This is going to be my last letter, I'm afraid. My hope is that when the time comes for you to tell Catherine about her adoption that she'll be able to forgive me for giving her up. She'll see that she was better off with you and Russell. I don't know if her sister could ever forgive me, however. I left her to be raised by her father because I wasn't fit to be a mother. Nevertheless, I'm concerned that was a terrible mistake. And now it's too late to fix it."

"A mistake?" Mary asked. "I wonder why."

"I don't know, but I want to find her, Mary." She dropped the letter in the drawer and felt her heartbeat kick into overdrive. "I want to find my sister. I've lost too many years already, and I don't want to lose another minute."

Mary stood and held out a hand. "We will, I promise. First, you and I need a good night's sleep. We'll start our search in the morning."

Catherine took her friend's outstretched hand and let her pull her to her feet. She swayed a bit but didn't fall over. She figured that was good, at least. "Thank you for being here," she said, emotion clogging her throat. "And for helping me through all this."

"Oh, geez." Mary rolled her eyes and started for the door. "Don't start getting all mushy on me."

Tired and emotionally worn out, Catherine still managed to laugh at her friend's belligerent tone. "I love you too," she called out as she followed Mary out of the room.

"Ditto. Now get to bed before you fall on your face. I really don't want to carry your ass."

Catherine shook her head as she watched Mary head to the guest room, where she'd stayed on hundreds of occasions before. "See you in the morning."

"Morning, yeah." She yawned, then added, "I'm going to want pancakes."

"You got it," Catherine tossed back. After Mary disappeared inside the room, Catherine opened the door to her bedroom and flipped on the light. That's when an important nugget of truth hit her. She had a sister. "I'm not alone," she whispered to herself. Soon, she would be meeting Gracie in person, Catherine vowed. She wouldn't just be reading about her in an old letter. For the first time in months, Catherine smiled.

3

It'd been six weeks since she'd found the letters in her mother's bedside table. Now, as Catherine stood on the porch of what appeared to be an old abandoned warehouse, fear skated up and down her spine. She checked the address once more to make sure she had the right place. The numbers definitely matched. As she reached up to knock on the door, her phone buzzed. She grabbed it out of her purse and looked at the name of the caller. She grinned and hit ANSWER.

"I haven't met her yet," Catherine quickly said, trying to keep her voice down. "Stop calling."

She heard Mary curse. "What's taking so long, woman? The waiting is killing me."

If Catherine wasn't so nervous she would've laughed at Mary's anxious tone. "I'm standing on Gracie's porch now." She looked at a few cracked bricks above the door frame and said, "At least I think it's her porch. Anyway, I'll call you with all the details later. I promise."

Mary heaved a deep sigh. "Fine. But don't leave me hanging."

Catherine chuckled. "I wouldn't dream of it."

They said their good-byes, and Catherine had barely managed to get her phone put away when the door suddenly swung open. For the first time in her life she was face-to-face with her sister. God, the pictures in the e-mails didn't lie. They really could be twins. They had the same red hair, the only difference being Gracie's was fine and wavy. Catherine's hair had always been pin straight and thick. Same green eyes too. Their build was even similar. Curvy. Gracie was shorter by an inch or so though. Still, it was strange. Like looking at a different version of herself.

After Catherine had found out about Gracie in the letters, it'd only been a matter of searching the Internet. She'd located Gracie on a social networking site. It'd all been a whirlwind since.

"Catherine," Gracie said in a quiet voice. "You're finally here."

Despite telling herself not to, Catherine found herself crying. "Finally," she said, her voice shaking.

Without another word, Gracie stepped onto the porch and wrapped her in a tight embrace. For several seconds, Catherine just stood there, too stunned to move and both of them crying. She swiftly snapped out of it and returned the hug for all she was worth. After several seconds, they both stood back. Catherine was the first to speak. "I'm so glad I came."

"Oh, me too." Gracie winced and slapped a hand against her forehead. "I'm making you stand out in the cold. Geez, I'm so sorry. Please, come in."

"Thank you." As Catherine stepped inside the warehouse her gaze quickly scanned her surroundings. She stopped dead at how gorgeous the place was and said as much. "Your home is beautiful."

"A little surprising considering the outside, huh?"

Catherine laughed and felt heat rush to her cheeks. "A little."

Gracie winked. "I had the same reaction my first visit here. Wade owns the place, but his sister is the one who did all the interior design. She's a genius."

"No kidding," Catherine mumbled as she looked around the large, open room. It was warm and inviting. Some of her jitters disappeared. High ceilings and white oak hardwood floors flattered the Asian-style, burgundy L-shaped couch and matching round chairs. She liked the steel appliances in the kitchen. She noticed an interesting wrought iron spiral staircase that led to a second floor. The modern design was very different from her parents' big Victorian home in Georgia.

"Speaking of Wade, there are a few people that want to meet you. I hope you don't mind."

Catherine smiled. "Is your fiancé still trying to figure out if I'm on the up-and-up?" She knew Wade, the man who only a few weeks ago had asked for Gracie's hand in marriage, was a private investigator, and he'd been a little suspicious of some woman coming out of nowhere and claiming to be Gracie's long-lost sister. But she'd thought the background check he'd run on her had been sufficient proof. Maybe it hadn't been.

Gracie waved a hand in the air. "No, no, nothing like that. But everyone *is* curious about you, and they've been dying to meet you."

Catherine relaxed at once. "I understand completely. Besides, I'm anxious to meet them too."

Gracie nodded. "The excitement is natural, but I still didn't want to bomb you with the entire bunch at once. I wanted to have you all to myself when we finally met in person. So we've decided to sort of filter them in a little at a time."

Catherine put her purse on a chair next to a long, barlike countertop before replying, "I wanted to meet you alone too. A friend of mine wanted to come with me on this trip, but I asked her to stay home. I guess I didn't want to share this first moment with anyone else."

"Your friend Mary? The one you told me about in your e-mails?"

Catherine crossed her arms over her chest and nodded. "The one and only."

"She could've come. I would love to meet her."

"You will soon enough." She chuckled. "She's a handful."

"Can anyone crash this party or is it by invitation only?"

They both turned at the deep baritone. Right off Catherine recognized Wade from the pictures Gracie had sent, but the real-life version was quite a sight. The man was big, a little dangerous looking, and gorgeous as all get-out with his messy dark hair and ornery grin.

Catherine realized she was simply standing there staring and moved to apologize. "Sorry, I didn't mean to go mute, there."

Wade shrugged and stepped forward. "Seeing you in person sort of threw me for a loop for a second as well. You and Gracie look so much alike it's downright eerie. That Southern accent tends to give you away though."

Catherine smiled, and looked over at Gracie and nodded. "I know what you mean. I feel like I'm looking into a mirror."

Wade held out his hand and said, "Welcome to the family, Catherine."

Catherine happily took it and thanked him, her heart soaring. She'd made the right decision in coming here. She knew that now.

Wade released her, then wrapped a strong arm around Gracie's middle before pulling her in close. "Yes, welcome, Catherine," Gracie added.

"Thanks, and uh, sorry for staring at your fiancé." She winced. "Great first impression, there."

"Aw, don't worry about it." She chuckled. "He has that effect on a woman. Wait until you meet Jonas and Dean."

"Why wait?" Another voice chimed in.

Wade and Gracie moved to the side to let whoever owned

the voice into the room. She heard Wade mumble something to the big, dangerous man, but she couldn't make out what. Catherine froze in place as he approached her. He had the same dark hair as Wade. She couldn't help noticing he appeared to be a little more muscular than Wade though. The black T-shirt seemed to be straining to contain him. And he looked almost angry. His dark brown eyes stared at her as if he wanted her gone. Like yesterday.

"Catherine, I'd like you to meet Dean, Wade's younger brother and Deanna's twin."

This was the sweet-natured brother that Gracie had talked about? Really? The man in front of her didn't seem to fit the description at all.

"It's nice to meet you, Catherine," Dean said as he stepped forward and extended his hand.

She hesitated a second, and she watched his gaze narrow. Feeling challenged for some odd reason, Catherine stiffened her spine and plastered on a smile. Taking his hand in her own, she gave it a firm shake before replying, "It's nice to meet you too. Gracie has told me a lot about you."

He didn't release her right away, and Catherine couldn't understand why her body began to riot out of control. She took the initiative and tugged. A slow, sexy smile changed his entire demeanor. For an instant Catherine couldn't look away. It wasn't until he let go of her that she was able to pull her attention back to Gracie and Wade.

She was stunned to realize Gracie had said something. Unfortunately, the only thing Catherine had heard was the sound of her own heart galloping. "I'm sorry?" She glanced over at Dean and saw the knowing smirk on his face. She itched to smack it off.

"I was saying that Jonas and Deanna will be along shortly. For now, I thought I could put on a pot of coffee and we could talk?"

"Sounds wonderful. The flight seemed extra long. Maybe that's because I haven't had a decent cup of coffee since leaving Georgia."

Gracie went behind the counter and started rinsing the carafe. "I wish you would've let Wade and me pick you up at the airport. We really didn't mind."

"I know, but it's fine. Plus, I managed to rent a very pretty red coupe. I love the little thing already." She didn't say it, but she'd needed the time alone to shore up her nerve. As sweet as Gracie had been in the many phone calls and in the e-mails they'd shared, Catherine had still worried that she'd change her mind about wanting to meet her.

As if sensing the train of Catherine's thoughts, Gracie turned and said, "Well, just so you know, I'm really glad you came. I'm glad you got in contact with me. And I'm really glad that I have a sister."

"Me too," she said, her eyes stinging a little. Sister, wow. There it was again. She'd never get used to it. Then she remembered the letters tucked into her purse. "Oh! I nearly forgot about the letters."

Gracie held up a hand. "No rush. We can get to them later. We have plenty of time."

"Yeah, we'll get to those later," Dean added. When she looked over at him, she saw the truth written all over his face. He didn't believe her. Didn't trust her. For some odd reason the knowledge hurt.

4

Dean didn't want to be attracted to Catherine, but damn if that wasn't exactly what was going on. Her Southern accent was sexy as hell, but she had a slightly snooty attitude, as if he didn't deserve to breathe the same air as her. The thought pissed him off. If anyone should be grateful, it should be her. He didn't trust her. Didn't believe for a second that she was only here to visit her long-lost sister. There was more to it, and he intended to find out what it was.

The instant he'd seen her picture on Gracie's computer he'd been intrigued by her. She had an innocent look to her. As if she'd been sheltered from life's dirtier side. But Dean knew that looks could be deceiving. He'd expressed his concern to Wade, but his brother wouldn't listen to reason. As far as he was concerned, Catherine was who she claimed to be, Gracie's sister and nothing more. Jonas had even done a search on her. Nothing had come back save for an article about Catherine's prize-winning roses. She had no criminal record. She lived with her parents in Atlanta, Georgia, until her parents had died in a car accident. That's when she'd found the letters about her biological mother. It was only then that she'd learned she had a sister living in Ohio. All of it sounded great. But Dean still felt there was something Catherine wasn't telling. He knew too well that a woman could put on a facade to get what she wanted. The question was, what did Catherine want?

When Catherine brought up the subject of her adoption, Dean spoke up. "Speaking of your parents, you told Gracie that your parents never revealed to you that you were adopted, is that right?"

She swallowed several times before answering. "Yes. I think Mama was going to tell me, but she never found the right time. I'm still trying to deal with that."

"You learned the news through a friend?" he prompted her. Dean could see it was a sore spot for Catherine, but there were too many questions and not enough answers.

She nodded. "Our family doctor. He was a friend of my parents for years."

"A very good friend if your parents trusted him with such a big secret."

"No, like me, he was never told the truth. He was Mama's doctor, so he knew she'd never given birth to a child. He'd examined her, you see."

Dean frowned. "And that sort of thing can't be misjudged? He's absolutely sure she never gave birth?"

"Dean, enough with the questions," Wade growled.

Catherine held up a hand. "No, please, it's fine. Keeping these things in the dark is what caused all this to begin with. Gracie and I missed out on a lifetime of memories because of this secret. It's high time it's brought to the light."

"But we're going to make up for that," Gracie said, adding her weight to Team Catherine.

She smiled at Gracie. "Exactly." Catherine turned her attention back to him, the smile disappearing in an instant, and said,

"Even if Doctor Cabel had made a mistake, the letters from Gracie and my biological mother are proof, don't you think?"

"And why didn't Gracie's father know about you?"

Gracie glared at Dean. "I told you about that, Dean. Catherine explained that the letters indicate we have different fathers. It's not so unusual for a woman to have children with two different men."

"Of course not, but—"

"No buts, Dean," Wade said, his voice brooking no argument. "Enough with the interrogation. There will be plenty of time to go over all the facts later. For now, let Gracie and Catherine have some time to visit."

Dean looked over at Gracie and saw the worry on her face. He felt like an ass. "Sorry, Gracie. Sometimes my mouth gets ahead of my brain."

Gracie went to him and pulled him in for a hug. "I know you're concerned," she whispered for his ears alone, "but it's going to be fine. You'll see."

He nodded and patted her on the back. "Of course it will be."

As she pulled away he was pleased to see a smile on her face. She was going to be his sister when Wade married her. He wanted to see her happy, always. In the meantime, he intended to see that Catherine didn't do anything to dampen that happiness.

"Anyone want a refill on the coffee?" Gracie asked.

"Did someone mention coffee?" a female voice asked from the doorway. Dean turned to see his sister, Deanna, and Jonas striding in. Dean watched as Jonas helped Deanna off with her coat. Christ, it was still weird to see the two of them together. Jonas had been friends with Wade for years, ever since their military days, but he'd only recently gotten together with Deanna. Jonas seemed to make her happy though, and as long as that never changed Dean was fine with it.

"Damn, it's cold out," Jonas grumbled. "Spring is definitely in hiding."

Wade turned to Catherine and said, "In early April, Ohio can be pretty cold still. It warms up, though, by the middle of the month."

"Don't worry, I came prepared." She plucked at her top and said, "I brought along lots of sweaters."

"Two cups of coffee coming right up, guys," Gracie said, "but first I'd like you both to meet Catherine," Gracie said, her voice all but brimming with happiness.

Catherine got out of the chair and moved forward to accept a handshake from Jonas and a hug from Deanna. Dean's gaze unerringly went to Catherine's ass. She wore a pair of skintight jeans and a loose, fuzzy black sweater. The high-heeled boots didn't escape his notice either. She was all sexy hills and valleys. Dean had the overpowering need to reach out and grab her, to pull her against him and feel how well she fit. He tamped down on it and glanced over to see Wade watching him and frowning. Shit.

"So, who here is hungry?" Gracie said as she clapped her hands together in front of her. Jonas said he could eat a horse, and Deanna and Catherine both mentioned that they could eat a few bites. When Wade offered to cook, everyone sent up their agreements. Wade was a damn good cook.

Dean didn't speak, because all his concentration was focused on his baffling reaction to Catherine. She turned to him and her eyebrows rose. "Aren't you hungry?"

He thought of just how easily he could devour *her* and replied, "Famished."

"You didn't say anything."

He let a grin slip across his face. "I was distracted."

Her cheeks heated as if she could read his dirty thoughts as clear as day. "Oh," she murmured.

Wade slapped a hand on the counter, effectively pulling Dean's attention away from Catherine's alluring green eyes. "How about chicken Parmesan."

Dean was about to agree, but he remembered they were still missing a member of their little clan. "Shouldn't we wait for Mom?"

"She's on her way," Deanna offered. "She called and said she was running late from work."

Catherine moved back to her seat and wrapped her hands around her mug, then tapped out a little rhythm on the side. Dean had noticed her doing it before. There was something about the gesture that captured and held his attention. "I can't wait to meet her," Catherine said. "I've heard so much about her from Gracie."

"Are you sure it's not too much your first day here? I mean, everyone would've been content to wait a day or so. To give you time to adjust."

"Gracie's right," Jonas said with a grin. "We can be a lot to take in all at once. We're better in small doses."

Catherine laughed, and Dean's heart sped up at the sweet sound. "It's fine, really. I love it that you all came to meet me. I'm honored."

Deanna went to the coffeemaker and started brewing another pot, while Wade started preparing dinner. Gracie asked Catherine a question about some book that was recently released, and soon the pair was lost in a conversation about some author's hot heroes. Dean looked over at Jonas and caught the man staring at him. He made a motion with his head before heading into the other room. Dean stood and followed.

Once alone, Jonas whispered, "You satisfied that she's who she says she is?"

Dean tucked his hands into the front pockets of his jeans. "I believe she's Catherine Michaels. I believe she was adopted and that Gracie is her sister. They look too much alike not to be related."

Jonas quirked a brow. "Then what's with the looks you keep sending her when you think no one is watching?"

"I just don't trust her," he gritted out. "I won't rest easy until I know for certain that she wants nothing from Gracie except some sisterly bonding time."

"What the hell else could it be?"

"I don't know, but aren't you the least bit suspicious? Hell, she comes out of nowhere and drops this bomb on Gracie and we're all supposed to just embrace her?"

"We ran a check on her, Dean. She came back clean. She doesn't even have an outstanding parking ticket."

Dean ran a hand through his hair. "I know, I know. It's just a feeling. Something about her puts me on edge."

Jonas rubbed his jaw. "Yeah, I noticed. However, maybe this has nothing to do with her being some sort of con artist."

Dean stiffened and stepped closer to Jonas. "What do you mean?"

"Hell, man, you're attracted to her. You've been watching her like a hawk that just spotted a field mouse."

Christ, he'd been that transparent? "Look, I won't deny she can fill out a pair of jeans. So what's your point?"

Jonas shook his head. "Whatever. All I'm saying is that you need to chill." He pointed a finger in the direction of the kitchen. "Wade's about half a step from kicking your ass. This reunion is important to Gracie. She's been looking forward to it since she first spoke to Catherine."

"You're right." Dean sighed. "Damn it."

Jonas grinned, which made Dean want to punch him. "I usually am, buddy."

Dean shoved at his shoulder. "You're also a pain in the ass."

Jonas laughed as he headed back into the kitchen. When Dean followed, he purposely kept his gaze away from the delectable Catherine Michaels. She was going to be visiting all week. Surely he could keep himself in check that long. How hard could it possibly be?

5

Catherine had been curious about Dean from the moment she'd met him the night before. At Gracie and Wade's, he'd seemed to have a chip on his shoulder when it came to her and she wanted to know why. She'd even told Mary all about him when she'd called her to tell her how her first face-to-face with Gracie had gone. Now, as she stood on his front walk in the bright noonday sun, she had to wonder if her curiosity would get her into a world of trouble. Unfortunately, there was no going back now. She was already here. Besides, he wasn't an ogre. Hadn't Gracie said he was a sweet guy? Surely they could come to some sort of understanding.

Catherine wanted things to work with her sister and that meant that Gracie's family needed to accept her. Even though Gracie hadn't married Wade yet, his family had made it clear that Gracie was indeed one of them. Besides, the only other alternative was to ignore the man for the duration of her stay. She couldn't very well do that without coming off as rude. A little voice inside her head said there were other, more intimate reasons for not wishing to ignore the sexy man, but Catherine squashed that little voice into oblivion.

As she strode forward and stepped onto the front porch, Catherine began to have second thoughts all the same. Maybe he would tell her to go fly a kite. Maybe he'd resent her for showing up unannounced. When Catherine had talked to Gracie about Dean's obvious animosity toward her, Gracie had come up with the plan for Catherine to meet him one-on-one. On his own turf. It was Saturday, and Gracie had sworn he'd be home, but what if he was busy? Or worse, busy with a woman?

"Oh, God," she mumbled. For all she knew he'd greet her with a shotgun. "Maybe I'll just call. We can have a nice, safe chat over the phone."

As she turned around to leave, she heard the door creak open behind her. Catherine froze in place. Her feet simply refused to move. Okay, she had two options. Run full steam ahead back to the safety of her rental car, or face the man. When she heard a low, deep voice whisper something from behind, Catherine screwed up her courage and turned around. Dean stood there, leaning against the door frame, an annoying frown marring his handsome expression. He had comfortably worn jeans and a loose, heather gray T-shirt. And he was barefoot. Dang, the man was delish.

"And just where do you think you're going?"

Catherine had the sense that she was facing down her executioner. She held on to her purse tighter, as if for self-defense, and forced herself to look him in the eye. "Hi. Um, I hope I'm not interrupting you."

"Nope." He stepped back and asked, "Do you want to come in?"

"Thank you." Catherine stepped around him and entered the house. It was a pretty ranch style. The interior wasn't as interesting as Wade's, but it was spacious and comfortable. Lots of windows and a cathedral ceiling made the room appear larger than it actually was. The big, brown suede couch facing a large flat-screen television looked inviting. The kitchen was at the back of the house but it was open to the living area, and she could see something cooking on the stove. She looked up at him and asked, "Were you having lunch?"

"Yeah."

That one word and nothing more. Catherine slumped, as it became crystal clear that Dean wasn't going to be in an understanding and compromising mood. "I'm sorry. I shouldn't have come."

When she turned to go, a strong hand wrapped around her upper arm, effectively halting her in her tracks. "I don't mind sharing lunch with you. You like chicken and noodles?"

His tone was as unyielding as the hand holding her in place, but the fact he was willing to be at least a tiny bit civilized gave her hope. Catherine smiled. "I love it. But only if you have plenty, of course."

Dean snorted and released her. "My mom made a ton of it. It'll take me a week to eat it all."

Catherine unzipped her black wool coat and laid it over the back of a brown, leather recliner sitting near the door. "Mama used to make enough food for an army." Her heart squeezed at the memory. "Daddy was always getting on her about making him fat, even though he barely had an inch of fat on him."

"You miss them," he stated as he moved toward the kitchen.

It wasn't a question, simply an observation. Catherine felt compelled to respond anyway. "Every day." She put her purse on the chair and followed him. "At first the grief swamps you. It gets easier as time goes on, but not by much."

He nodded as he spooned up a good portion of the steaming soup into a round, white stoneware bowl. He placed it on the square oak table and waved a hand toward her. "I lost my dad a few years ago. It's tough."

Catherine pulled out a chair and sat, but she was too inter-

ested in the conversation to care about the food. He was opening up a little. She decided to see it as a good sign. "I'm sorry.
How did he die?"

He placed a napkin and spoon on the table next to her bowl.
"Heart attack. None of us saw it coming."

"When it's sudden, comes out of nowhere, it makes you feel
as if you've been cheated. There's no chance to say good-bye."

"Yeah," he growled as he turned back to the stove to ladle
up a helping for himself. As he moved to sit in the seat across
from her and picked up his spoon, his dark chocolate gaze
caught and held hers. "So, did you come here to talk about the
death of a loved one?"

She squinted at him. "You like to get right to the point, don't
you?"

"Usually, yeah. And right now you're stalling."

She watched him eat. He didn't wolf down the food, but ate
each bite slowly, as if he wanted to savor it. "I thought we were
having a nice conversation," she said, distracted by the way his
tongue darted out to lick up a bit of broth. "You know, two
adults enjoying each other's company."

He placed the spoon on the table and swiped a napkin over
his mouth. "Here's the thing," he said. "I don't trust you.
That's not likely to change just because you want it to. So, if
that's the reason you're here, then you might as well leave."

She dropped her spoon, and it hit the bowl with a clang,
bounced off, and landed on the table. "What's your deal?" she
shouted as she lost her grip on her temper. "Everyone else
seems okay with my presence here. Everyone except you.
Why?"

"You came out of nowhere and insinuated yourself into
Gracie's life. Maybe all you want is some bonding time with
her, but I can't help but feel there's more to it than that."

She threw her hands up in the air. "What more could there
possibly be?"

"You tell me, Catherine."

"All I want is to spend time with her. I didn't have the luxury you had growing up."

He sat back and crossed his arms over his chest. "And what luxury might that be?"

"The luxury of growing up with your siblings. You got to see Wade graduate from high school. You watched Deanna go from a little girl to a beautiful, intelligent woman." Her throat closed up for a second and she had to swallow hard before she could say the rest. "Gracie's childhood was stolen from me, Dean. We never got to talk about boys late into the night. She and I never swapped clothes and makeup. Even arguing over whose turn it is to do the dishes was lost to us. All the things sisters do, she and I missed out on that."

He cocked his head to the side, his expression as unreadable as ever. "And that's all there is to it?"

"Oh, my Lord, what is it with you?" she said, her voice rising even more as anger began to take the place of common sense. "Do you think I'm after her money? Because I can tell you that I have plenty of my own. Not only did my parents have a nice-sized insurance policy, but I'm a website designer. I do just fine, trust me."

"See? That's just it, Catherine, I don't trust you. I thought we already established that."

Frustrated and ready to commit cold-blooded murder, Catherine shot out of her chair. "Obviously this was a huge mistake. I never should have come here. I'm sorry I bothered you." But before she could take more than a few steps, Dean was there, holding her still with one arm wrapped around her middle from behind. She stiffened. "Let me go," she bit out from between clenched teeth.

He tsked. "Nope, I'm not through with you yet."

"I don't give a damn." She tried to pry him loose, but he wouldn't budge. "Let me go, or I start screaming."

He chuckled and whispered close to her ear, "You're awfully damn naive, do you know that?"

She grasped onto his hand and tried to remove it, but the man must have been made of steel. "What do you mean by that?"

"You're in a strange man's home, sweetheart. I'm bigger, stronger, and I could do anything I wanted to you right now. Screaming wouldn't do a damn bit of good, because the nearest neighbor is half an acre away."

Yeah, okay, that was a scary thought. "B-but Gracie trusts you."

He pulled his arm away, but before she could run to the front door he was spinning her around to face him. "And that's enough for you? How do you know that I'm not some rapist or murderer?"

His brown eyes weren't filled with menace. In fact, unless she missed her guess, Dean looked concerned. "You wouldn't hurt me," she shot right back. It was a leap of faith, but Catherine had always had good instincts. She had no reason to stop trusting them now.

"If you hurt my family, I'll do that and more," he murmured. "Make no mistake, Catherine, I protect my own."

"Gracie is my family too, Dean." She swatted his chest. "Get that through your thick head."

"She's your biological *half sister*. Practically a stranger to you."

"I know what she is, thank you very much." Her eyes narrowed. "Boy, you don't have any faith in your brother's opinion or his abilities, do you?"

His head shot back as if he'd been slapped. "What's that supposed to mean?"

"Your brother trusts me. He ran a check on me. Don't you think he knows what he's doing? He is a private investigator, after all."

"Of course Wade's good at his job, but his first priority is to see Gracie happy. Finding out about you sent her over the moon. Love is clouding his judgment of you right now."

It hurt to think that Wade was only being kind to her for Gracie's sake. She'd thought his feelings toward her were genuine. "I see," she said in a low voice as she looked down at the hardwood floor. "I didn't realize."

Dean took her chin in his palm and tugged until she was looking into his gaze once more. "Look, Wade does like you. Hell, everyone thinks you're terrific. I'm the only paranoid one in this outfit. Okay?"

She nodded. "The thing you need to remember is that I know how Gracie grew up. We've talked about her dad. His alcoholism and neglect. She had it rough. I don't want to add to Gracie's pain, Dean. I only want to get to know her. To be a part of her life. Is that so bad?"

He was quiet for several seconds, but finally he released her and stated, "I can live with that."

Catherine couldn't believe her own ears. "So you trust me?" She held her breath, afraid of his answer.

He shoved his hands in his front pockets. "Let's just say I'm willing to play nice and leave it at that, shall we?"

It was more than she'd had when she'd come over here, but it still hurt to think he didn't trust her. It shouldn't bother her so much, but instead of letting her disappointment show, she nodded. "Works for me."

"Now, since you didn't get to finish your lunch, how about we skip right to dessert."

The fact that he wasn't shoving her out the door sent a little thrill through her bloodstream. "Dessert?"

He bobbed his eyebrows. "Mom made chocolate cake. You in?"

Catherine forgot everything else at the mention of chocolate. It was her one guilty pleasure in life. "Oh, I'm definitely in."

6

Dean was having a very hard time keeping a straight face. He really didn't want to offend Catherine now that they'd reached some sort of understanding, but it was downright comical the way she dug into her dessert. It was as if she'd never had cake before. Each bite got special attention. He was beginning to get a little jealous of her devotion to the damn thing. He could leave and she wouldn't even notice. "You really like cake, huh?"

The fork stopped midway between the plate and her mouth. She glanced across the table at him. "Am I making a spectacle of myself?"

He winked and pushed his plate away, content to watch her. "Not really."

She gently placed the fork back on the plate. "You're lying. I am making a spectacle of myself." She closed her eyes tight and muttered, "Oh wow, now I'm embarrassed."

"Don't be," he whispered, pissed at himself for saying anything. She'd let down her guard for a minute and he'd blown it. "I appreciate a woman with a healthy appetite. Hell, you should see Deanna go to town."

She rolled her eyes. "Your sister is tall and thin and as pretty as a model. I don't believe for one second that she puts cake away like it's her last day on earth."

Dean placed his elbows on the table and leaned closer. "Didn't you notice when she ate Wade's chicken parmesan last night?"

She frowned. "No, I guess I didn't. I was on sensory overload, I think. Meeting and getting to know everyone, it was a lot to take in. I don't know if you know this, but the Harrison bunch can be pretty overwhelming to a girl who grew up as an only child."

"Finish your cake and I'll tell you a secret about Deanna."

She looked down at her plate and shrugged. "Heck, who am I kidding? I'm not about to let good chocolate go to waste."

As she picked up the fork, Dean said, "Good, because I don't really have any secrets to tell."

As Dean watched her, he became all too aware of how close they were—a few feet of oak was all that separated them. With her preoccupied, Dean let himself look her over. He'd already noticed the way her hair spilled down her back, the softness beckoning him to reach out and smooth his palm down the length. The sweater she wore today was tight. The V-neck hinted at a delicious amount of cleavage, and the dark green shade suited her green eyes. Catherine had the prettiest emerald-green eyes he had ever seen. Almond shaped, like a cat's eyes. No doubt about it, she was beautiful. But could he trust her? The jury was still out on that one.

"You're staring at me," Catherine said as she finished off the last of her cake.

"Men tend to stare at pretty women."

Her head shot up and her eyes went wide. "Did you just pay me a compliment?"

He chuckled. "Don't let it go to your head."

"I wouldn't dream of it." She wiped her mouth on a napkin,

then stood and brought her plate to the sink. Dean sat back, content to stare at the sway of her hips. The jeans she wore today weren't quite as tight as the others had been, but they were no less sexy. He watched her bend over to pick up the fork she'd dropped, and Dean nearly drooled at the view he was provided of her ass. When she placed the utensil in the sink and turned to lean against the counter, Dean was afforded a lovely view from the front.

"So tell me, Dean, do you often serve cake to strange women, or is this a unique experience?"

She was digging into his personal life. Dean was content to play along because he sure as hell intended to dig into hers. "With so many pretty ladies in the world?" he replied. "It'd be downright selfish of me to give all my chocolate cake to just one, don't you think?"

Her lips kicked up at the corners. "I see your point, but is there a special one in the bunch?"

He quirked a brow. Subtlety wasn't Catherine's strong suit. "Are you trying to find out if I'm single, Catherine?"

Her nose shot up in the air. "Well, yeah."

He liked how blunt she could be when the need called for it. "Yes, I'm unattached and plan to stay that way." Linda's deceitful face clouded his vision for a second before he managed to snuff it out. "I'll leave marriage and babies up to my brother and sister." No way would he ever consider going down that road again.

She moved to sit back in her chair, then leaned her arms on the table and asked, "Why? You don't want to be a father someday?"

Red flags went up in Dean's head. Too damn personal. He decided it was time to flip the spotlight back onto her, the way he liked it. "What about you? Do you have a man back in Atlanta?"

She shook her head, and Dean felt all the blood in his body

go south at the knowledge that she wasn't already claimed. "I haven't had much luck in the dating department."

"That's hard to believe. How is it that a guy hasn't caught you and wiggled a ring onto your dainty finger?"

She glanced down and began tapping out a rhythm on the table. "Eh, I've dated," she answered, "but nothing too serious. And lately all my concentration has been on dealing with my parents' estate."

"Why do you do that?"

She stopped and looked up at him. "Huh?"

He pointed to her fingers. "You tap whenever you're thinking about something or nervous."

"Oh, that. It's so automatic sometimes that I don't realize I'm doing it. I'm sorry. My friend Mary says it's annoying."

"Not at all." He shrugged. "I only brought it up because I was curious."

There was a lull in the conversation, and Dean wondered where Catherine's mind had drifted off to. It was a unique experience, sitting across the table with a woman on a Saturday afternoon and chatting. Usually if he wasn't in bed with a woman, then he had little use for them. It was a callous attitude and he knew it, but it was one he'd been content with, until now. Somewhere over the years he'd become a complete ass.

"I took piano lessons when I was little," she explained, yanking him out of his depressing thoughts. "My piano teacher, Mrs. Clover, wasn't a very nice woman. I can still hear her angry voice scolding me for not hitting the proper keys. I didn't take more than a few lessons, but that's when I developed the tapping thing. Like a nervous tick, I suppose."

Dean could easily picture Catherine as a young girl. Cute red pigtails and light brown freckles dotting her nose and cheeks. It pissed him off when he imagined her being reprimanded by some incompetent teacher. "Sounds like your teacher had no business being around kids."

"Mama said pretty much the same thing at the time." She propped her head on her fist and said, "I suppose for the most part Mrs. Clover was a decent-enough teacher, but she always made me so nervous."

"Are you nervous with me, Catherine?"

"No." She hesitated a moment before saying, "Yes."

He didn't want that. He wanted her at ease. "You don't need to be nervous around me, sweetheart."

She snorted. "You don't like me very much. You've admitted as much. That tends to make a person nervous."

He shook his head. "No, I never said I didn't like you. I said I don't trust you. There's a difference."

She rolled her eyes and sat back in her chair. "That doesn't make me feel loads better."

"I'm sorry." Dean wanted to reassure her, to tell her something that would put her mind to rest, but it'd be a lie.

She pointed to him. "Time," she said. "That's what you need. Time to see that I'm not the devil you think I am."

She captivated him. Sitting across his table so determined to prove him wrong. He hoped she did, because then he'd be able to do more than look at her delectable siren's body. The little green-eyed beauty had no idea how tempted he was in that moment. His bed wasn't all that far away. Within seconds he could have her in it. But nothing had changed since the moment he'd met her. She was still a stranger attempting to insinuate herself into his family, and he still didn't know if that was a good thing or not.

Dean decided it was time to change the subject. "So, what do you and Gracie have planned while you're in town?"

She turned her head and looked at the time on the stove before answering. "We're meeting later today to do some shopping. She wants to show me around the area a bit."

"That sounds like fun."

"It'll be my first time to shop with my sister." Her voice shook a little. "It's a little surreal still."

"I can imagine." He paused before adding, "And if I know Gracie I bet she has a whole list of things in store for the two of you. She'll run you ragged if you aren't careful."

She laughed, and Dean's cock stiffened. God, she had a cute laugh. "Yeah, she's already mentioned taking me to some nightclub tonight."

Every muscle in Dean's body went rigid. "A nightclub?"

She nodded. "The Pit, she called it. Gracie says it just opened recently." She cocked a brow at him. "Have you heard of it?"

For some reason the thought of Catherine at a nightclub bothered him. She'd be surrounded by men, and they'd all want to get in her pants. To hell with that. "Yeah, it's a nice place, but are you sure that's such a good idea?" he asked. "Two women alone and all?"

"Oh, Wade is going with us. I think he likes to make sure Gracie's safe. Gracie says he's not quite over the stalker thing yet." She swiped a stray crumb off her sweater. "I can't blame him really. I wouldn't be either."

Dean recalled the ugly incident several months ago. "They both landed in the hospital. It's not something any of us will soon forget."

All the color left her face. "Oh, God. Gracie told me about some of it, but not that part. I suspect she glossed over the uglier details."

"What *did* she say?"

"Only that some sicko had been stalking her." Her brows scrunched together. "The creep broke into her apartment and trashed it. And before Wade could catch him, the guy kidnapped her. But Wade and Jonas saved her."

"They did save her, but not before Wade got shot and Gracie got cut up. Scared the daylights out of all of us."

She slapped a hand over her heart. "God, that's awful! Gracie must have been so scared."

"Yeah," he muttered. "So be careful at the club tonight. Like I said, it's a nice place, but there are drunken assholes in the nice clubs too."

She cocked her head to the side. "Are you worried about me?"

Dean narrowed his eyes. "I'm worried about Gracie," he answered, which wasn't quite the truth. "She'd be upset if something happened to you."

"Oh," she said in a faraway voice, "of course."

He'd made her sad. Well, hell. *Great going, asshole.* Seeing her sad made him uncomfortable. "Catherine?"

"Yes?"

"I might have lied," he growled. "I'm sorry."

He eyes widened. "You did?"

"It's not only Gracie I'm concerned about. I don't want anything to happen to you because . . . well, just because." Christ, how had he gone from wishing she'd disappear to wanting to see her smile? The woman was dangerous to his peace of mind.

For several seconds she didn't speak. Finally she asked, "Um, so Gracie said you own your own construction company."

He chuckled at the abrupt subject change. "Yep. It does a pretty good business these days actually."

She stood and walked around the room. He noted the way she avoided his gaze. "Did you build this house?"

"This one and several others around here." Catherine was an enigma. Blunt and sure of herself, but there was a touch of vulnerability there too, Dean thought.

She smoothed a palm down the granite countertop and hummed her approval. "You do excellent work."

She was doing her best not to look at him, and Dean didn't like it. "Thanks, but I'd rather you look at me."

Her head swiveled around and their gazes locked. "Why?"

He got to his feet and crossed the room. Once he was within inches of her, Dean murmured, "Because I like it when you look at me with those pretty green eyes. Got a problem with that?"

"I-I think I need to get back to the hotel. I need to get ready for my shopping trip with Gracie. Besides, I've taken up plenty of your time already." Her gaze quickly darted away again, as if suddenly finding his refrigerator fascinating.

"Do you plan on buying something pretty to wear to The Pit while out shopping today?"

His question had the desired effect. She turned her head and looked up at him. "Maybe," she whispered. "I didn't really bring anything along on this trip appropriate for a nightclub."

Dean imagined her wearing a little black dress, one that showed off her figure to perfection. He thought of how sexy she'd be out on the dance floor, her hips moving to the beat of a slow, seductive song. His dick hardened beneath the fly of his jeans. Without thinking, he said, "And maybe I'll see if Wade and Gracie have room for one more tonight."

She crossed her arms over her chest. "You want to go out with us? Seriously?"

Dean shrugged, becoming preoccupied with a smear of chocolate icing on the corner of her mouth. "Is that a problem?" As dumb as it would be for him to get involved with Gracie's sister, Dean was starting to realize he might not have a choice in the matter. She was a temptation, one he wasn't sure he wanted to resist.

Catherine swallowed several times before replying, "No, it's not a problem at all. I just didn't figure you for the nightclub type." She paused for a few seconds, then a frown replaced her confusion. "Or is this just another way for you to keep an eye on me because you don't trust me around your brother and Gracie?"

The reminder that he didn't trust her made the idea of getting involved the dumbest one he'd come up with in a long time. Still, she intrigued him, and it'd been a damn long time since a woman had managed that feat.

Not willing to delve into his reasons, Dean answered, "If I come tonight it'll be because I want to be there."

She laughed and shook her head. "You like to play your cards close to the chest, don't you?"

Dean took hold of her arms and pulled her close, close enough to smell her pretty, floral scent, but not so close he lost all control. "You have a little chocolate on you," Dean murmured as he tipped her chin up and kissed her. Catherine went rigid. He angled his head and let his tongue dart out to touch one corner of her mouth. When she relaxed against him, her arms moving to wrap around his neck, chocolate was all but forgotten. And so was his control. All Dean wanted to do was devour her. Inch by inch.

His tongue touched the side of her mouth and licked slowly back and forth. He tasted the chocolate, but it wasn't enough. He wanted a deeper taste. He wanted the flavor of Catherine in his mouth. Something to tide him over until he could see her again. He tugged until their bodies were aligned. Her soft curves fit him perfectly, and Dean took a moment to relish the fact. Naked, they should definitely be naked. He ached to feel her silken skin against him.

When he slid his tongue over her bottom lip and gently nipped, Catherine gasped. Dean took the advantage and delved inside the dark recesses of her mouth. She moaned and dug her fingers into his hair. Her tongue shyly explored his, teasing him with the possibility of more. When his hands cupped and squeezed her buttocks, she pressed her lower body into his. Dean knew she'd feel the heavy weight of his cock. He felt the instant Catherine came back to reality. Her body stiffened and she dropped her hands away. Dean pulled back and looked down at her. Her eyes were wide open and staring at him as if he'd sprouted horns.

"It's gone," he said by way of explanation, as his gaze went to her swollen lips.

"Huh?" she asked, her voice unsteady.

He smiled. "The chocolate."

"Uh, right." She licked her lips, then added, "A napkin would've worked too."

He tsked. "You'd want me to waste perfectly good chocolate?"

She shook her head. "You're determined to keep me on my toes, aren't you?"

Instead of answering, Dean pointed to the stove. "Are you going to be late?"

Catherine's gaze shot to the green readout. "Crap." She sprinted out of the room and grabbed her purse. As she took hold of the doorknob, she stopped and looked back at him. "Thanks for . . . lunch."

He grinned and leaned against the wall. "It was my pleasure, believe me."

The last thing Dean saw before she rushed out the door was the alluring shade of pink in her cheeks. "That woman is going to be bad for my health," he muttered.

7

"He kissed you?" Gracie asked as she skimmed a rack of dresses.

The store Gracie had taken her to was small but had a large variety of party dresses and eveningwear. Catherine stared at a display of skirts, but all she saw was Dean. The heat in his gaze as he stared down at her after the kiss. Her body temperature spiked all over again. "I don't get it," she admitted. "One minute he's telling me he doesn't trust me, like I have some diabolical plan in mind for you, then he's kissing me. The man is beyond annoying."

Gracie stopped and frowned over at her. "But he really kissed you?"

"See?" Catherine threw her hands in the air. "You're as baffled as I am."

She shook her head. "Well, I suppose the trip was a success to some degree, then. I mean, clearly he must not hate you the way you suspected or he never would've kissed you."

"No, he doesn't hate me." She snorted. "He just doesn't trust me."

Gracie pushed her purse higher on her shoulder. "But if that's true, then why'd he kiss you?"

"Because I had chocolate on my mouth, he said." Catherine's gaze caught a dress on the rack Gracie was picking through. She picked it up and looked at the tag. "Damn, wrong size."

"Uh-huh. And he's coming to the club tonight."

"He said he *might* come. I doubt that he'll show up though. Kiss or no kiss, he doesn't want me around, Gracie." She slumped. "He'd love it if I took the first flight back to Atlanta." She cocked her head. "That might have been what he wanted in the beginning, but now I wonder if that's changed."

"A kiss didn't fix the problem. No more than the conversation with him did." Catherine bit her lower lip. God, she swore she could still taste him there. Strong and masculine, but tender too. "He still doesn't trust me."

Gracie shrugged. "If you're so sure, then you probably aren't interested in what Wade said about Dean's bizarre attitude toward you, huh?"

Oh, now that got her attention. "Spill it, sister."

"Sister." Gracie grinned. "I'll never get used to hearing that."

Distracted from the topic of Dean and the kiss for a moment, Catherine smiled. "Me either. It feels so natural too. Like I've known you my entire life."

Gracie reached out and took her hand and gave it a squeeze. "I know what you mean."

A few seconds went by, the two of them simply soaking in the moment. When a woman wanted to get through the aisle they were standing in, Gracie released her hand and together they moved to a different aisle. It wasn't until they reached a rack of assorted items that Gracie said, "Wade thinks that Dean is fighting an attraction to you."

Catherine instantly recalled the rigid length of Dean's erection when he'd pressed against her in the kitchen. The feel of him had gone straight to her head. Like tequila. Dangerous stuff. "I admit he seemed to enjoy the kiss, but I don't think an instant out of time explains all the attitude I've been getting from Dean." She stopped, then added, "I mean, he's been this way since before I met him yesterday."

"True," Gracie conceded as she picked up a black skirt. "What about you? Are you attracted to him?"

"I don't know," she said. Immediately she knew that was a lie and opted to tell the truth instead. "Yes. But he makes me crazy with his accusations and distrust. And he reminded me that you and I were half sisters, which I know we are, but it doesn't feel that way to me."

"It doesn't feel that way to me either." Gracie picked up a pretty black dress with dark green accents around the bodice and held it out toward her. "So, since he's making you so crazy, maybe tonight you should return the favor."

Catherine took the dress from Gracie and read the tag. Right size, and the price wasn't even too bad. "How could I possibly make that man crazy? He's so in control of himself. I get the feeling he never lets down his guard."

Gracie wagged her eyebrows and pointed to the dress. "By looking extra hot tonight. At the very least you'll have him squirming a little, which he deserves for giving you such a hard time."

Catherine laughed. "I don't know if I can pull that off, but I like the way your mind works all the same."

"We're going to drive those Harrison men insane. Just wait and see." She nodded toward the dress and said, "Try it on."

Catherine held it against her body. It was shorter than her normal style. She'd be showing a lot of leg. "What can it hurt?"

"That's the way I see it. He shows up, you get to make him drool. If he doesn't, then there will be plenty of other men at the club to choose from. Either way a win-win." Gracie picked another dress out and checked the tag. "Ouch. Too much."

Catherine leaned over and checked the price. "I'll buy it for you. It's what sisters do for each other, right?"

Gracie hesitated a moment before replying. "Only if I get to buy you some pretty shoes to go with that dress."

Catherine laughed. "Deal."

The wild beat of the music wasn't the only thing that had Catherine's heart pounding. As Dean pulled out a high stool for her, so like the perfect gentleman, and held it while she sat, Catherine wondered what he was up to. He moved the stool nearest to hers a little closer, then sat. Unfortunately that put them within touching distance. Every so often their legs brushed against each other, sending electric sparks shooting up Catherine's entire body. The man was lethal. It wasn't until Gracie had asked the men to go get them drinks that Catherine felt like she could begin to breathe normally again.

Now, as she watched Wade and Dean walk toward them, carrying a bottle of beer for her and club soda for Gracie, Catherine thought maybe she'd gotten in over her head. They were both gorgeous men, but it was Dean who held all her attention. He wore a pair of black trousers and a white button-down shirt with the sleeves rolled to the elbows. His silky dark hair had even been combed into submission. The hot looks he kept giving her were driving Catherine's libido into a frenzy.

"Are you glad he decided to come with us?" Gracie asked, leaning close to be heard over the din of the music.

"I'm not sure," Catherine admitted. "Dean's been fairly hostile toward me from the start, but tonight he seems different. He seems . . ." She broke off, unable to put her thoughts into words.

"Predatory?" Gracie helpfully supplied.

"Yes, that's it. Predatory." She looked at her sister and asked, "What do I do with predatory?"

Gracie chuckled. "You dance." She stepped off the stool and

held out a hand. "Come on, let's put these new heels to the test."

Catherine stood just as the guys came back to the table. Wade placed Gracie's club soda in front of her, but Dean didn't seem so inclined to hand over her beer. She pointed at it and asked, "Are you keeping my beer hostage?"

He placed it on the table and slid it toward her. Catherine became spellbound by the way his fingers wrapped around the longneck bottle. When she moved to take it from him, their fingers touched. It was brief, but enough to leave her breathless.

"Where are you two going?" Dean asked, his gaze holding hers captive.

Gracie leaned up and kissed Wade on the cheek, then whispered something in his ear. Wade looked over at Catherine and winked. "We'll watch your purses."

"Thanks," Catherine shouted back. Dean asked again, but before she had a chance to answer, Gracie was tugging her onto the dance floor.

Glancing to her right, she saw a high platform where women danced. Was she just old fashioned or were women dressing decidedly skimpily these days? One woman in particular caught her eye. Her bra was totally exposed through a lavender-colored mesh shirt. The skirt she wore rode her buttocks, and if she moved just the wrong way, she'd be baring her entire backside. Judging by the happy glow on her face, she didn't seem too worried. The woman danced right along with everyone else, bumping and pushing into others as they bumped and pushed against her.

When had dancing turned into a contact sport?

With her eyes trained on the women on the platform, she started to feel a little overdressed. There was a lot more skin exposed than there was covered in this room. Catherine looked down at her own dress. The black lightweight fabric teased her thighs each time she took a step and the heels were tall, but not so much that she risked breaking her neck. She'd spent a great amount of time taming her hair into a sleek, straight mane down her back. But she couldn't tell if Dean had noticed her efforts or not. Now that she looked at the other women, Catherine thought he'd have to be blind not to notice *them*. Were his eyes on the other women even now? Was he watching the woman in the mesh shirt as she swayed and moved to the beat?

Catherine ruthlessly pushed the little green monster out of her mind. She had absolutely zero reason to be jealous because she had no feelings for Dean. None. Zip. He was attractive and he was Gracie's soon-to-be brother-in-law. Nothing more. So what if he'd kissed her and she'd responded with her own small bit of passion. Could she really help it? There wasn't a female on the planet who wouldn't respond to Dean's luscious mouth and his stroking tongue.

And if any of the women here wanted to taste him for themselves, they'd have to go through her first.

With that firmly in her mind, Catherine moved a little to the beat. It wasn't long before she was forgetting big brooding men with chips on their shoulders and succumbing to the rhythm of the song.

8

As the song ended and another one started, Catherine started to feel someone watching her. She turned in time to catch a man at the far end of the dance floor, staring. When their gaze connected he quickly looked away. Catherine danced closer to Gracie and, speaking into her ear, she said, "There's a guy on the other side of the room watching me."

Gracie chuckled and kept dancing. "A lot of guys are watching you."

Catherine shook her head. "Maybe, but this one is creeping me out."

Gracie stopped dancing and asked, "Which one?"

"Short blond hair and long-sleeve blue shirt." Catherine looked again, and sure enough his gaze was trained on her. "It's the way he's staring."

Not even bothering to appear nonchalant, Gracie turned her head to see who she meant. When her gaze came back to hers, she said, "Ew, you're right. He is creepy."

Catherine shifted, putting her back to him. Gracie obviously sensed her unease and sidled up next to her. She strained to be heard over the loud beat. "If he bothers us, Wade and Dean will take care of it."

Catherine didn't know if she liked the idea of Dean "taking care of it." "Dean and I came here together, but we aren't together together. He's not required to fend off unwanted men on my behalf."

Gracie said something, but it got lost as the song picked up tempo. Catherine looked again, hoping the stranger was gone. Of course that would've been too easy. He watched her as if she were a midnight snack. It made her skin crawl. He must have moved closer, she realized, because now he was no longer on the other side of the dance floor. In her distraction he'd moved around until he was barely twenty feet away. A cold feeling moved through her veins at the intense look in his eyes.

He wasn't a bad-looking man. Catherine supposed women would find him handsome, with his curly blond hair and scruffy facial hair. He wore a pair of low-riding blue jeans and worn, black work boots. Several gyrating bodies were all that stood between them, but Catherine was glad for at least that much of a barrier.

Gracie leaned close. "Just forget about him. We're here to have fun."

Catherine knew that Gracie was right. She didn't want anything to damper her first night out with her sister, but the heebie-jeebies weren't letting up. "I'm trying, but it feels as if he's touching me. I don't know what it is about him." A voice in the back of her mind reminded her that she didn't feel the same ick vibe when Dean looked at her. His gaze sent her heart fluttering and her nerves dancing. This stranger made her want to take a shower. There was no crime in looking at a woman, Catherine reminded herself. He hadn't made any advances.

"Would you rather head back to the table?"

"No," she said, firming up her resolve to have a good time, despite the creep. "We're here to have fun. Screw him."

Gracie smiled and went back to dancing. When another up-beat song started up, Catherine forgot her worries. The light-haired stranger no longer mattered. Dean's distrust toward her even took a backseat. Everything faded as the music surrounded her and carried her away.

Catherine heard Gracie yell something about the tune being one of her favorites. She smiled and realized the romantic tune was one she loved as well. One more thing they had in common. The song was soft, with a woman's lilting voice that made Catherine picture herself in the arms of a lover. She closed her eyes and imagined Dean. It startled her. Thinking of him that way made her remember the delicious kiss from earlier in the day. The music, the soft lights, all of it coaxed out her uninhibited side. She let herself float along with it as the rhythm took hold. In her mind, Catherine saw the planes and angles of Dean's stern face, his soft, talented lips and the intense brown eyes that seemed ever trained on her. God, how she wanted his lips pressed to hers in that moment. If she were honest with herself, Catherine would admit that she wanted his entire body pressed to her. Since she couldn't have that, then at least the music would help her fantasize a little. Her imagination would simply have to be enough for tonight.

As she swayed and moved, her eyes drifted closed. Catherine wondered how good his hands would feel, and soon her own hands were traveling down her body, barely grazing but enough to spark off an erotic thought or two. She touched her own neck, imagining his lips caressing her there. She wondered if he would take his time, kissing and nibbling on her before moving farther south.

Catherine's fingers hooked beneath the hem of her skirt and lifted slightly, unaware that she was giving a tantalizing glimpse of her upper thigh. She felt the satin of her own skin beneath her fingertips. She quivered. Would his hands be calloused? A working man's hands? As the song began to wind down, she wondered if she'd ever find out what Dean's touch was like.

Dean didn't need this right now. On top of her looking good enough to eat, Catherine danced like a goddess. Damn, he should've known the minute he'd kissed her that he'd have a hard time keeping his distance. He nearly salivated at the loving way her short black dress cupped her ass cheeks. Dean had to clench his fists in front of him on the table to keep from leaping out onto the dance floor and taking her into his arms. As he glanced around the room he noticed several other men watching her with lust in their eyes, and that alone had him wanting to drag her off. He'd take her somewhere private, somewhere he could get more than just his hands on her soft curves.

Wade nudged him, and Dean forced his gaze off Catherine long enough to see what he wanted. "Yeah?"

"So what's this about Catherine coming to your place?"

Dean frowned, knowing an interrogation was coming. "It was no big deal."

Wade quirked a brow and gave him one of those big brother "I can see right through you" looks.

"She wanted to clear the air," Dean said, keeping it simple. The kiss they'd shared was no one's damn business. "To see if she and I could form a truce or something."

"And did you?"

He thought of how good she'd tasted and had to bite back a curse. "I'm here, aren't I?"

"Oh, you're here." Wade sat back in his chair and crossed his arms over his chest. "But I'm still trying to figure out if it's because you came for the terrific company or simply to keep tabs on Catherine. Judging by the way you've been watching her dance, I'd say it's somewhere in between. Am I right?"

"Look, you all want me to like her, to accept her as a part of this family, I get that. You've made your position very clear, Wade. But—"

"She *is* a part of this family," Wade said, his voice rising over the blast of the bass and the roar of the crowd. "She's Gracie's sister and that makes her a really big part."

Dean shoved a hand through his hair and leaned closer. "She's still a virtual stranger. You and I both know that exchanging a few phone calls and e-mails doesn't mean you know a person inside and out."

"Yes, I'm aware, and that's what this visit is for. So they can get to know each other."

Dean was tired of banging his head against that particular wall. When he turned and looked at Catherine, his anger dissipated. She looked like a wood nymph. Her long red hair flowed down her back as she danced around the floor, completely oblivious to the riot of emotion inside him. Dean took another swig of his beer and placed it on the table, then sat back and watched the show. She swayed to the beat of the music, as if completely lost in it. She moved with passion. He wondered what was going through her mind. Was she imagining a lover's touch? When her hands went on a journey over her body, Dean's dick thickened beneath his trousers.

A movement to her right caught his attention, and he saw a man striding across the dance floor. He was headed right for Catherine. That quickly, his conversation with Wade was forgotten. All Dean could think about was keeping the other man from touching her. He heard someone call his name, but he ignored it. As he crossed the room, maneuvering his way through the gyrating bodies, Dean came up directly behind her and placed his hands on her hips. She went rigid.

He leaned close. "Come home with me."

Catherine tipped her head back to look at him. "That's it? You think I'll simply surrender and fall into your arms?"

Dean barely noticed when the song ended and another, slower

tune started up. All his concentration was on the softness of the woman beneath his hands. He wanted to feel the satin of her skin. He wanted the dress gone. "It'd be nice if you would, yeah."

She shook her head and turned in his arms. "That isn't a good idea."

When she wrapped her arms around his neck, Dean wanted to shout in triumph. She wasn't melting against him, but it was still a damn sight better than a knee to the crotch. "Not even if it's what we both need? What we both want?"

She looked over his shoulder, and several seconds passed before she said, "You don't understand."

He took hold of her chin and urged her gaze back to his. "Then help me understand."

"Dean, I'm not the type to give in to my wishes and wants," she explained. "Flights of fancy aren't me."

He nudged her legs apart so he could wedge one of his between them. When he felt her shudder, he grinned. "Don't you ever allow desire to rule the show every once in a while, sweetheart?"

She shrugged. "Not when those desires stand in the way of what is most important."

Dean smoothed a palm down her hair, enjoying the silky texture. "And going home with me, letting me make you feel good, that stands in the way, huh?"

"Yes," she muttered, "because you don't trust me, and I can't go to bed with someone who doesn't trust me. Besides the fact you're going to be Gracie's brother-in-law soon."

"You're Little Miss Practical, I get it. Hell, I admire a quality like that in a woman." His hand moved down her back until he was barely grazing her ass. "And you're listing all the right reasons why we shouldn't get involved. But none of it matters, not right now. Only you and I matter." He coasted his hand lower until he felt one rounded buttock beneath his palm. "Can you honestly tell me that you don't want me? That you don't feel the chemistry between us?"

"Yes, I feel it," she ground out. "But it scares me. You scare me."

He hadn't expected such a strong response, and he certainly didn't want her afraid of him. "Why? I thought we already established that I'd never hurt you?"

"Actually I believe you said that if I hurt your family you'd do far worse." He started to speak, but she held up a hand, halting him. "That's not the point though. I'm leaving in a week, Dean. Getting involved now would be insane."

He leaned down and pressed his lips to hers, then whispered, "So, take what you can get of me. Get your fill, sweetheart. Before it's too late."

The song ended then, and Dean watched her take a deep breath before looking up at him. She seemed to be studying him, and it made Dean uncomfortable. Her silent intensity washed over him. Catherine's green eyes held so many secrets, and Dean wasn't sure if he'd ever learn them all. The only thing he knew for certain was that she did things to him. Things no other woman had been able to do in a long time.

Dean dipped his head and pressed his lips to hers briefly, then murmured, "I want you in my bed. I want so many damn things, Catherine, but if it really isn't what you want, then tell me and I'll leave you alone. You have my word."

Catherine dropped her head to his chest and muttered something against his shirt. He wrapped his hands around her upper arms and pulled her off him. "What did you say?"

"I said, I do want you."

It dawned on Dean that the music had changed, the tempo was faster, the romantic tune was gone, but the mood was still there. He was still as edgy, still as ready, and Catherine was still standing in front of him, staring at him as if she wasn't sure whether to run in fear or surrender to the passion arcing between them. And Dean wasn't about to leave it to chance.

He took her face in his palms and touched his mouth to her soft lips. She moaned, and the sound went straight to his cock. The people surrounding them dancing to the music were forgotten. Her taste was like honey, and he wanted it. Craved it. Nothing was going to stand in his way of getting a great big helping of it either.

9

As Dean nudged her lips apart and delved inside, Catherine caved. She should've guessed that the man played dirty. Of course, she hadn't really expected him to ask her to go home with him either. Geez, one minute he acted as if she was a nuisance, and the next he was making love to her mouth. Catherine thought she heard someone whimper. It took her a moment to realize the sounds were coming from her. She knew without a doubt that if she didn't pull away he'd be able to have her right there on the dance floor. She wasn't into public displays of affection, so why wasn't she pulling away? Simple, her mind had taken a leave. Her libido now ruled the show.

She was giving in too easily and she knew it. So much for the thrill of the chase or putting up a little resistance. The knowledge that she was acting completely out of character should've had her yanking herself out of his arms. Instead she moved closer, bringing their bodies into full contact. She could smell his strong, masculine scent, and it was delicious. The rigid length of his cock was a heavy weight between them. She wanted more of him.

She wanted to know what his muscled chest felt like beneath her curious hands. She ached to run her tongue over his salty skin.

Catherine understood now what it was about a man that made women lose their heads. It was that all-too-enthralling maleness. Dean's aggressive attitude, the way he'd swooped in and all but ordered her to come home with him, it'd hadn't been a turnoff. She'd liked it. For the first time in her life, Catherine imagined surrendering to a man. She wondered what it'd be like to let Dean have complete control.

She ran her tongue over his lips and felt his body stiffen. Rising up on her tiptoes, she took a better taste, licking and nibbling at him as if he were a candy bar. Catherine raked her fingers through his hair and groaned. God, she loved his hair, so thick and soft.

When she angled her head, deepening the touch, Dean tore his mouth from hers. "Home," he growled against her open mouth.

Apparently he'd had enough of the PDA. The idea of being alone with Dean scared her a little though. He was so intense, and Catherine wasn't sure she could handle him. "I'm scared," she admitted.

He shook his head and frowned down at her. "You don't—"

A deep, male voice broke into their intimate moment. When Catherine looked to see who it was, she cringed. It was the stranger that had been staring at her earlier.

"Miss, would you care to dance?" The polite question would normally get a polite rejection, but Catherine was still creeped out by the way he'd watched her. When she started to speak, Dean spoke over her.

"No, she wouldn't," he said in a tone that brooked no argument.

The man's eyebrows rose, but his gaze didn't waver from hers. "The lady can speak for herself, can't she?"

Catherine squirmed under his scrutiny, but his rudeness didn't sit well with her Southern manners. "My dance card is full, thanks."

Dean's arm tightened around her. It was a possessive move, as if he were staking a claim. Catherine should've been perturbed, but she was too busy being grateful for his presence to think about her need for equality and independence.

When the guy still didn't get the message, Dean said, "The lady's with me. Get lost."

Okay, that was going too far. Her anger came rushing to the surface, and she oh-so-casually stomped on Dean's foot. He simply frowned down at her, completely unfazed. Mental note, the man was made of stone. Still, Dean was a better alternative than the man standing in front of them. So, she stayed silent. For now. She'd have a little talk with him later about his poor choice of words.

Finally, the stranger turned his attention to Dean. "I don't see a ring on her finger."

Dean dropped his arm from around her middle and stepped closer to the man who seemed to be itching for a fight. "You really don't want to push me," he warned.

Catherine could practically feel the tension mounting. She was about to intervene in the hopes of heading off a fight when Wade and Gracie suddenly showed up by their sides. She felt instantly better at having Gracie there. The stranger, who was clearly a few bricks shy of a full load, appeared not to even notice Wade's big, menacing form. When he turned to her and smiled, Catherine felt sick to her stomach.

He inclined his head. "Maybe some other time then."

As he walked off she heard Dean call him a not-so-complimentary name. She poked him in the ribs and he glared at her. "Don't give me that look," she said, pointing a finger at him. "What's with the 'the lady's with me' crap?"

"The ass wasn't going to stop until he knew you were off

limits. I sort of got the feeling you wanted him gone." He quirked a brow. "Was I wrong?"

Catherine felt a headache coming on. "No, you weren't wrong," she gritted out. "That's why I chose not to dance with him."

"I—"

"Dean."

Wade's tone had them both going silent. Dean looked over at his brother and said, "I'm a little busy, bro."

Catherine didn't know Wade well, but even she could see he wasn't a happy camper. Whatever he had to say, it wasn't going to be good.

"I can see that." Wade looked at Catherine for a second before going back to glaring at Dean. "But we need to talk."

"It can wait," Dean said, stepping closer to Wade, which effectively cut off Catherine's view of Wade's face.

"No, it can't," Catherine heard Wade reply, his tone rising.

She could well imagine Dean's anger in that moment. When she felt a soft hand on her shoulder, Catherine looked to her left to find her sister standing there, concern causing her brows to scrunch together.

"Maybe we should let the guys talk a minute," Gracie said into her ear.

Catherine nodded. There was simply too much testosterone for her peace of mind. She was about to let Gracie tug her to the other side of the room, back to their table, but Dean stopped her with a hand on the back of her neck. She glanced back at him in question.

"Don't go too far," he gently ordered, a small smile playing at the corners of his mouth. It was the sexiest thing Catherine had ever seen. After she nodded, he released her. When he began walking toward the restrooms with Wade, Catherine found she couldn't look away from his drool-worthy body. There was something completely wild and untamed about Dean. It turned her on something fierce. She sighed as she realized her night wasn't quite going to turn out the way she'd hoped.

Catherine turned her attention to Gracie. "Okay, what's going on?"

"Come on," Gracie persuaded as she dragged her to the stools they'd vacated earlier. Once they were seated, she said, "Wade thinks Dean might not have good intentions where you're concerned."

Catherine rolled her eyes. "Dean asked me to go home with him, if that's what you mean." Gracie's eyes widened. "But I'm a big girl, Gracie," she rushed to say. "I don't need Wade's permission."

Gracie looked troubled. "No, it's not that. It's just that Dean has made it clear how he feels about you being here. Wade is worried that he's not thinking clearly. He doesn't want you to get hurt in the cross fire."

After being an only child her entire life, Catherine wasn't terribly comfortable with having a pseudo big brother butting into her private life. "If you're concerned that Dean is using me, don't be."

"No, it's not that. Well, maybe it is." Gracie threw up her hands. "I'm not sure. It's just that Dean's been acting so strangely since you arrived. And then out of the blue he acts like he can't keep his hands off you."

Catherine sighed. "Yeah, he's confusing me too, but I can deal with it. Dean isn't trying to charm me or anything. He's been completely honest from the start."

"But you said yourself he doesn't trust you. Is it wise to start a relationship with him?"

Catherine didn't even have to think about the question to know the answer. "No, it isn't. But I'm sort of tired of being the wise one."

Gracie crossed her arms in front of her on the table and leaned closer. "What do you mean?"

She thought about her parents' death and dealing with all the details of their estate. "For the last two months I've been working my tush off to get things straightened around since my parents died. There hasn't been a whole lot of *me* time. I figure I'm due."

A waiter came over and asked if they wanted another drink. They both declined. After he moved to the next table, Gracie said, "So, this thing is merely a fling between you and Dean? There's nothing else?"

"I don't know." *Geez, that sounded lame.* "But I'd like to find out. Do you think I'm terrible for wanting to go home with him so soon?"

Gracie reached over and took her hand in one of hers. "Of course not. I know all about attraction at first sight, believe me. But what about the trust thing? Doesn't it bother you?"

"Heck, yeah, it does, but I'm determined to prove him wrong on that score." Catherine squeezed her sister's hand. "For the remainder of my visit I plan to whittle down his defenses until he cries uncle."

Gracie laughed. "Well, my money's definitely on you."

Catherine was about to say something else, but Dean and Wade came back to the table, effectively ending the conversation. She looked at them. Neither man was smiling, but they weren't sporting black eyes either. "Everything okay?"

A muscle in Dean's jaw twitched. "Dandy."

His attitude left Catherine more uncertain than ever. Had he changed his mind about her?

Dean reached out and took her hand in his and leaned close. "Ready to go?"

Apparently not, Catherine thought as she allowed Dean to help her off the stool. Like the perfect gentleman, he even helped her into her coat. She noticed Wade's arm wrapped around Gracie's shoulders, but when she looked into his eyes, eyes so like Dean's, he was staring at her with concern. Warmth filled her.

He cared about her. Like a brother might care for a sister. Catherine suddenly felt blessed to have him in her corner. She smiled in appreciation, and he gave her a wink. When Catherine saw the worry in Gracie's expression, though, she went to her and hugged her close. "I'm going to be fine. I'll call you in the morning, okay?"

Gracie nodded, and a small smile slipped across her face. "You and I have plans, remember?"

Catherine's eyes lit up at the reminder. "How could I forget? I've been dying to see that 3-D movie since they started advertising it."

Gracie clapped her hands in front of her. "And we're going to Genji's restaurant for dinner afterward. I love their yum-yum sauce. I'm buying!"

"Ha!" Catherine snorted. "We'll see about that."

Dean tugged on her hand, and Catherine got the hint. He was anxious to leave. Anxious to be alone with her.

Her heart sped up at the notion.

After grabbing her purse and saying their good-byes, Catherine let Dean practically drag her out of the nightclub. When they reached his red four-wheel-drive truck, he unlocked it and held the door open for her. She took a chance and looked into his eyes. The heat she witnessed turned her on like nothing else, but it also sent a bolt of fear through her.

"Here, let me help," Dean murmured as he reached down and took hold of her waist to lift her onto the seat.

Catherine could feel the heat of his touch clear through her dress. "Thanks."

His smile was pure sin. "Seat belt," he gently ordered before slamming the door shut.

Once they were on their way, Catherine decided to lay it all out on the line. "I'm not sure what I'm doing here," she admitted. "I'm not even sure why I agreed to go back to your place with you."

He reached across the middle console and took hold of her hand. "Aren't you?"

She shook her head and looked out the windshield. The streetlights seemed to be going by way too fast. The man was definitely in a hurry. "I won't deny that I want you," she softly replied. "But to go home with you when I don't even really know you. I feel like I'm easy or something. Even though I'm not," she rushed to reassure. "I mean, I never go home with a man on the first date. Not to imply that what we had tonight was a date exactly, it's just that—"

"Catherine," Dean said, stopping the speeding race car of her mouth. "It's okay. I don't think you're easy. In fact, it's not exactly my MO to take a woman home so fast either." He spared her a look, one that she couldn't quite read in the darkness. "How about we just agree to share a nightcap and see what happens from there. Okay?"

She cocked her head, wishing she could see him clearer. "Why are you so sweet one minute and the next you're looking at me as if I'm the bogeyman? Or in my case, the bogeywoman." She clutched her purse tighter. "I just can't figure you out."

He chuckled. "First, there's no such thing as the bogey-*woman*. Even if there were, I don't think you'd resemble her in any way. You're way too pretty to be something so nasty. Second, I can't help the way I feel. I'm into you, sweetheart. My head is telling me it's a bad idea, that I shouldn't trust you. Thing is, my head isn't running the show right now."

Catherine both hated and loved Dean's brutal honesty. One thing for sure, she'd never have to wonder if he truly meant what he said. "And my head is telling me I should go back to my hotel room," she blurted out, giving him her own dose of candor. "To go to sleep like the good girl I was raised to be."

Dean chuckled. "How about we let the bad girl in you decide how the evening should end?"

Considering she wasn't even sure she had a bad girl side, Catherine had to give that some thought. Or tried to. With Dean stroking the back of her hand with his thumb, Catherine kept getting sidetracked with ideas of how good that thumb would feel on other parts of her body. In the end, Catherine decided it was high time her nearly nonexistent inner bad girl got to come out and play. "Your house," she finally said, throwing caution to the wind for the first time in her life.

She heard Dean curse before squeezing her hand gently. "You won't regret it, I promise you."

Catherine hoped that was true, but she had a terrible feeling that nothing would be the same once the night was through.

10

Dean shut the front door behind her, and the sound echoed in the dark room. Every nerve in her body started a riot. She nearly leaped out of her skin when he flipped a switch next to the door and light flooded the room.

"Don't be so skittish," he murmured as he helped her off with her coat. "I'm not the big bad wolf." After he placed her coat on a chair by the door, he held out his hands. "See? No claws."

She smiled as his teasing managed to relax her a fraction. "Sorry, but the nervousness seems to be here to stay."

He shoved his hands in his pockets. "Then how about something to relax you? I make a mean hot chocolate."

She tossed her purse on top of her coat. "I don't know a single woman on the planet who would pass that up."

"Hmm, chocolate cake earlier and now hot chocolate." He winked. "I'm beginning to see how to get around your defenses, Miss Michaels."

His use of the word Miss sent a shiver down her spine. "Ew,

don't say Miss. Makes me think of that guy at the club tonight."

He turned toward the kitchen. "Yeah, he was a real pain in the ass."

Catherine pulled out a chair at the table and sat. "Actually, I had noticed him earlier. He'd been watching me. It felt weird."

Dean took down two mugs and placed them on the counter. Catherine became pleasantly distracted by the way his trousers molded to his buttocks and thighs, but the look he shot her over his shoulder sent her dirty mind into hiding. She frowned. "What?"

"Why didn't you say anything about that before?"

"Uh, first off, it's not a crime to look at a woman, Dean. Second, you don't need to fight off unwanted suitors for me."

Dean shook his head as he went to another cupboard and grabbed a can of hot chocolate mix. "I should've kicked his ass anyway. As it was, I wanted to kick his ass. I was just trying not to make a scene your first night out."

She laughed. "I appreciate your restraint, truly."

As he went about making their drinks, Catherine went back to watching him move around the kitchen. Damn, the man was built. Every hard inch of him made her mouth water. As gorgeous as he was, Catherine couldn't forget the fact that he didn't trust her. Of course, now that they'd spent some time together, maybe he'd changed his mind. There was one surefire way to find out. Ask him. The coward in her couldn't bring herself to form the question. She didn't want to ruin the moment by bringing tedious things like reality into it.

As he placed a steaming cup in front of her, Catherine hummed her approval. "This looks yummy."

Dean handed her a spoon. "Do you want marshmallows?"

Catherine quirked a brow. "Do you have the mini ones?"

He wagged his eyebrows, and Catherine nearly melted on

the spot. "Yep," he replied. "Whenever Deanna comes over she insists on them."

He went to grab them, and Catherine couldn't help but wonder about Dean's relationship with his twin. "What's it like? Being a twin, I mean."

He placed a bag on the table between them, then sat down with his own cup. "I guess like any other brother and sister, only we share the same birthday."

Catherine helped herself to the marshmallows. "Really? There isn't a deeper connection or anything?"

She watched Dean plop several into his own mug and stir before answering. "I guess there is a deeper connection, yeah. There have been times over the years when we've known when the other was in trouble. Like a few months back, when Deanna was held at gunpoint. I could feel something was wrong." He shrugged. "It sounds strange, I know, but I could feel her fear."

Catherine had taken a small sip of her drink, but the pain in Dean's voice caught all her attention. She didn't like the idea of him hurting. "From what I heard, Deanna is lucky to be alive." Catherine remembered Gracie telling her about the horrifying event. Deanna had been hired for a remodeling job, but the client had turned out to be a drug dealer. When a teenage boy had overdosed, the boy's distraught father had shown up with a gun to exact his revenge. Deanna had simply been in the wrong place at the wrong time.

Dean raked a hand through his hair. "Waiting on Jonas to disarm the guy were easily some of the longest minutes of my life."

Catherine reached across the table and covered his hand with her own. "I can't imagine. You must have felt so helpless."

Dean's gaze went to their hands, and Catherine couldn't tell what he was thinking. As he slowly turned his hand over and entwined his fingers with hers, Catherine's heart skipped a beat. "It's something I never want to repeat," he whispered. "That's for damn sure."

She took another sip of her hot chocolate and moaned at the creamy flavor. "This is delicious, by the way. You could sell it and make a fortune."

He chuckled and picked up his own, then took a long drink. God, even watching his throat work was sexy. After he placed his mug back on the table, his gaze went to hers. "Enough about the chocolate. I want to know more about *you*."

Catherine started to pull her hand away, but he held on tighter. When their gazes connected, Catherine's blood turned to molten lava. Dean stared at her as if he wanted to devour her. She left her hand where it was. "What do you want to know?"

He pushed his mug to the side and leaned in closer. Catherine could smell his scent, and like before it turned her on. "Anything. What do you like to do in your off hours? Any hobbies?"

She laughed. "Seriously?"

One side of his mouth kicked up in a playful half grin. "Why not? It's a place to start."

"Okay. I either spend time with my friend Mary, or I read. I love books. It's something Gracie and I have in common." She tilted her head to the side. "What about you? Do you like to read?"

"Eh, not all that much." He paused a second, then asked, "Your friend, what's she like?"

"She's different. Bold, lovable, a real risk taker." Catherine shrugged. "The opposite of me. We're as close as sisters though."

Dean slid his thumb back and forth over her knuckles, creating a maelstrom of need inside her. "I'm not sure about the risk taker part," he murmured, "but you can be pretty bold. Hell, you've put me in my place more than once."

Catherine liked the way Dean described her, even if it was

inaccurate. "I don't think you're talking about the right person."

"Hmm, we'll leave that for another day. For now, tell me about your job, web design. Do you enjoy it?"

Oh, now, that was a subject she could sink her teeth into. "I love it. It can be demanding and clients can be difficult at times, but it's nice to set my own hours. And there's a lot of satisfaction when I finish a project and the client walks away happy."

"Web design requires a fair amount of knowledge with coding, doesn't it? You must be good with computers."

She swirled her finger around the rim of her mug, gathering several droplets of foam, then licked it off. "I know enough," she answered. "But I'd like to go back to college to learn more."

He frowned. "I'm having a hard time picturing you sitting alone at a computer all day. How'd you get into it?"

The fact Dean couldn't imagine Catherine in such a way was more proof that he had her pegged all wrong. More proof that she needed to show him that she wasn't the woman he thought she was.

"I started out thinking it was computer engineering that I wanted to do," Catherine replied. "I ended up in information technology instead."

He looked her over and murmured, "I'd never figure you for a geek."

Her eyes grew round. "I am not a geek!"

"You sure as hell don't look like one," he growled, as he tugged on her hand and brought it to his mouth. He brushed each fingertip with his lips, one by one, until she was panting. By the time he placed her hand back on the table, Catherine's pussy throbbed. "Don't taste like one either."

She had to clear the lump out of her throat before asking, "Tasted a lot of geeks, have you?"

He winked. "I confess, you're my first."

"Oh, I—"

"Catherine?"

Catherine's breathing increased. "Yes?"

He nodded toward her hot chocolate. "Are you finished with your drink?"

She looked down at the half-empty mug. If she said yes, they'd be moving their little party into the bedroom. Did she want that? Part of her screamed "hell, yes," but another part told her to do the right thing and leave. Getting involved with a man who didn't even trust her couldn't end well, could it?

Suddenly Dean released her and stood. When he came around the table and crouched in front of her, she had the desperate urge to wrap her arms around him and drift into the passion she witnessed in his warm brown eyes. But the good, Christian girl her mother had raised would never be so bold.

Large, strong hands wrapped around her thighs and squeezed. "I know you're bothered by the trust thing. I wish like hell I could let it go, I do. But it's there and I can't shake it."

"But you still want me," she stated. She needed to lay it all on the line.

"I want you so badly right now I'm about to self-combust here," he admitted in a rough voice. "Tonight, forget about the rest."

He moved one hand beneath her dress. The roughness of his palm scraped against her skin and set butterflies flitting through her stomach. He slid higher, until he was a bare few inches away from her pussy, and Catherine lost the ability to think clearly.

As if knowing how much he affected her, Dean gently ordered, "Just feel, sweetheart. Let yourself go."

"Dean." His name came out as a moan. Catherine hardly recognized her own voice.

"Mmm, fuck, yeah, I love the way you say my name," he

whispered, his hand inching ever closer. When he came into contact with her panties, he stilled. "You're wet for me, huh?"

She slapped a hand over her eyes. "Yes," Catherine admitted as she tried to grapple for control.

Dean's hand cupped her mound. She pried her eyes open to see the dark desire etched into his handsome features. His nostrils flared, and a muscle in his jaw twitched. "I'm dying to see these pretty panties, Catherine."

Catherine shook her head. "I don't know what I'm doing. I'm not . . . not the type to play like this with a man. I've never been the adventurous sort."

Dean slowly moved his hand up and down her pussy, caressing her through the silk. "And I've never fondled a woman in my kitchen before, but now I can see the appeal."

As Catherine sat in the hard wooden kitchen chair, Dean's hand covering her pussy and teasing her beyond reason, she said the first thing that popped into her head. "I want to be adventurous, Dean. With you. Tonight."

"Hell, yeah," he growled as he pulled his hand away and stood. Before she could take another breath, he had her cradled against his chest. "I'm going to need plenty of room for what I have in mind, sweetheart."

A bout of insecurity hit from out of nowhere as Catherine imagined getting naked in front of Dean. He was so fit, without an ounce of fat on him. She, on the other hand, had more than enough fluff for the two of them. She buried her head in his chest and groaned.

Dean stopped. "Look at me, Catherine," he ordered, his tone almost angry. For whatever reason Catherine couldn't disobey him. "You're beautiful," he whispered, when their gazes connected. "Sweet and shy and sexy, and I can't wait to get this dress off you so I can touch this hot body."

"I'm the epitome of imperfection," she admitted in a last-ditch effort to get him to see her for who she really was: the average gal with a little extra to love and not the gorgeous creature he'd described.

"My cock disagrees with you." He touched his lips to hers in a brief caress, leaving her body craving so much more. "Let's listen to him, shall we?"

Despite the heat of the moment, Catherine found herself grinning. "So far he's had some pretty great ideas."

He chuckled. "Exactly."

They didn't say another word as Dean stepped through the doorway to his bedroom. When he flipped on the table lamp, Catherine knew she was about to get her hands on paradise. The notion sent her libido into a spin.

11

"Wow, this room is . . . big." Two of Catherine's bedrooms would fit in Dean's room, with space left over. It surprised her to see that it was all done in jewel tones too. "I sort of feel like I've stepped into a sheikh's palace."

He put her on her feet next to the bed. "Been to many palaces, have you?"

"No, but I'm pretty sure they look a lot like this." Her gaze wandered around the room and landed on a water fountain. Actually, it was a rain curtain. It drizzled down in perfect slim streaming lines, only to be caught in a pool below. On another wall, she noticed an entertainment system big enough to make her eyes bulge. The plasma widescreen alone would cost a pretty penny. "That's cool," she said.

"Thanks. I made the entertainment cabinet myself. Took some doing; the mahogany was pricey."

"You're wonderfully talented." She turned toward him and caught sight of him leaning against the bedpost, and about fainted. He was sinfully sexy and he was all hers. At least for this one night. Catherine was determined to make the most of it.

The bed, she noticed, was an enormous, four-poster canopy style. All dark wood and draped in a gauzy white cotton fabric. It seemed to be its own little bit of heaven. "You do like to have plenty of room, huh?"

"Oh, yeah," he murmured.

Catherine noticed another thing. Off to one side stood an easel, and there were pictures strewn all over the place. She crossed the room and picked one up off the floor. It was a sketch of a landscape. "This is really good, but why are they tossed about like this?"

"It's just something I mess around with. It's no big deal."

Catherine shook her head. "I definitely disagree. I wish I had this sort of talent. Heck, I can't even draw a stick figure."

"Catherine," Dean growled.

Her name and nothing more, but it was enough to elevate her temperature. Catherine placed the sketch on the easel before turning around to face him. He was watching her, much like an eagle watched its prey. A slight smile crossed over his face, and her knees went weak. "You're very sexy," she blurted out.

He crooked a finger toward her. "Come here," he softly ordered.

Catherine couldn't move. Nerves kept her feet rooted to the spot. She glanced down at the floor and saw several sketches, and that's when it hit her. What did she really know about the man? Well, besides the fact he was her sister's future brother-in-law and he thought she was a scheming liar. She thought of his questions in the kitchen and realized that while he'd gotten to know her a little better, he was still very much a mystery to her. She hadn't even known he was an artist until now.

"You know so much about me," Catherine said, putting her thoughts into words.

"I wouldn't say that. I know some things, yeah." When his

eyes traveled the length of her, Catherine felt seared clear to her bones. The look of arousal in his gaze was unmistakable.

Still uncertain, Catherine crossed her arms over her chest and said, "But I don't really know *anything* about you. You're very adept at keeping the focus on me, I've noticed."

He shrugged. "That's because you're far more interesting." He paused before adding, "This conversation would be better with you over here, by the way."

She firmed up her resolve. "I want to know more about you."

He straightened away from the bedpost and held a hand out to her. "I'll tell you whatever you want to know. Later. For now, I want you to come over here, Catherine." His voice was soft, but it was a command all the same.

Catherine narrowed her eyes. "Later? You promise?"

He nodded. "I'm an open book, sweetheart."

Catherine wasn't so sure about that. It dawned on her that whenever the conversation came back around to him, he always managed to get it back on her somehow. Still, he'd promised, and Catherine intended to see to it that he kept it. She dropped her arms to her sides and crossed the room.

Once she was within a few feet of him, Dean wrapped one arm around her and pulled her close. "I think I could come up with something much more stimulating to do than talk about me right now, don't you?"

She didn't have time to respond before his mouth was once again covering hers. The kiss was rough and demanding, forcing her lips apart. He didn't bother to wait for her to open them in her own time. He took possession of the soft interior in a way that had her body swaying against his rock-hard chest. Catherine gave in to the need coursing through her and wrapped her arms around his neck.

She sank into his kiss, giving in to the sweet demands her feminine core was suddenly making on her. For once in her life,

Catherine didn't want to think about her next move. She wanted Dean to take the choice from her altogether. And he seemed all too happy to do so.

When he sucked at her lower lip and probed her mouth with his insistent tongue, Catherine's pussy throbbed. Without warning, Dean bent low and lifted her into his arms, carrying her as if she weighed no more than a child. He placed her on top of the soft downy blankets with such gentle care that Catherine felt her heart melting. He was so big, so strong, and yet he was tender. He came down beside her and propped his head up on his elbow, staring down at her with such reverence that it shook her.

"Why are you looking at me that way?" Catherine asked, putting thought to words.

He touched a finger to her jaw and murmured, "How am I looking at you?"

She locked gazes with him, her jaw firming as she tried to explain the way his eyes seemed to see right into her soul. "You stare at me, and it's as if you can see my every thought. It's disconcerting."

"You're beautiful, Catherine. I'm the type of person who likes to stop and savor when I see something beautiful. Is that so wrong?"

Her cheeks burned at the praise. "See, there you go again, making me all nervous and jittery with your compliments."

He frowned down at her, as if truly bewildered. "Why can't you see the truth? The first time I saw your picture on Gracie's computer I thought you were sexy as hell. Even then I had a feeling I wouldn't be able to keep my hands off you. At the bar, you danced like a siren, so alluring and kissable. I was spinning out of control watching you move. Hell, it was all I could do to bide my time until I could be alone with you." His penetrating gaze pinned her in place, as he asked, "In many ways you're very innocent, aren't you?"

She blinked, trying to digest everything he'd said. She chose to ignore the praise, because she couldn't believe it. No one had ever said things like that to her before. "I have been with men, Dean."

"Still, I have a feeling you're too innocent for a guy like me."

"A guy like you?"

"In the bedroom, I like variety," he murmured. "Do you understand?"

She wondered at that. "No, I don't. Not really."

"You know, handcuffs, paddles, even some role-playing." He winked. "That sort of thing."

"Oh," she said, as X-rated images zipped through her head at the speed of light.

He chuckled. "I take it you've never done any of that?"

She shook her head, feeling very much like a country bumpkin. "I did say I wasn't the adventurous type, remember?"

"See?" He wagged his eyebrows. "Now I want to dirty you up a little."

She laughed. "You're the teacher and I'm the student, is that it?"

He tapped her nose. "You'd look hot in one of those little plaid skirts."

"I can see I'm going to have to tread carefully around you," she teased. "Otherwise you'll corrupt me."

"A little corruption can be fun," he whispered, then he was there again, taking his lips on a sensual journey over her mouth and cheeks. When he kissed his way down over her chin to her neck, Catherine groaned—and promptly surrendered.

Dean had had his fair share of women. Beautiful woman who'd left him gasping and willing to please and be pleased. But there was something about Catherine that set her apart. He couldn't seem to resist her. The predator in him had recognized her vulnerability; it seemed to taunt him to swoop down and snatch her up.

The instant she had walked into Wade and Gracie's home, Dean should've known his days were numbered. Her shiny red hair and lush curves had him impatient to find out for himself whether she was as soft to the touch as she appeared. Dean had always hated women who were too thin. He liked something to hold on to, something to play with, and Catherine had exactly what he craved.

"You do realize that now that I have you here, I won't be letting you go anytime soon," he whispered.

Her gaze narrowed. "What do you mean?"

"This won't be a one-nighter." Dean could see Catherine's willful thoughts in the expressive features of her beautiful face. "I know we both thought so at first, but I've changed my mind. I'm not going to let you simply walk away from me when morning arrives."

"Dean, I—"

He swallowed her words with a quick, hard kiss. Dean didn't want to listen to her protests. He wasn't even sure why he'd brought it up. Besides, the time for words was over. Instead, he intended to hear her cries of pleasure soon. A hell of a lot of pleasure. He wanted Catherine to forget the fact that he didn't trust her. That he may never be able to give her anything more than a few hot moments between the sheets.

Using one hand, Dean began to inch down the side zipper on her dress. He looked into her anxious eyes and growled, "I'm tempted to rip this flimsy thing right down the middle."

Catherine stiffened. "Don't even think it. Gracie bought if for me."

He came down to within a breath of her lips. "As it happens, I like revealing you a little at a time." Dean swept his tongue across Catherine's soft lips. She parted them on a sigh, and he knew it was an invitation to taste her deeper. As he slipped his tongue inside, Dean tasted a hint of chocolate along with a generous amount of Catherine. Her arms came around his neck, pulling him closer. God, she was so damn sweet and tempting, and he wanted more of her.

He lifted an inch. "I want my tongue on other parts of your sexy body, sweetheart."

She licked her lips a few times. "You do?" she finally asked.

He grinned at the breathless way she spoke. "I want to lick your pretty breasts. To taste and tease your nipples into stiff little peaks."

"God, Dean," she moaned, closing her eyes tight. It was as if she thought that would hold back the need.

"After I've had my fill, I'll move lower. Take your pussy into my mouth and feast on your tangy juice."

"You're making me crazy!"

"Good," he growled. "I want you so crazy that you'll beg me to fuck you."

He moved the zipper the last few inches south until finally Dean had her dress open. He saw a hint of red satin, but it wasn't enough. Within seconds, he was tugging it over her head and tossing it onto the end of the bed. He leaned back and looked at her from head to toe. Her bra and panties were a deep shade of red. The color suited the creamy shade of her skin. Between her breasts he spied several freckles that he ached to taste.

"So damn pretty," he murmured, then he dipped his head and licked a fiery path down the valley between her luscious breasts. Dean knew a sense of pride when her body bowed for him. She was so sexy. So eager. Her hands came up and clutched at his hair, pulling hard enough to sting. She brought his mouth more fully against her heated flesh, and Dean obliged by kissing each cute little freckle.

"Dean, please," Catherine softly pleaded.

"Your skin is as soft as silk, sweetheart." With a mere flick of his fingers the front closure on her bra snapped open, causing her full breasts to jiggle a little. "Jesus, I feel like a kid with a present." Seeing the mauve shade of her fat nipples in the soft light for the first time was enough to send him over the edge. "A truly lovely present," he gritted out as his cock responded to the sight.

"That's wonderful but, Dean?"

"Yeah?" He asked, only partly paying attention. He kept getting distracted by the tempting trail of freckles littering her breasts and stomach.

Catherine took hold of his chin and he was forced to look into her eyes. "Can you please stop staring at me and touch me before I explode?"

"Mmm, so demanding," he whispered as he lowered his head and sucked one perfect raspberry nipple into his mouth with ravenous haste.

"Oh, God, yes," Catherine replied in a husky little murmur. The sound sent fire licking through Dean's veins.

12

Dean nibbled at the precious swell of one breast, his need of her uncontrollable. As he moved over her body, crushing her to the mattress beneath, he used his knee to spread her legs wide, then wider still, and he felt her legs lift and wrap around his waist. "That's it," he praised her as he pushed his aching erection against her soft little mound, letting her feel what she did to him.

"Take off your clothes," she gently demanded.

"Soon," he promised, then using both his hands, Dean cuddled and shaped her perfect tits, squeezing one while tasting the other. Catherine writhed shamelessly beneath him. He groaned his approval and released her nipple with an audible pop before moving to the other hard peak. He licked and sucked on her, knowing he could live forever and still need more of her. Dean skated down her body, using his tongue to feel his way, until he was level with her navel. His eyes glazed over when he caught sight of a small gold hoop.

He flicked it with his index finger. "What have we here?"

She peeked down at him, a slight blush covering her cheeks. "Mary made me do it."

"Remind me to thank her then," he uttered in a gruff voice as he let his tongue dip into the sweet indentation, toying playfully at the delicate jewel.

"Oh, Dean, that feels . . . oh, God." Her voice quivered. "I-I need you. Please, quit teasing me this way!"

Dean lifted his head at her restless tone. "I want this to last, Catherine," he explained. "I want your pleasure to go on and on. No way in hell am I going to rush this first time with you."

She groaned, her frustration evident. Dean was unaccountably charmed by her not-so-ladylike pout.

He slowly slipped his hand down her body, committing her curves to memory. When he reached the warm skin of her thigh it was his turn to groan. He skimmed beneath the stretchy, red material of her panties, pleased when he noticed she was already so hot and wet, but it wasn't enough. He wanted to feel her with nothing in his way. He wanted her soaked and eager to take him into her body.

Dean lifted up so he was kneeling between her widespread thighs, and took no time in getting rid of the last bit of silk separating him from paradise. He stared down at the perfection of her luscious body and wanted to praise God for such a work of art. The neatly trimmed tuft of red curls covering her hidden treasures was the sweetest sight indeed. "I want to kiss you here."

"I need your touch there so badly, Dean."

Dean's cock grew painfully hard at Catherine's hungry tone. She craved something adventurous tonight. He knew it was at least half the reason she'd agreed to come home with him. Dean was content to indulge her. In return, he would take a large helping of the sweet dessert he'd craved ever since first seeing her picture.

Without another word between them, Dean left the bed, his

body temperature spiking into the red zone when she whimpered, clearly unhappy that he was no longer lying on top of her. He was tempted to lie back down between her long, shapely legs and sip her honeyed heat, but Dean had a way of doing things, and he wouldn't be denied.

"Stand up for me, little Catherine."

She hesitated for a brief moment, then she rose from the bed, her body as fluid and graceful as a dancer. Dean stepped forward, so he was within touching distance, and then murmured, "I want you to undress me."

Catherine's expressive green eyes stared up at him, the desire he witnessed there nearly sending him to his knees. As Dean's words seemed to register, Catherine's face changed. Now she looked every inch a virgin. It was amazing that one minute she could look like a sly, sexy kitten that had just caught a mouse, then the next so uncertain.

He took hold of her wrist and brought it to his chest. "Start here, sweetheart."

She nodded, and Dean watched her swallow a few times. When the fingers of her right hand stroked slowly over his pectorals, back and forth, her eyes drawn by some imaginary force to the path her hand made over his body, Dean felt his muscles jump beneath his shirt, and he wished her to get on with it.

He wanted her.

Yesterday.

Catherine appeared to have no such intentions though. She seemed intent on massaging his chest and shoulders. Finally, her fingers drifted lower over his abdomen, and Dean flung his head back on a groan. Desire and pain mingled and pushed him precariously close to the edge of control. He was strung as tight as a rubber band, and all she had done was touch him. Over his clothes!

"Mmm, you have the body of a god, Dean," Catherine

whispered. "My first impression was that you looked danger-ous."

Dean's pride came roaring to life in a flash, but the latter de-scription of him didn't sit right. "Dangerous?"

Catherine licked her lips and sighed so loud even Dean heard it. "Yeah, but not in a serial killer way."

"Then in what way am I dangerous?"

"In a big-bad-wolf sort of way, I suppose." She shrugged as she continued to tease her fingers over his chest. "Not that I'm opposed to wolves. I just don't quite know what to do with one."

Dean chuckled at the odd conversation they were having. "Well, if you undress me, then you'll be able to pet me. That's a good start, right?"

She nodded, and her gaze traveled over him. Hell, he wasn't a vain man, but in this one instant Dean was heartily thrilled she found him appealing.

As her fingers delicately tugged at his shirt buttons, pulling them free one by one, Dean's blood pressure skyrocketed. She pulled the hem free of the waistband of his trousers, then pushed the material wide, revealing his chest. Dean took over a second, yanking at the offending material and tossing it to the floor. Now, if he could just move her along a little faster, maybe he would be able to prevent exploding in his pants.

"You are magnificent, Dean. No way am I really here, with you. This has got to be a dream," she murmured. "A really, really lovely dream."

When her fingers encountered his skin, Dean felt scorched. He was forced to count to ten to keep from flinging her to the floor and shoving his heavy cock inside her waiting pussy. Catherine leaned forward and placed a tiny kiss to his left nip-ple, then nipped it with her teeth. Suddenly, it was too much. A haze of dark lust engulfed him.

Dean shoved her away, startling her out of her sexual musings. "You're taking too long," he said by way of explanation. He swiftly stripped out of the rest of his clothes, all the while Catherine's gaze traveling his entire length. When she hesitated on his swollen erection, Dean watched in predatory delight as her eyes went round and her tempting mouth formed a perfect "O." Dean imagined his heavy cock sliding between those succulent lips. He ached to watch her lick and suck and swallow his hot come. Christ, he wanted her a million different ways. It was insane, but he had never felt so out of control for a woman, not even in his youth.

"On the bed," he growled.

His rough words jarred her out of her curious musings, and her eyes shot up to his. "I—I'm not sure I'm ready. I mean, you're so intense and . . ."

Dean could see her shutting down and he wanted to kick himself. He stroked a finger over her plump lips and murmured, "It'll be okay. Don't go shy on me now, sweetheart."

"Well, I did say that I wasn't really the adventurous type, remember?"

"Yes, and I like you just the way you are," he told her as he wrapped his hands around her upper arms and pulled her close. Their bodies touched for the first time without any barriers separating them, and Dean knew he'd died and gone to heaven. "I like that I can turn your body to fire with a mere touch."

"But do I do that to you?"

Ah, so that's what the problem was. He cupped her chin in his palm, forcing her to look at him. "Are you worried you'll disappoint me?"

"I don't know . . . maybe."

"That could never happen, sweetheart," Dean said, as he bent his head and kissed her, licking her soft lips, starved for the unique taste of her. When he lifted his head he noticed Catherine's entire face had gone warm and drowsy with want. He could easily become accustomed to seeing such a lovely sight every night.

Catherine pressed a hand over her lips for a few seconds, as if attempting to contain the kiss. Finally she whispered, "I love the taste of you."

Dean couldn't help the grin that spread across his face. "There's more of me to taste, believe me." Catherine's gaze drifted downward once again, her cheeks going all rosy when she spotted his cock. "You're staring," he murmured, unaccountably charmed by her.

"I'm not sorry."

He laughed. "If I'm ever going to get you past leering at me like I'm a slab of meat, then I'm going to have to take matters into my own hands."

"Oh?"

"I wanted this to be slow and sweet. But I can't wait another minute to have you." Dean took no time in lifting her and placing her in the middle of the bed. Her cry of surprise had his dick swelling another inch.

Catherine lifted to a sitting position and smiled. "Do you know you get very aggressive when you're turned on? Out goes the gentle Dean and in comes the wild beast."

He stepped close to the side of the bed and stared down at her. "Does it bother you?"

She bit her lip and shrugged. "It's sort of sexy," she whispered, as if admitting some deep, dark secret.

Dean wanted to respond, but he was rendered mute when Catherine's hands went to the smooth expanse of her belly. She massaged one palm over her skin, and Dean was mesmerized. Slowly, the hand moved upward, sliding over each breast, kneading and plumping them, then her head fell back as she pinched the raspberry tips. Dean trembled with barely leashed sexual energy. Did she know she was baiting a tiger with her little teasing show? Catherine slipped her delicate fingers over and around the fleshy orbs, and he went rock hard.

"You don't know what you're doing, Catherine," he ground out. "You really shouldn't tempt me."

She opened her eyes at his words and smiled saucily, causing his gut to clench. "Well, you keep talking about wanting to go slow with me. That you want this to be sweet. I don't need that tonight. I only need you. So very badly."

"What are you asking for, sweetheart? Tell me."

"You know," Catherine said, her gaze narrowing in anger. "Don't make me say the words."

Dean placed one fist on the bed and leaned close until they were nose to nose. "In here, in my bed, you say the words," he demanded.

He chin came up and fire lit her eyes. "Fine then," she muttered. "Fuck me, Dean. I want you to fuck me, hard. I want you to send me to the moon."

Dean didn't bother to respond. At once, he was on top of her, pulling her arms above her head and pinning her to the mattress. Catherine gasped and stiffened. Dean didn't give an inch as he used a knee to push her supple thighs wide and rocked against her wet pussy. He felt her slowly relaxing beneath him. She squirmed a little, but when he lowered his head and sucked one stiff nipple into his mouth, Dean was rewarded by a deep moan from Catherine.

Dean took his time, laving and suckling on one breast, then moving to the other. Then he did it all over again. Soon, he could feel her lower body lifting, grinding against his hips, seeking fulfillment. He lifted immediately and demanded, "You do not come until I allow it, Catherine."

"My body might not care if you allow it, Dean," she replied, her voice breathless.

"Mmm, your body knows who the boss is, though, sweetheart."

She swatted the back of his head. "Pretty arrogant, don't you think?"

He chuckled. "Not arrogant, just greedy. I don't want some quick orgasm out of you. I want the mother of all orgasms."

She shook her head and rolled her eyes. "That's the most ridiculous thing I've ever heard. An orgasm is an orgasm."

"Give me a chance to prove you wrong there," he said. "Do as I say. Exactly as I say."

She hesitated, her gaze searching his, before she smiled. "Seeing as how I have nothing to lose, I suppose it doesn't hurt to submit."

"Good thinking," he whispered as his gaze roamed over her tits, reddened from his five o'clock shadow, and he knew she was made for him. Only him. Dean took a few seconds to enjoy the sight of such a beautiful creature before he moved to his knees. He inched his way up her body until he straddled her face. "Suck my cock, Catherine," he murmured. She licked her lips and stared at the head. When she closed her eyes tight, he had a feeling she was trying to take back control of the passion zipping back and forth between them. Dean wouldn't let her. He wanted her to give herself to him completely.

He took his cock in his fist and rubbed it over her lips, back and forth, drawing a bead of moisture to the bulbous tip. "Don't you want a taste?"

As she licked her lips, taking in the sticky fluid, Dean nearly shoved her lips open. When her hands grasped his buttocks and pulled him closer, a haze of lust covered his vision. Catherine's gaze locked with his as she angled her head and sucked his dick into her hot little mouth.

Nothing seemed to matter beyond the feel of her sweet lips wrapped around him so tightly, her tongue stroking him as if he was her tasty treat.

"Catherine." Her name, thickly garbled, was all that emerged from his lips.

She kept her eyes trained on his while he placed one large hand at the back of her head and pulled her farther onto him. Dean could feel the head of his dick at the back of her throat. She gagged a little, and he quickly pulled back. "Fuck, sorry," he muttered.

Catherine didn't respond. She merely wrapped her lips around his dick again and hummed in pleasure. The vibrations moved over his entire length, driving him to the very brink. Having Catherine love him this way somehow seemed even more intimate than any other. She had the power to bring him to his knees, begging. Her hand came up and cupped his sac, squeezing gently, and Dean was forced to shut his eyes and concentrate on not coming too soon. He threw his head back on a groan as Catherine allowed her hands and mouth to play with him. Her tongue probed the slit in the tip, and her hand massaged his balls. If he wasn't so anxious to taste hot pussy, he would've gladly let the pleasurable torture continue until he gave her a mouthful of his cream.

He was both relieved and displeased when she slid her mouth backward and off him. "Kiss it," he growled. When she obeyed, letting her lips give a loving kiss to his tip, Dean nearly came. She started to suck him in again, and Dean had to stop her with a gentle pull of her hair.

"What? You didn't like it?"

"I fucking loved it," he gritted out. "Too much."

When she smiled like the Cheshire cat, Dean silently vowed she would know the taste of his come. Soon, she would be drinking his hot seed. For now, he wanted to feel the tight clutch of her pussy with his lips and tongue. He wanted her tangy juice coating his mouth and chin.

13

Catherine couldn't think straight, could barely breathe as Dean moved to lie on top of her and pressed his lips to the pulse in her neck. "Oh, yeah," she moaned, digging her fingers into his mass of dark hair to hold him firm while he suckled her skin. She ached to feel those lips and that tongue lower. So much lower.

As if she'd spoken the thought aloud, Dean inched downward, touching off several spasms as he went. When his tongue flicked over one hard nipple, Catherine nearly shot off the bed. She forgot her misgivings. All her worries about what a huge mistake she was making vanished. Her body only craved Dean's touch. It'd been so long since she'd let herself go. Since she'd tossed caution to the wind. And it'd been way too long since she'd derived any real pleasure from a man.

With slow, sweeping movements, designed to drive her wild no doubt, Dean ran his tongue back and forth over her areola, then he sucked her nipple into his warm mouth and savored it. He hummed in satisfaction, and the raspy vibration of his voice tormented her oversensitive skin further. His hands on either side of her body effectively pinned her to the bed. She was surrounded by his lethal strength, and she reveled in it.

While he switched to her other breast, Catherine marveled at his patience; he appeared to have great stores of it. Dean seemed to be settling in for a Thanksgiving feast with the way he laved at her skin and toyed with all her hot spots.

As she urged him lower with a tug on his hair, Dean obliged by moving his loving torture south. Her body knew what was coming and reacted with a flow of moisture to her pussy. God, every inch of her seemed ready for him to take her.

"Please, Dean," she shamelessly begged.

A grunt was her only indication that he'd even heard her plea. Every inch of skin he encountered received a kiss until by the time he had reached his destination, Catherine was on fire.

He sat back on his haunches and stared down at her naked body. "You're beautiful, you know."

She could barely think, let alone speak. A quivery "thank you" was all she could muster.

Dean passed a hand over his face and grumbled, "Damn it. Wade's right, I never should've touched you. I should've kept my distance. You're way too nice for someone like me."

Okay, that brought her back to reality. Catherine reached down and smoothed a palm over his thick hair. "You aren't exactly a loser, Dean. And I'm not here against my will either."

Dean cupped her mound in his palm. "Whatever," he said, "All I know is I'm not stopping now."

"Thank goodness for that." She tried to maintain her cool composure, but when his middle finger found its way through her curls and sank all the way to the knuckle inside her heat, she gave up any pretense of control over her own body.

"Mmm, just look at you." He groaned. "This hot, wet pussy needs to come, and I'm going to seriously enjoy hearing you scream when you do."

When a second finger joined the first, Catherine succumbed

to the passion riding her body. Her hips began to move, matching his pumping rhythm, and her blood flowed hot in her veins. Dean thrust his fingers in and out several times. Catherine moaned. When he brought both digits all the way out, she wanted to beg him to come back, but her words died in her throat as she watched him suck her juices off.

"Tangy," he whispered. "And so damn delicious."

As he spread her legs wider and dipped his head between her thighs, teasing her clit with his tongue, Catherine arched upward and cried out his name.

"Fuck, yeah, sweetheart," he mumbled against her mound, then all at once Dean was there, holding her down with an arm over her stomach, while he sipped at her pussy.

Catherine writhed under his pleasurable assault, but when his tongue dipped in and out, she was swept into a different plane of existence. He suckled her clit and she lost control, bucking wildly beneath him. Dean nibbled and flicked it several times with the tip of his tongue until Catherine burst apart, shouting out her orgasm as her come flowed into his mouth.

Neither of them moved for several seconds after her orgasm ended, as little aftershocks kept her on the very edge.

When Dean lifted his head, Catherine heard him curse. Her eyes drifted open and their gazes met. "You're so damn hot," he growled.

Catherine couldn't respond, didn't know how. No one had ever said something so sexy to her. The words were short and succinct, but it was all Dean and she loved it. As Dean swept his rough palms over her breasts, praising her body with his touches, Catherine climbed the cliff of desire all over again. Her legs trembled and her pussy throbbed for Dean's touch.

He moved and grabbed a condom. After he ripped the wrapper and rolled it down his thick erection, he covered her with his large, powerful frame. "Wrap those silky legs around my waist, pretty Catherine." She immediately complied, lifting and bringing them closer together. "That's good," Dean said against the shell of her ear. She felt him inch his way into her tight heat. He moved slowly at first, a little at a time to allow her body to become accustomed to his size, until he was fully imbedded inside her pussy.

"Oh, God," she groaned.

He stilled, every muscle going rigid. "Too much?"

"No!" Catherine tightened her legs around his waist, keeping him firmly inside her. "Please don't stop now. You feel . . ." Catherine left the statement hanging, unable to describe the incredible pleasure-pain of his cock stretching and filling her.

"No way in hell," he promised, as he moved gently in and out. "Son of a bitch, you feel good. So tight and hot," he said, then he moved back, sitting on his heels. "Lift up for me. I want to suck your nipples."

Catherine pushed herself upward and wrapped her arms around his neck to keep from falling back to the bed. Now she was practically sitting in Dean's lap, his cock seated deep. When Dean leaned forward and sucked one peak then the other, Catherine surrendered and smashed her tits against his face. Dean bit her nipple and laved at each one with slow precision, deriving several whimpers from her.

"Reach down and make yourself come," he quietly ordered. "Do it now, sweetheart. I won't have the control to hold myself back much longer."

Catherine rose up and down on his shaft, fucking him slowly, leisurely, then she slipped her right hand between their bodies and began playing with her clitoris, flicking and tugging the swollen button over and over. As her orgasm began to build, Dean pulled out all the way, then he wrapped his hands around her waist and shoved her onto his engorged length once more. "Yeah, that's what I need. God, I love the way your body wraps around my dick. So tight. So mine."

Catherine's blood raced and her legs tightened around his

hips as she continued to rub and pump her clit. Once. Twice. Her pussy clenched. It was too much. It was all she needed, all she could take. Throbs turned to spasms as Catherine moaned and threw her head backward, coming apart and shattering into a million pieces once more. Dean was right there with her as he shouted her name and found his own release. Hot come filled the condom as his cock pulsed and emptied into her limp body.

By the time Dean loosened his hold on her, Catherine had come back to earth. He placed a kiss to her forehead and cheeks, and Catherine melted a little more. "You're amazing," he said as he took hold of her head on both sides. "You make me crazy."

Catherine didn't know how to respond. Crazy didn't seem so much like a good thing to her. And she was too exhausted to bother removing herself from Dean's firm embrace. She wanted to ask him to explain his statement, but she just couldn't muster the strength.

Instead she opted to kiss him. He quickly took over, slipping his tongue into her mouth and angling her head for a better fit. His hands sifted through her hair and held her still for his intimate invasion. Catherine tasted his warmth and masculinity. It was a flavor she wanted on her tongue over and over again. She was afraid she would crave his flavor now.

Lifting away, his hands still wrapped in her hair, Dean said, "What you do to me . . . it's not like anything else. I don't know what it is, and putting my feelings into words is sort of foreign to me. All I know is that it's unique."

Was Dean saying he cared for her? Catherine was much too afraid to hope, so instead she blurted out the first thing that came to mind. "Sex, Dean. It was great, but is it really any more than that?"

He was silent, staring at her with eyes that saw way too much. She looked away, unable to face the awful truth. That he enjoyed her body but may never trust her enough to want more from her.

"It's more than sex."

The hard tone of his voice had Catherine swinging her head back around. His eyes had gone cold. Great, she'd made him angry. Worse, she didn't know what to say. Her emotions were all mixed up when it came to this man. Unable to think straight, Catherine lifted off his lap and went into an adjoining room, hoping it was a bathroom. She flicked a switch on the wall and saw a faucet. At least she'd gotten one thing right.

Catherine closed the door and looked around the room. Beige walls, double black sinks, and recessed lighting. The natural slate tile around the tub and inside the shower only added to the character and class of the room. She'd noticed the warmth of the tiled floor beneath her bare feet and wondered if it was heated. As she stared longingly at the huge Jacuzzi-style tub, Catherine wished she could take a long, hot soak. But she was too anxious and uncertain. Instead she opted for a quick washup.

Her hair was a wreck, and she had red splotches all over her skin from Dean's touches and kisses. She looked . . . thoroughly loved. She shook her head and left the bathroom, but when she came back into the bedroom, Dean was already sprawled out on the bed with the covers up to his waist. She wanted to join him, but was she supposed to do that? This was her first one-night stand and she didn't know the rules.

Catherine crossed her arms over her breasts, suddenly feeling very naked. "I suppose I should go home," she offered.

Dean watched her in silence for a few seconds before extending a hand to her. "Stay," he said, his voice low and rough.

She couldn't discern his mood and she wasn't sure staying was a great idea, but she really didn't want the evening to end either. When she crossed the room and slipped under the covers, Dean reached over and turned off the light. A long time passed, neither of them talking or touching, and Catherine felt hollow and cold. She wanted him to hold her. She wanted to feel his warmth surrounding her. To sleep in his arms, his strength and heat enfolding her in a safe cocoon.

Suddenly, Catherine felt an arm around her middle as Dean effortlessly dragged her across the expanse separating them. He pulled her into his body, her back against his chest and slung one muscled thigh over her legs. "You're a stubborn woman, Catherine Michaels, and I have a feeling you're going to turn my world upside down."

Catherine's eyes burned with unshed tears, and her voice shook when she admitted, "It wasn't just sex to me either."

Dean's lips brushed the back of her head. "Sleep for now, sweetheart. We'll figure this thing out, I promise."

Catherine didn't bother to dispute him, even though she knew firsthand that to believe in a promise was like buying into false advertising. The consumer always ended up the loser.

14

Catherine woke to warmth. Too much of it actually. Usually she froze half to death at night, so why was she so warm? As she shifted around, Catherine realized her bed was lumpy and hard. What the—but then it all came slamming back at her. The nightclub. The man. The sex. Oh, God, the really great sex.

Something wet swept across her cheek, and Catherine wiped her cheek and frowned. She pried one eye open, then nearly came out of her skin when she saw a large mass of fur and teeth staring her in the face.

"Uh, nice doggie." Catherine deliberately kept her tone soft in the hopes of not riling the animal. The dog, a Rottweiler if she wasn't mistaken, only continued to stare at her, his tongue hanging out of one side of his mouth. She couldn't tell if the big animal was happy or hungry. She peeked around the bulky body and noticed the mutt's stubby tail wagging back and forth. "Okay, that's a good sign." Deciding to take a chance that the large toothy creature was friendly, Catherine reached out a hand, palm up, and let him investigate. He sniffed her first, then as if satisfied with her scent he proceeded to lick her.

"Now that we have the meet and greet over with, I can honestly say you are a really intimidating dog." When he plopped his large head on her stomach, all but begging to be petted, Catherine smiled and gave in. His fur was soft and shiny, well cared for. Dean had a dog? Why hadn't she seen him before? "You're a big pushover, aren't you?" She frowned as something else occurred to her. "And where is your owner?" Dean was nowhere in sight. She stretched her arms above her head, yawning herself awake, and wondered if he'd sent the dog in his place so he wouldn't have to deal with the awkward morning after. "He's not getting off that easily," Catherine said to the dog as she gently pushed the Rott off her stomach and legs. When feeling came back to her limbs, she breathed a sigh of relief. "Good, I'm not paralyzed. Things are looking up." When she stood, the cool air in the room brought goose bumps to the surface. She'd slept naked. It'd been great while she was cuddled up to Dean, all warm and cozy. She let a grin slip over her face as she recalled the way he'd woken her in the middle of the night to make love to her. Twice. It'd been pure bliss both times.

"Okay, sleeping with the man was probably not the smartest thing I've ever done," she mumbled to herself. Try as she might, Catherine couldn't quite bring herself to regret it either, even though she had no idea what it meant for their relationship, or lack thereof. Dean had been passionate and sweet and totally overwhelming. It'd been so perfect it was scary.

But not exactly smart.

Catherine looked at the dog, his big body sprawled out on the bed and sending her curious looks every so often, then said, "Still, aren't I allowed one stupid act in a lifetime? I've been under a lot of stress." When the dog only closed his eyes and began to snore, Catherine decided she wasn't going to get any answers standing naked in the middle of the room and talking to a Rottweiler. Might as well find something to wear.

She sighed as she glanced around the room for a chest of drawers or an old T-shirt flung over a chair. When she spotted a closet, Catherine crossed the room and pushed at the sliding door. She saw several long-sleeve shirts. Would he be upset if she helped herself? She shrugged and grabbed a black one. After she had it on she fixed the collar, and that's when a familiar scent hit her. She tugged the shirt up to her nose and inhaled. Dean. His strong, masculine scent filled her nostrils. God, it was intoxicating.

She went into the bathroom and caught sight of her reflection in the large, rectangular mirror that sat above the counter. "Holy mother, I look like crap."

Her skin was scraped raw from where Dean's whiskers had abraded her skin. He'd kissed every inch of her face, and now she had a rosy-cheeked look—which was not a pretty sight for a redhead. The juncture between her thighs began to throb at the memory of his sexy mouth kissing every inch of her body. He'd been so talented with that mouth of his. She wanted to experience it again. "One-night stand, my butt," she muttered. She'd need several weeks to get the man out of her system.

Of course if something wasn't done with her hair, she would end up scaring the daylights out of the poor man. She never had been one of those women who woke up looking refreshed. No, usually she woke looking like something the dog had dragged in. She thought of the big Rott on the bed in the other room and laughed.

She turned on the cold water and splashed her face several times. It helped to take some of the redness out of her cheeks, but her hair was way beyond repair. She'd need a shower to fix such a pathetic mess, but she didn't want to waste another second. She wanted to find Dean. Then maybe they could share a really long . . . good-bye kiss. *Now, that wasn't at all a pleasant thought.* She shook the thought away and did her best to wipe away her leftover makeup, then used some toothpaste and her finger to scrub her teeth. Catherine tried to finger comb her hair, but if anything it got worse.

"Wow, what would Mary say if she could see you now?" Catherine asked her reflection.

At the thought of her dearest and oldest friend, Catherine grinned from ear to ear. If Mary could see her now she'd be floored. Catherine never strayed from the straight and narrow, whereas Mary happily kept to the curves.

Catherine left the bathroom behind and headed toward her cell phone, which she'd left on the bedside table. She picked it up and dialed. Mary answered on the first ring.

"This better damn well be good or you're dead meat."

"Good morning, hon," Catherine said by way of greeting.

"Cat?" Mary asked, more alert now. "What's wrong?"

"Everything is fine. Better than fine, in fact."

"You did something naughty."

Catherine slumped onto the side of the bed. "How can you possibly know?"

"You had the same tone when you stuck a tack on Christopher Blythe's chair in the tenth grade."

Catherine remembered the incident well. Christopher had tormented her to the point she'd lost it and decided to turn the tables and give the jerk a taste of his own medicine. "Lordy, that was probably the last time I've done anything wild and impulsive."

Silence from the other end, and then, "Impulsive, huh? Spill."

"I slept with Dean," Catherine blurted out as she picked at the hem of Dean's shirt.

"You did?" Mary asked in a bewildered tone. "I thought you said he hated you?"

"He still doesn't trust me, and I'm not sure sleeping with the man was a good idea, but I don't regret it." She squared her shoulders as she imparted that little truth. "Not one glorious minute of it."

Mary laughed. "You slut, you!"

"I'll tell you more later. For now I have to try and escape with my dignity intact. This morning-after stuff is for the birds."

"Hold your head up high, hon, and he'll be begging for more of your hot bod."

She laughed at the crazy notion. Deep down, Catherine worried that she may never see Dean again. That maybe he'd avoid her like the plague now that he'd gotten what he wanted from her. "I'll call you when I get back to the hotel. Go back to sleep."

"Oh, I intend to. Keep me posted."

"I will." They said their good-byes and hung up. She put the phone back on the stand and headed out of the room. When she entered the kitchen she spotted Dean sitting at the table. He didn't have a shirt on. His shoulder muscles caught her attention, and she had to force herself not to drool. She noticed he'd pulled on a pair of navy blue striped pajama pants. He was adorable, and she wanted to cross the room and straddle him. She didn't, of course. The bold Catherine was gone. In the bright light of day she was back to being her usual boring self. Lovely.

She shored up her nerve, cleared her throat, and stood a little straighter. "Dean?"

He turned in his chair, and suddenly two sets of eyes were on her at once. Catherine inhaled sharply as she saw Deanna seated across the table. "Catherine, what are you—" She stopped midsentence as her gaze moved downward. Dean, the big idiot, merely sat there staring. If Catherine didn't miss her guess she thought the look he sent her was one of disapproval. What was that about?

Too late it registered in Catherine's mind exactly why they both seemed shell-shocked. All she'd bothered to put on was Dean's black shirt, which hit her midthigh. Crap.

Abruptly, Dean stood just as Catherine swiveled on her heel, ready to retreat from the weird spot she found herself in, when she felt Dean's hand on her shoulder, halting her flight. With one sinewy arm he pulled her up against the front of him. Catherine stumbled and tried desperately to dislodge herself, but his hold only tightened. He chuckled low under his breath, and Catherine wanted to strangle him.

She turned around, ready to blast him, but Dean descended on her, kissing her in the most passionate way. Forgetting they had an audience, Catherine went up on her tiptoes and flung her arms around his neck, then sank body and soul into the kiss. In an instant, her body was ready for him. Liquid fire flowed through her veins. His hands grasped onto her arms in a rough, bruising hold. She would have even more marks on her, but she didn't care. She wanted this. She ached for him. Catherine pressed her lips to his, enjoying the taste of him first thing in the morning. He pried her mouth open with his tongue and slipped inside the dark recess. Dean played, their tongues tangling and dueling. Unfortunately, her brain kicked in and kicked her libido to the curb. Catherine tore her mouth away from his, momentarily caught by the way he licked his lips and stared down at her as if he wanted to take their little party into the bedroom. His dark, hooded eyes sent a shiver up her spine. Dean looked determined, and despite the fact that Deanna was mere feet away, Catherine had the urge to finish what Dean had started. Another voice intruded on her wayward thoughts, forcing her back to the here and now.

"Uh, sorry to pop in like this. I honestly didn't know Dean had company."

Dean cursed under his breath, then slowly released her. He turned his attention to his twin, and Catherine could swear she saw smoke coming out of his ears. "You need to learn to call first, little sister."

If the sudden burst of laughter was anything to go by, Catherine would say that Deanna didn't seem at all fazed by Dean's belligerent attitude. "I'm family, Dean. We get special privileges."

Dean shoved a hand through his hair, clearly losing his patience. "How about you leave and come back later," he muttered. "Much later."

As the pair of siblings argued, Catherine saw her chance to slip out of the room. Standing mostly naked in the kitchen while Dean argued with his twin was simply too much for her Southern sensibilities. As she turned to go, Dean caught her arm. "Where are you going?"

"Clothes, Dean, clothes," she shot right back.

"I'm only going to have to take them back off. May as well stay the way you are."

Her face heated and she heard Deanna snicker. "Dean, you're embarrassing me," she said under her breath.

"Dean, we really do need to talk. Give Catherine a few minutes to pull herself together."

Finally, the voice of reason, Catherine thought. Dean didn't bother to acknowledge his sister though. The infernal man cupped her cheek and whispered, "I loved every minute of last night, sweetheart."

Unable to form a clear thought, Catherine stammered, and before she could take her next breath, Dean swept her off her feet and into his arms. He held her against the solid wall of his chest and strode right out of the room, leaving Deanna calling his name.

Catherine looked into his eyes and witnessed his fixed expression. He was every inch the possessive male. "Dean, you can't leave your sister out there. Think about what you're doing." She was mortified, but turned on too. She wanted him so badly that she was terribly afraid she wouldn't protest if he tried to get her into bed.

"You look so goddamn good in my shirt," he groaned as he walked into the bedroom. "Deanna has terrible timing."

Catherine had to agree with him there. Still, things had gone too far as it was. She pushed at his chest and said, "Put me down and go back out there and visit with your sister."

Dean blinked several times, as if coming out of his lust-filled haze, and frowned down at her. "You're lucky she's here."

His arrogant words brought her feminine pride to the forefront. "Oh really?"

"Really. I'm this close to bending you over the bed and fucking you until we both cry uncle."

Her pussy flooded with liquid desire at the coarse language. His voice, so silky smooth, held promises of sensual delights. Putty, that's what he'd done to her. Turned her into putty. "I tend to . . . scream. It would end up embarrassing for both of us."

Dean smiled, sending her heart into a tailspin. "I do so enjoy it when you scream." With obvious regret, he put her back on her feet in front of the bed. "Don't take too long." His gaze landed on the dog. The big animal seemed completely oblivious to the turmoil going on around him. Dean quirked a brow. "Did he scare you?"

"At first." She shrugged. "I figured out pretty quick that he's something of a softy."

Dean laughed. "He's my neighbor's dog. He stopped by earlier to ask if I could dog sit while he's out of town for a few days." He frowned and rubbed his jaw. "I should've warned you. Sorry about that."

Something about the stiff way the words had come out told Catherine that Dean didn't apologize all that often. When she leaned down to scratch the big animal behind the ear, she thought of how nice it would've been if she'd known they weren't alone in the house. "I don't mind waking up to find the dog, but walking into the kitchen in this—" She plucked at the shirt. "And finding your sister sitting at your kitchen table is not something I ever want to repeat."

"Yeah, I wasn't thinking."

"I gathered that." The dog began to snore, catching her attention once more. "This big lug and I came to an understanding. So, no harm done."

"Oh? And what's that?"

"We decided I was A-OK and that he didn't have to eat me."

"His name is Duke," Dean said as he tugged on her hair. Her gaze caught his. "Duke might not want to eat you, but I intend to get my fill of you later."

And there went her pulse again, pounding out an erratic rhythm. "Sister. Kitchen. Go."

Dean winked, then he was gone. Catherine slumped onto the bed. "What have I gotten myself into?"

15

The sight of Catherine as she'd stood in his kitchen would be forever tattooed onto his brain. Hell, his black shirt had never looked so good. Her curves had pulled the material tight. Her tangled mass of red hair falling down around her shoulders all but begged him to sink his fingers in and get good and lost. Her bare legs and feet had been the final straw. He'd forgotten about Dee. All he could think in that moment was getting Catherine back to bed where he could love that voluptuous body for the next few hours.

"Uh, earth to Dean," Deanna said. "Come in, Dean."

His morning definitely wasn't going as planned. He'd envisioned waking up to Catherine all cuddled close and slowly rousing her up with his kisses. Instead, the doorbell had woken him and everything had gone to shit. He never should've answered the damn door.

Dean shook his head and went straight for the coffeepot. He grabbed the glass carafe and brought it to the table, then poured himself another cup. He had a feeling he was going to need it. "Want another?"

"No, I'm good." Dean barely had the pot back on the warmer when Deanna began to hammer him with questions. "You and Catherine, huh? When did that happen? Does Wade know?"

Dean crossed his arms over his chest and stared down at her. "Not that it's any of your business, right?"

She pointed a finger at him. "Hey, you nosed into my business when I started seeing Jonas. Turnabout is fair play, brother."

He supposed she had a point there. He took his seat and looked down at his mug, uncertain how to respond. "Last night. That's all there is to Catherine and me. And yes, Wade knows. He's not thrilled, but he knows."

Deanna leaned across the table and in a quieter tone she asked, "One night? She's Gracie's sister, Dean. Not some hot little piece you picked up at a bar."

He rolled his eyes. "Christ, Dee, don't you think I know that?"

"Then what are you doing messing around with her? Do you care about her?"

He thought of how perfect they'd been together and he was tempted to say yes, but he couldn't let himself be blind to the fact that he still didn't trust Catherine. A single night of sex hadn't changed his mind about her. "Look, I'm not sure if she has something up her sleeve. Everything points to the fact that she doesn't, I know, but—"

"She's here for one reason, Dean—to get to know her sister. Why can't you accept that?"

Dean had no answer for that. The hair on his neck stood up whenever he thought of trusting her, and he needed to know why. "There's something she isn't telling. I can feel it."

Deanna shook her head and looked away, but not before Dean saw the sadness in her eyes. She was worried about him, and he hated it. He reached across the table and took her hand in his. "It's going to be fine."

She snorted. "It's not you I'm concerned about. Catherine is a sweet person. Kind, gentle. Her adoptive parents are dead. All she has is Gracie."

His chest tightened when he thought of all that Catherine had been through. He didn't like to think of her hurting and in pain. "What's your point?" he bit out, getting angry and not sure why.

"My point is that she's vulnerable right now, and all you're going to end up doing is confusing her."

Dean shoved his chair back and stood. Christ, when had things gotten so damn complicated? "Look, I know you mean well, but you need to butt out of this one, Dee. This is between Catherine and me. No one else."

"Fine, but you might want to ask yourself why you're so drawn to her. She's not like the other women you've dated."

He pushed his mug away, no longer interested in the hot brew. At the mention of other women, Dean immediately thought of Linda. She'd seemed sweet and gentle too. So had the two women he'd dated before Linda. Right up until they'd kicked him in the gut. "And what would you know about my personal life?"

"I know enough to know that you pick women who know the ropes. You don't date a woman because she makes you laugh or can engage in intelligent conversation. You date for one reason only."

"Christ, Dee, you make me sound like a world-class prick."

Deanna stood and went to him. "No, you're not a prick," she replied softly, "but you are a guy who guards his heart with a double-edged blade."

"Whatever," he ground out. "It doesn't change the fact that you need to mind your own business."

"Only if you'll promise to be careful. She deserves that much, don't you think?"

"The only thing I can promise is that before she goes back to Georgia I'll have my answers."

"Answers? Is that what this was all about?" The questions hadn't come from his sister. Dean cursed under his breath and turned to find Catherine standing on the other side of the room, dressed in her wrinkled dress and staring at him as if he'd kicked her puppy. Fuck. He started for her, but she put up a hand, green fire shooting from her eyes. Damn, if looks could kill he'd be a dead man.

"Don't," she said, her voice a little unsteady. She dismissed him altogether and looked toward his sister. "Can you please take me back to my hotel?"

"Uh, sure."

"Catherine," Dean growled.

To Dean's horror, Catherine's lower lip quivered. "Please, you've said enough."

Dean felt like someone was ripping his heart out of his chest when Catherine left the kitchen. He watched as she pulled on her coat and waited for Deanna by the door. His sister pulled him down for a hug and whispered, "I'll talk to her."

He shook his head. "My mess," he said around the rock suddenly lodged in his throat.

"My fault," she whispered right back.

When Deanna released him and went to pull her coat on, Dean started across the room. He couldn't let Catherine leave. Not like this. But damn if he wasn't quick enough. Catherine made it out the door and partway down the sidewalk, hell bent on getting away from him, before he could reach the living room. Deanna looked at him and shook her head in sympathy, then took off after her.

Dean was forced to stand by and watch as they pulled away. He willed Catherine to look back at him. She didn't. Damn,

116 / Anne Rainey

he'd screwed up royally this time, and he desperately needed to fix it. He wouldn't let her walk away that easily. If she didn't listen to reason on her own accord, then he'd just have to tie her pretty ass to the bed and force her to listen.

Catherine waited until she was inside her hotel suite before she let the tears fall. Her purse dropped to the floor by the door, and her legs shook as she headed to the couch. God, she'd been such a fool thinking Dean might've actually wanted her. The entire time he'd only been working her, hoping to get under her defenses so he could learn all her deep, dark secrets. If only he could see the truth, that there weren't any damn secrets.

Deanna had tried talking to her in the car on the way back to the hotel, but Catherine hadn't heard half of what she'd said. Her ears were still ringing from Dean's vow to get answers. Catherine's stomach knotted as she recalled the way she'd hurried to get dressed. She'd been so anxious to get back to Dean. Her body had burned and her insides felt scorched by the sinful promises he'd spoken before leaving her next to his bed. Her mind had taken a pretty X-rated turn as she'd imagined what other sexual adventures Dean might have in store for her. Catherine had conjured up all sorts of things as she'd slipped into her badly wrinkled dress and uncomfortable shoes. As she'd stepped into the kitchen, overhearing Dean talking about her as if they hadn't just spent the entire night loving each other, Catherine's libido had all but shriveled and died.

"I'm such a pathetic fool," she groaned as she closed her eyes and breathed deeply. Several deep inhales and exhales later, she felt more in control and less like she would shatter at any given moment.

"Get hold of yourself," she gritted out. "He's just a man and it was one night. You've managed worse situations." When she opened her eyes and stood, she became aware that she still wore her coat. She tossed it onto the couch before kicking her shoes off. She thought about calling Mary. She was always good for a shoulder to cry on, but Catherine didn't really want to talk to anyone about Dean. The pain was too sharp at the moment.

As she went into the bathroom, Catherine turned on the light and got a good look at herself in the mirror. "God, I look like . . . sex. Messy, frantic, lust-filled sex." It had been fantastic, too, right up until the bubble had burst thanks to Dean's big mouth. "Distrustful Neanderthal," she muttered as anger finally took the place of pain. Dean had been great, but it was over. Time to move on. What she really needed was a long, hot shower, then she'd call Gracie. Her sister was the reason she'd come to Ohio in the first place. Dean didn't have a thing to do with it.

Having given herself that pep talk, Catherine stripped out of her clothes and stepped into a hot shower. In her mind, she heard Dean's last words, though, and she felt the stab to her heart all over again.

The water went cold before Catherine's second crying jag was over. She got out and wrapped a towel around her body. As she tucked a lock of hair behind her ear, Catherine heard a knock on the door. She frowned and left the bathroom, wondering who it could be.

When she looked through the peephole, she frowned and pulled the door open. Gracie and Wade stood in the hallway. Catherine easily saw the worry on Gracie's face. "Deanna called you, huh?"

Gracie nodded. Catherine let them in and closed the door behind them. She wanted to reassure them, but before she got the chance, Gracie was pulling her into her arms and giving her a big hug. Catherine had to force back the emotion clogging her throat. When Gracie pulled back she said, "I could kick Dean for this, I swear."

"No need," Wade chimed in. "I'll beat the crap out of him and solve all our problems."

Catherine's heart swelled at the way the pair rallied around her. She smiled, hoping to keep the conversation light. "It's fine, really." She looked down at her towel-clad body and said, "Let me just get dressed, then we can go see that movie."

"Are you sure you still want to go? We don't have to if you aren't up to it, I mean."

"I definitely want to," Catherine said, and meant it. Dean wasn't going to spoil the little bit of time she had with her sister. Catherine quickly left the room. As she entered the bedroom she closed the double doors and went about getting dressed. By the time she had on jeans and a brown scoop neck blouse, Catherine's hair was nearly dry. She decided a ponytail would be the quickest fix. Within minutes she reentered the living room. "Ready?"

Wade and Gracie's gaze landed on her, and she knew they weren't quite buying her act. "Catherine, we can both see you aren't fine."

She waved a hand in the air. "He said some hurtful things, but it doesn't matter. Dean didn't make me any promises. I knew what I was doing when I went home with him. I'm a big girl. I can handle a little rejection." *God, please let them believe me.* Catherine had zero desire to dig around in her bruised heart at the moment. She'd had enough crying for one day.

"I don't know what Dean's problem is," Wade bit out, "but I'm putting a stop to it."

Catherine heard the severity in Wade's tone and it shook her. "I don't want you and Dean fighting because of me. Please, I couldn't stand it if I was the cause of some family feud." She'd never been a weak woman. In fact, she was usually pretty confident, but with Wade ready to fight her battles and Gracie's need to shelter and protect, Catherine was more than a little shaken. She'd never experienced that sort of loving devotion.

She'd always known a parent's love, but it had been different. This made her feel cherished, even though she hadn't known either of them for very long.

On impulse, Catherine went to Wade and hugged him. "Thank you," she said. His arms wrapped around her in a tight bear hug, and that's when she knew. He did truly care. Like a brother might care for a sister. It felt good to have him in her corner. She stepped back and looked over at Gracie and saw the tears shining in her eyes. "I can't tell you how much it means to know that you two are here for me."

"That's what family is for," Gracie said with a small smile.

"I know, but this thing between Dean and me, it's complicated."

Wade laughed. "You're trying to tell us in a nice way that our help isn't required, aren't you?"

Catherine winced, knowing how ungrateful she seemed. "Something like that. Although it is appreciated."

"Okay, but I still want to punch him."

She shook her head. "If violence is needed, I'll be the one dishing it out."

Gracie nodded. "Get him, sis!"

"Darn straight," Catherine said, feeling a fraction better. For the first time since Dean had opened his big mouth, Catherine felt a real smile coming on. "Now, how about we go see that movie?"

Gracie still appeared unconvinced, but in the end she relented. "I hope he's at home rotting in his own misery."

Catherine didn't want to think about what Dean might be doing. That road led to disaster. She grabbed her coat and purse, and the three of them left the suite. Wade dropped Catherine and Gracie off at the mall, giving them time alone, and promised to swing by and pick them up after their movie to take them to dinner.

Fifteen minutes into the flick, Catherine discovered she was actually having a good time. She'd learned that Gracie had the same love of movie theater popcorn as she did. They shared a big tub, and it wasn't until the credits were rolling and the lights came back on that Dean's hurtful words came back to her.

"Come on," Gracie said, as she tugged her out of the theater. "It's time for some girl talk."

They entered a little café on the second floor of the mall, and Gracie ordered them both a cup of coffee while Catherine found a table for them near the back. After they were seated, Catherine said, "Clearly putting on a brave front is a waste of time."

Gracie blew on her coffee, then said, "I was always terrible at hiding my emotions from Wade. He can see right through me."

"I don't know why Dean is so bent on thinking the worst of me." Catherine squeezed her eyes closed tight. "He's so hard-headed."

Gracie snorted. "He's a Harrison, so that explains the hard-headed part."

Catherine thought of the conversation she'd had with Deanna in the car on the way to the hotel from Dean's house. "Yeah, I can see it runs in the family. Deanna was intent on making me see that Dean didn't mean what he said. The thing is, I heard it with my own ears."

"Deanna didn't tell us what happened exactly. She only said that Dean spoke without thinking and that you got hurt because of it. That alone was enough to send Wade into a tizzy."

Catherine took a sip of her coffee. It was too hot to drink yet and she ended up burning her tongue. She barely noticed though. "The night we shared was so wonderful, Gracie. Dean was attentive, gentle, rough, and completely insatiable."

Gracie winked. "So far, so good."

"He seemed to really want me. The way I wanted him. It felt

right, but I'd been deluding myself because all he'd wanted was answers. The sex was nothing more than a means to an end."

Gracie's brows scrunched together. "Are you saying he was only using you?"

Catherine nodded. "He said as much. The joke's on him though, because I have no answers to give him. The idiot won't listen to reason, of course."

"God, Catherine, I can't imagine how you must feel." Gracie frowned. "I'm surprised he'd do something so callous. I really thought he was into you."

"Yeah, he's really great at pretending, I guess." She thought of how many times he'd come, and doubt started to seep in. A man couldn't fake that sort of thing. He'd turned to her again and again, wanting her with such intensity.

"Are you sure he wasn't just spouting off? Men sometimes say things when they're angry that they don't mean. Women too, for that matter."

Catherine wasn't sure of anything anymore. "It seemed like he sincerely enjoyed our night together." She looked across the table at her sister. "Should I give him a chance to explain?"

"At this point, I don't see how it can hurt." She paused before adding, "Not that he deserves it."

Maybe Gracie was right, but Catherine had a terrible feeling that if she wasn't careful, Dean was going to end up breaking her heart.

16

After Catherine had left, Dean had done some serious think-ing. He'd hurt Catherine with his careless words. He needed to make it up to her, if that was at all possible. But he also couldn't shake the feeling that he couldn't trust her. That she wasn't telling him the full truth about her parents, her adoption, all of it. He, better than anyone, knew how easily a woman could lie. Hadn't Linda acted the part of the perfect girlfriend? She'd pre-tended to be so in love with him, even going as far as wanting to have his babies. Dean would've gone on believing her too, if he hadn't come home early and found her in bed with Jimmy. Then there were the women who'd lied and used Dean before Linda had entered the picture.

He didn't know if Catherine was capable of such deceit. He wanted to believe she wasn't. Dean ached to have faith in her the way everyone else did. The bottom line was, if he was ever going to have more than one night with Catherine then he needed to find out one way or the other whether she was the innocent long-lost sibling she claimed to be. That thought had brought him to Deanna and Jonas's house.

Dean pounded on the front door and waited. He needed to talk to Jonas. He knew the idiot was home, because his black Charger was in the driveway. He couldn't reach him on his cell, and no one was answering on Deanna's house phone either. Dean was starting to think Jonas was avoiding him. When the door swung wide, revealing Jonas barefoot and wearing a pair of gray sweatpants and a white T-shirt, Dean frowned. "Why aren't you answering your damn phone?"

Jonas crossed his arms over his chest. "Because I'm seriously pissed at you at the moment."

"What the hell for?" He rubbed his hands together to stave off the cold and asked, "Can I come in, or are you planning on letting me freeze to death?"

To Dean's consternation, Jonas actually appeared to give that some thought. When he stepped back and let him enter, Dean was only too pleased. Jonas slammed the door shut behind him and proceeded to glare. "Deanna is upset because of the way you're treating Catherine. I really don't like Deanna upset."

Dean looked around for his sister but came up empty. "Where is Deanna anyway?"

"She went shopping with your mom. She needed to get her mind off her asshole twin."

Dean winced. "Look, that's why I'm here. I want you to run a search on Catherine."

Jonas threw his hands in the air. "Why the hell would I? In case you forgot, we already did a background check on her when she first contacted Gracie claiming to be her sister. Get it through your thick skull that she's clean, Dean. The. Fucking. End."

Dean unzipped his Carhartt and tossed it over a chair. "Then you need to dig deeper. I know it sounds crazy, but there's something she's hiding. I can't move forward until I know what it is."

"Why are you so sure she's hiding something? Don't you think Wade or I would've gotten the same vibe from her if that were true? We're the private investigators here, not you, and our instincts say she's harmless."

"You and Wade want her to be harmless. You don't want to find anything on her because you care about her. My head is less clouded by my feelings."

Jonas quirked a brow at him. "Oh, really?"

Dean squared his shoulders, ready for a fight. "Really."

"From what I hear, your feelings are plenty involved, seeing as how you spent the night with her."

Dean took a step forward, closing the distance between them. "Don't even go there, Phoenix. What happened between Catherine and me is off limits."

Jonas fisted his hands at his sides and shot right back, "I sort of thought so too, until I saw Deanna cry earlier today."

Dean felt as if someone had punched him in the stomach. He couldn't have heard right. "She was crying? Because of me?"

Jonas rolled his eyes. "Haven't you figured out that she loves you and wants to see you happy? She came home in tears after dropping Catherine off. It was all I could do to get her to tell me what had happened."

Dean shook his head, unwilling to think of how much pain he'd caused everyone already. "Catherine and I had a little misunderstanding. I'm going to fix it. Deanna doesn't need to worry about me."

"Yeah, well, she does. So if you don't get your head out of your ass soon, I'm going to lose my temper and do something we'll both regret."

He had to bite back a smile at Jonas's protective attitude toward Deanna. Dean's admiration for the guy went up a few notches. "Then help me find out more information on Catherine. Once I know for sure that she has nothing to hide, I'll gladly let this whole thing go."

Jonas sighed and shoved a hand through his hair. "Deanna won't like it if she finds out we're digging around in Catherine's life. She considers her part of the family already."

"Look, if you won't do it, I'll find someone who will."

Jonas was quiet a moment before asking, "You aren't going to stop, are you?"

Dean shook his head. "Not until I can see the proof of Catherine's innocence with my own eyes."

"I'll do it, but I think you're making a big mistake," he said. "She's not the con artist you think she is. You could really fuck this up, Dean."

Dean was starting to think the same thing. On all counts.

"Give me a few days. I'll be in touch."

"Thanks," Dean muttered as he grabbed his coat and headed for the door. "I owe you one."

Jonas snorted. "If Deanna gets wind of this we'll both be up shit creek."

Dean cursed under his breath at the thought. His twin wasn't a pretty sight when she was angry. "Let's make damn sure she doesn't find out, then."

Jonas nodded and shut the door in his face.

It wasn't until Dean was behind the wheel that he thought of Jonas's words. *You could really fuck this up.* Pain shot through his chest when he thought of never seeing Catherine again. Never touching her soft skin, never kissing her awake. Never slipping inside her welcoming body and making slow, sweet love all night long. No, he wouldn't let that happen. He would talk to Catherine. Grovel if necessary. She'd gotten under his skin, and Dean aimed to keep her there. In the meantime, what was the harm in having Jonas get him some answers? It was peace of mind, nothing more. It would all work out, Dean would make damn sure of it.

* * *

It'd been more than two full days since Catherine had seen Dean. She'd avoided his calls, even though it'd been the hardest thing she'd ever done. When he'd stopped by her hotel suite a few times, Catherine hadn't answered the door. It hadn't been until she'd spied the pretty bouquet of daisies on the floor outside her room that she'd cried like a baby. Her heart was breaking, which was insane because they'd only spent one night together. She wasn't supposed to fall for a one-night stand. They barely knew each other, so why did she feel such an overwhelming connection to Dean? It made little sense.

The time she'd spent with Gracie had helped to take her mind off the big jerk. She'd had fun going to the historical museum on Monday. Ohio was swiftly growing on Catherine. So much so that she'd begun to think of living in the Buckeye State. To be closer to Gracie would be wonderful. Unfortunately that would put her closer to Dean as well.

Now it was five o'clock on Tuesday, and Catherine had the evening to herself. She'd killed some time by doing some updates on a few clients' websites, but she'd finished them too quickly. She still had the evening to herself. She contemplated going down to the hotel spa and getting a massage, maybe a mani-pedi as well. She felt like pampering herself a little. The distraction would do her good, and maybe the massage would loosen up a few of the knots in the back of her neck.

As she reached for the phone to call the front desk, a knock on the door stopped her. Her heartbeat sped up at the thought that it might be Dean. God, she missed him. It wasn't fair that she could long for a man who saw her as some sort of fraud.

When she rose up on her tiptoes to see through the peephole, she all but swallowed her tongue. Dean stood outside her room, and he had the look of a man who'd had just about enough. His gaze zeroed in on the peephole, right at her, causing Catherine to stagger backward.

"I know you're in there, Catherine, and this time I'm not leaving."

His voice was loud enough to have everyone on the floor wondering what was going on. Catherine sighed, knowing she couldn't avoid him forever. It was time to face the man, once and for all. She took a deep breath and turned the knob. The vision of him sucked all the air out of her lungs. He had on a pair of low-riding jeans, a black pocket T under his Carhartt, and a pair of black work boots. He was carrying a grocery bag in his right hand. Damn it, she could've stayed strong if he'd looked like crap. Maybe. As it was, Catherine knew it was only a matter of time before she caved.

On the other hand, she resembled something out of a horror movie. Her hair was piled up in a messy bun on top of her head, and she had on an old pair of jeans that so did not flatter her figure. The worn, baby-blue T-shirt she only ever wore to bed was the icing on the cake. Great, the ball was in his court already.

"It's about time you stopped hiding from me," he said as he strode through the door and pulled off his coat. After he tossed it onto the couch along with the bag, he turned and glared at her.

Catherine's cheeks burned with embarrassment. She closed the door, then took a second to gather her courage. "I wasn't hiding," she lied as she turned toward him. "I simply didn't want to see you. There's a difference." She pointed to the computer and decided to use work as an excuse. "Besides, I had some work to tend to."

He moved closer to her, and Catherine found herself backing up. "You were hiding," he reiterated, his voice as hard as steel.

Catherine wasn't about to get into a debate with the man. "I have plans tonight, Dean, so make it fast."

He grinned. It reminded her of a panther, once it had cornered its prey. "I talked to Wade and Gracie a little bit ago, Catherine," he said, as he took another step in her direction. "You don't have plans with them. They're on their way out to dinner with one of Wade's clients."

Her head shot up in the air. "My plans might not include my sister, but I have them nonetheless." Okay, she hadn't actually made the massage appointment yet, but Dean didn't need to know that.

Dean stopped dead and cocked an eyebrow. "If not them, then who do you have plans with? You haven't been in Ohio long enough to make friends."

Was that jealousy she detected in his tone? Hmm, interesting. "I don't see as how that's any of your business."

In two strides, Dean was in front of her, his hands wrapped firmly around her upper arms. "Everything you do is my business, sweetheart," he murmured. "Who do you have plans with?"

Too late Catherine realized her mistake. Baiting a man like Dean was simply suicidal. He was too possessive and predatory. "No one," she finally admitted. "I was going to make an appointment with the hotel spa, that's all."

He relaxed his hold, but he didn't release her. "Why wouldn't you answer my calls?"

She jerked out of his arms, angry that he'd even ask such a ridiculous question. "You can't guess?"

He cupped her cheek in one calloused palm. "I hurt you." His voice was low and rough. "I'm sorry, sweetheart."

Finally they arrived at the crux of the issue. Catherine debated the merits of shutting him down by simply refusing to hear his side of things, but she remembered her conversation with Gracie about giving him a chance to explain. Besides, didn't she deserve to know the truth? The way Catherine saw it, she had a right to know if the night they'd shared meant anything to him. "Tell me something, Dean, and I want the truth."

He shoved his hands in his front pockets. "I'll always be honest with you, Catherine."

She wasn't so sure of that, but she let it slide. "Did you sleep with me simply to gain answers?" she blurted out. "Is that what our night was to you?"

"Christ, Catherine," he growled. "Is that what you've been thinking all this time?"

Catherine tucked a wayward strand of hair behind her ear and plowed on. "You said yourself that before I went back to Georgia you would have your answers. What else am I to think?"

Dean shook his head and stared down at the floor. "I've been a world-class bastard to you and I know that, but I'd never use you."

Tears stung her eyes at the sincerity in Dean's voice. She had to look away in order to maintain her composure. A rough palm beneath her chin brought her gaze back to his. "What we shared, it was special to me," he said in a gentle voice. "It had nothing to do with getting answers and everything to do with you and me."

Catherine wanted so badly to believe him, which was of course the problem. "I don't know what you want from me, Dean," she said, giving him the plain truth. "You don't trust me and yet you're here. Why?"

"Because I can't stop thinking about you," he ground out, sounding none too happy about it. "I can't stop wanting you. Every moment of the day away from you has been an exercise in torture."

"Oh, God," Catherine moaned. It was too much. She couldn't hold up against an attack like that.

"Don't send me away, sweet Catherine," he murmured as

his lips brushed hers in a tender caress. "Let me make it up to you. Please."

"You don't fight fair," she complained, as tears began to stream down her cheeks. "Not fair at all."

He swiped at them with the pad of his thumb. "I'll do whatever it takes to get you in my arms again," he vowed. "Anything."

Catherine let her arms drift around his neck. His virile scent filled her senses and sent her libido into overdrive. "I'll be going home soon, you know. Back to Georgia." The idea of leaving Dean, of never again feeling the warmth of his embrace, made her heart ache something fierce.

"We should make the most of every minute, then, don't you think?" he asked, as he bent low and lifted her into his powerful arms.

She nodded, but before he could take her off to the bedroom, Catherine had enough of her wits about her to ask, "Does this mean you're staying the night?"

"If you'll have me."

Catherine could've sworn Dean's arms shook a little, but she must have been imagining it. A man as strong and confident as Dean would never show such an obvious sign of weakness. "Only if I can wake up next to you," she said, giving him a smile. "But what about Duke? Don't you need to get home to him?"

He shook his head. "My neighbor came home earlier than expected. So, Duke is back home."

"Oh, that's good, then." After settling that little dilemma, Catherine surrendered. She was completely off her rocker, but damn it, she wanted another chance with him. Another moment out of time to indulge the pleasure she would only find in Dean's arms.

17

As Dean placed Catherine on her feet next to the bed, he looked her over. He couldn't believe he was being given another chance. He didn't deserve it—no one knew that better than him—but he wasn't about to pass it up either. God, even with the crazy hair and baggy clothes, she was beautiful. It didn't matter what she wore because he'd already memorized every curve and valley. Her body would be stamped on his brain forever. Right now, with the two of them alone, he couldn't think of a better way to spend the rest of the night than to play. Maybe a game of memory . . . blindfolded.

Dean wrapped an arm around her, then glided his palm down until he was cupping one jean-covered cheek. Catherine jolted, and Dean couldn't prevent a grin. He had her full attention and he planned to keep it.

He grasped her around the middle with both hands, spanning her waistline. Catherine had curves, but his hands were big and his fingers almost touched together. She fit his body the way no other woman had. He watched her eyes heat up when he pulled her close, closer still, fitting her to him, and kissed her long and deep. The king-size bed was mere inches away. He walked backward, their lips locked together, until the backs of his knees hit the side of the bed and they both tumbled onto it, their mouths never breaking contact. Catherine's startled hiss brought him to a halt. She tore her mouth from his and stared up at him as if scandalized. As if she hadn't been the same woman who had begged him to let her come the other night. Several times.

"Dean?" she asked, her hushed whisper turning him on. Everything about her made him ache with hunger and need.

He grinned. "Catherine." He lifted up and took hold of her shirt, yanking it up until he could see her tempting belly button ring. He pulled the material over her head and tossed it away. Her bra went next. When her large breasts fell free, Dean groaned. "God, I missed you," he whispered before he blanketed her with his body. He dipped his head and sucked one already erect nipple into his mouth. She tasted like paradise, pure and simple. Catherine gasped and clutched onto the back of his head in a stinging hold. Her nipples were soft and pink, and Dean could feed on her for hours. He sucked and licked. She moaned his name, and Dean broke away long enough to admit, "I have to warn you. I haven't eaten much the past few days, and you, sweetheart, are a meal fit for a king."

"I-I certainly wouldn't want you to starve," she moaned.

"Mmm," Dean groaned as he flicked his tongue over and around one nipple before moving to the other, gently at first then rougher, demanding her flesh to beg for him. He cupped the round globe and pulled it up higher, kneading the supple skin. He heard her moan of delight. Dean took joy in her animated responses to him. He gave in to his primal cravings and bit down. She arched upward, eager for his touch. His hand answered her unspoken pleas. Letting go of her breast, he journeyed down until he found her precious mound. "Clothes, sweetheart," he mumbled as he quickly did away with her jeans and panties. His fingers delved at once, and his nostrils flared to life as he picked up her succulent scent. He found her clit swollen and throbbing. Damn, she was soaked. He fondled and toyed with the little nub until the teasing seemed to become too much. She cried out his name and came, exploding all around his finger. It was the sweetest thing to watch Catherine come totally undone at his hands.

Dean moved away and tore at the button fly on his jeans, freeing his erection. In the red haze of his lust, her pleading barely reached his ears. He looked down and saw her arms outstretched, waiting to embrace him, even as her body waited to welcome him in. But Dean intended to enjoy his beautiful little seductress.

"Hold that thought," he said as he moved off the bed and strode out of the room. He grabbed the bag he'd brought with him and carried it to the bed, where Catherine was now sitting up and looking at him with a question in her pretty emerald eyes. He took out the black blindfold he'd bought earlier in the day and held it up for her to see. She looked more confused than ever. They shared no words as he moved between her legs and placed the soft fabric over her eyes.

Her hands covered his in an instant. "Uh, Dean, I'm really not so sure about this."

"I am."

She clutched onto him tighter. "Dean."

Her anxiety could be heard in the quiver of her soft voice. She should know he wouldn't hurt her. He would never cause her pain. But then again, they'd only just met and he'd already made her cry. He had a lot to make up for.

"You don't have to worry that I would take advantage of you, sweetheart," he murmured. "My pleasure comes from yours."

"There was plenty of pleasure without the blindfold."

He chuckled. "Yeah, but this is more adventurous. And you

wanted adventure, remember?" Dean waited, and when she dropped her hands, he went back to securing the material in a knot at the back of her head. "Is it too tight?"

She shook her head. No words, only the sound of her rapid breaths could be heard.

"All you have to do is feel. Let yourself go, Catherine. Experience every touch, every throb, and every breath." A small shake of her head and Dean knew she was ready.

He moved out from between her legs, drawing a frown from her. But he wanted to give her more than a few moments of passion. He wanted to give her a part of himself. By the time he was finished, Catherine would have had more of him than he'd ever given any other woman. What she did with it would be up to her.

Dean fished around in the bag and brought out a bottle of wine. He inspected the label. It was a merlot, a good year. He used the bottle opener and uncorked it, then held the cork beneath her nose.

"What is that?" she asked as she inhaled.

"You tell me. What's it smell like?"

She sniffed again, then smiled. "Wine?" She paused, then added, "Uh, I'm not really a wine expert, Dean."

Unaccountably charmed by her, Dean leaned down and kissed her, the satiny softness of her lips fueling his already raging hard-on. "Experts aren't required for this game."

"If you say so," Catherine murmured, clearly unconvinced. Dean held the cork under her nose once more and allowed her time to take in the rich, seductive fragrance.

This time she took a deeper inhale. "Oak," she replied. "Maybe a hint of . . . cherry?"

Dean touched her thigh and felt her jump. The blindfold made every soft stroke more pronounced for her. "Very good girl," he whispered as he put the cork aside. He picked up the bottle and took out a glass he'd brought along, then poured a small amount. Dean put the glass to her lips and said, "Here, take a sip and tell me what you taste."

He watched her drink a small amount, then her tongue darted out and she licked her lips. Dean was having a hell of a time concentrating with Catherine sitting in front of him, her plump tits bare and her pussy inches away from his hand.

"It's good," she said, "and there's a hint of spice, I guess." She swiped her tongue over her bottom lip again, and Dean groaned. "Hmm, I can't quite put my finger on what else. Something fruity, maybe?"

"Ah, you do know wine," he murmured as he moved his hand higher up her thigh. "I don't drink much, but over the years I've developed a fondness for good wine." As he reached her sweet pussy, he flicked his thumb back and forth over the little nub he found there.

She threw her head back and moaned. "Dean, please, I need more. I need *you*."

Her voice had gone hoarse, and Dean was tempted to forget the game. He dipped his finger into the glass of wine and said, "Soon, I promise. First, open your mouth for me."

She hesitated only a few seconds this time. Dean slid his wine-soaked finger into her mouth and asked, "What's the fruit you taste?"

She closed her lips around his finger and licked it clean. The seductive sight had Dean's cock thickening. She pulled her mouth off him and shook her head. "I-I don't know." She swirled her tongue over her bottom lip, then said, "Blackberry maybe?"

Catherine's voice was a thready bit of sound in the quiet room, driving every one of his senses wild with need. He put the glass on the end table and plunged his wet finger into her slick, hot pussy. She moaned, and he covered her mouth with his, hungry for her taste. "Mmm," he whispered against her lips, "my two favorite things."

"W-what's that?" she replied as her hips began moving, arching into his hand as he fingered her.

"Your pussy and a good bottle of merlot," he answered. "Fucking delicious." Dean continued sliding a single finger in and out of her opening, driving himself mad, as he was already so hard he hurt. He wanted to thrust deep, drive his cock into her honeyed heat where he knew paradise waited.

"Oh, God, Dean," she moaned, "that feels so good. Please don't stop."

"I have no intention of stopping. You're like a fine wine to me, Catherine. I want to sip and savor you. I want to take in your scent and enjoy the essence of your sweet femininity. I want you, sweetheart, and I seriously doubt that will change anytime soon."

"Then quit stalling and take me, Dean."

Dean gave her what she craved. He slipped his finger out and spread her juices over her puffy pussy lips. "This is the spicy taste I want on my tongue," he growled. "No wine could ever compare to your luscious flavor." He licked her, slowly drifting his tongue over her distended clit. When her body bowed, Dean spread her legs wider, tasting her deeper. He cupped the ample softness of her breasts. She fit his mouth, his hands. Catherine was made for him, and he devoured her.

He licked and sucked, luxuriating in her gasps and moans. Her hands fisted in his hair, pulling him closer. He toyed with her little bud, nibbling on it the way he knew she liked, before teasing her nipples into hard points. He gave equal attention to her beautiful tits and wet pussy. Dean's cock dripped with pre-come as he played.

"Do you know that you drive me to the very brink of insanity?" he admitted. "I swear to God, I'm addicted to you. So quickly you've become a drug to me, Catherine."

Her hands tightened in his hair. "Then put your cock inside

my pussy, Dean," she demanded. "Right now, because surely you're in need of a fix."

Dean lifted his head and stared at Catherine's widespread thighs. She sat, blinded by the black cotton cloth, her sex dripping wet, breasts glistening from the suckle of his mouth. He wondered if she realized how open she was to him in that moment. Covering her eyes had unlocked a door for Catherine, and she'd unknowingly dropped the last of her inhibitions.

"You are incredibly sexy like this," he told her, his voice rough with emotion and passion both. "I could stare at you all night and I wouldn't get bored."

"Don't even think it, Dean." She reached between his legs, obviously searching for his cock. It took her several tries before she had it grasped in her tight fist. She squeezed, hard, drawing a growl from him. "I have the perfect spot for this. Don't force me to tie you down and do it myself."

Dean smiled at the thought. "I don't think I'd mind being at your mercy." Before she could make any more demands, he wrapped his hands around her hips and pulled her to the very edge of the bed. He knew she couldn't see what he was doing and she would assume he was following her orders. But he'd always hated being predictable.

Instead, Dean picked up the glass one more time and dribbled a tiny amount of wine over her swollen vulva.

She yelped. "Damn it, Dean, that's cold!"

He grinned. "Not for long, sweetheart," he growled as he dipped his head between her legs and lapped up the ruby liquid. She went pliant when his tongue and lips moved over her.

"Mmm, your spicy little pussy tastes so good with the wine. Adds just the right touch, if you ask me," he murmured against her dewy center.

He slowly trickled another few drops of liquid, this time onto her delightful berry nipples. She sucked in a breath and Dean watched as the tips turned to hard little peaks. He put the glass down and wrapped his mouth around one full breast, licking and suckling, before moving to the other to do the same. Her ragged groan went right to his bloodstream. She arched into him, clutching at the blankets for support.

"Would you like to taste my wine, sweetheart?"

She hesitated a moment, then a smile appeared as she nodded. His libido went into overdrive.

Dean stood, then took hold of her waist and pulled her off the bed. He placed her on her feet. She wobbled a little, but he steadied her. He took the bottle and poured a small amount onto the head of his cock and had to suck in a breath it was so cold.

"Get down on your knees," he instructed. "I'll guide you."

She gripped on to his hand and went to her knees. Once her mouth was a breath away from the head of his dick, Dean took hold of her hair and stopped her. "Far enough, now, open wide so you can take all of me." Again, her breathing quickened, but she silently obeyed.

Dean took his cock in a firm fist and brought the dripping tip to her waiting mouth. She tasted it with her tongue first, then took him all the way in, nearly bringing him to his knees.

"Christ, yeah, suck it," he gritted out as she lapped up all the flavored drink. Dean's vision blurred when she dipped her head and nuzzled his balls. A few swipes of her tongue on the sensitive underside of his cock and Dean was forced to stop her. He cupped her chin in his palm. "No more or I'll fill that hot mouth, sweets."

She sat back and smiled. "I like the taste of wine much better this way, I have to admit."

He chuckled. "Have I turned you into an alcoholic?"

She licked her lips and shrugged. "To tell the truth, the wine was sort of in the way of the flavor I really wanted."

Dean shook his head. "Little tease." He lifted her up and placed her back on the bed. Dean forgot about the wine when he watched her spread her legs, inviting him in. He bent his head and kissed her swollen pussy, then proceeded to lick and nibble until suddenly she was screaming out another climax. When she collapsed, all her muscles going slack, Dean took a moment to look at her. Her wet pussy and reddened tits were on display for him. She was a wicked temptation.

"Catherine." Her name was all he could muster. She didn't speak, merely opened her arms and waited. Dean moved on top of her, then thrust into her with a quick kind of force that had them both gasping for air.

He stayed still inside of her for a moment, enjoying the satiny clutch and the scorching heat that warmed him inside and out. Dean slowly pumped her tight channel, his movements growing faster and more furious as need swept through him, pushing all rational thought to the back of his mind. He ached for her. Only Catherine. She was a fire in his blood, and he had a primal need to bind her to him in some way.

Catherine lifted her hips, driving upward and forcing him deeper still. She came at him with her own brand of passion, her fingernails dug into his back as if marking her territory. He reached a hand between their bodies and touched off the beginning of a third orgasm for her. She screamed and wrapped her long legs tightly around his waist, squeezing, sending him over the edge. She shouted, and Dean pushed in and out several more times before he erupted, filling her with his hot come. Her inner muscles sucked onto his cock and milked him dry.

Mere seconds passed before Dean pulled out of her. With his body pressing hers into the mattress, Dean took a moment, transfixed at the sight of her sated body. She was still trembling from the orgasms he'd coaxed from her. A pleasant smile lit her face, and Dean wondered how he was every going to let her walk away from him when her visit with Gracie ended.

It hit him then, like a truckload of lumber. "Fuck, I can't believe I forgot."

She lifted her head and cocked her head to the side. "Huh?"

He got to his feet and raked his fingers through his hair. "I didn't wear a condom."

Catherine bit her lower lip and frowned. "I'm on the pill. And I received a clean bill of health the last time I went to the doctor."

"Same here."

One side of her mouth kicked up into a playful grin. "You're on the pill too?"

He reached down and plucked the blindfold off. "Smart-ass," he whispered, before kissing the temptation of her mouth. When he lifted it she was staring at him, her eyes half-closed. Her hair was a wreck and she had blotchy red marks all over her body, but Dean thought she looked more beautiful than ever.

"I've never experienced anything like that before, Dean," she admitted in a quiet voice. "Never."

Dean knelt down and, with one arm under her legs and the other supporting her back, he picked her up, cradling her close to his chest. "Me either," he said as her arms snaked around his neck to hold him tight. The look of sheer pleasure on her face speared his heart. He started out of the room. "Time to wash, sweetheart, and I plan on taking my time cleaning every inch of you too."

Catherine's stomach grumbled, and she blushed. "Apparently I'm hungry."

He kissed her nose. "I'll spring for room service."

"Sounds like a plan, but, Dean?"

"Yeah, sweets?"

"I'm going to want to wash you too. Every inch."

For the first time that he could remember, Dean actually got a little weak.

18

The next morning, Catherine was floating on a cloud. She and Dean had shared something profound the night before, and it went beyond hot and heavy sex. She knew it. Could feel it. There was something about the way Dean had looked at her when he'd slowly drawn the blindfold off, as if she meant something to him. Did he see her as more than a good time? He'd been so tender and loving when he'd washed her afterward in the Jacuzzi-style tub. As if he cared. He hadn't said anything to indicate he was becoming emotionally involved, but didn't actions speak louder than words? Catherine wanted to think there was more to their relationship than mutual desire, chemistry, and sating each other's needs.

In the past, Catherine had dated men who'd seen her as a comfortable companion. The wild, erotic stuff had only been something she'd read about in books. She'd never once experienced anything quite as intense as what she'd shared with Dean. And there'd definitely never been a deeper connection with any of the other men she'd dated. She wasn't sure what to think, and she had absolutely nothing to compare it to, which was sad when she thought about it. Heck, every man she'd ever gone out with had been Mr. Reliable. No frills and for sure no surprises. Yet Dean made her feel alive and sexy and wicked. Even a little bit cherished.

She'd known him only a few days. Good Lord, what kind of woman fell for a man she barely knew outside the bedroom? Could she be any more pathetic? She'd never believed in *love at first sight.* Until now.

When she thought of how many times she'd orgasmed, Catherine couldn't seem to help the smile that beamed across her face. Seriously, what woman wouldn't grin like a fool after a night like she and Dean had shared? Her orgasm meter had been dangerously in the red zone before meeting him.

At the moment, Catherine sat on the couch, dressed in Dean's black tee and a pair of white cotton bikini panties. He'd woken her early with a kiss, which had quickly turned to more. He'd ordered breakfast and they'd talked. Now, as he talked on his cell a few feet away, Catherine couldn't help but stare. The solid wall of his bare chest kept her spellbound. His jeans rode low on his hips and he was barefoot. He looked hot barefoot. He looked hot no matter what, Catherine admitted to herself.

When he ended the call and tossed the phone onto the desk, Catherine finally saw her chance to find out more about him. Maybe even spend the day together. "Who was that?"

"A guy who works for me," he explained, frowning. "There's a problem with some material that was supposed to arrive this morning. I'm afraid I need to go in and deal with it."

Catherine's hopes plummeted. There went her grand idea of spending the day with him. "Oh." She looked at her computer, which was still sitting open on the coffee table from the night before. "I suppose I could check e-mail and get some things done. And I'm meeting Gracie later. She's taking me to see the orchestra that's performing in town."

He crossed the room and took her face in his palms, a small

smile playing at the corners of his mouth. "Or you could come with me. Want to see my office? I promise to have you back in time for the performance."

Her heartbeat sped up at the thread he was tossing her way. A chance to see him outside the bedroom? Yeah, like she'd pass that up. "I'd love to! Just give me a minute to get dressed." She jumped off the couch and was headed for the bedroom when his deep voice calling her name stopped her. She turned and quirked a brow. "Yeah?"

He grinned and crossed his arms over his chest. "I'm going to need my shirt."

Feeling naughty, Catherine smiled and grasped the hem, then yanked it over her head. She tossed it at him, but it landed on the floor. Dean didn't even try to catch it. He only stood there, staring at her, a dark look in his eyes. Unsure if she'd done something wrong, Catherine started out of the room. A pair of strong hands stopped her.

"You're the devil," he whispered against her ear. "A delicious, red-haired devil."

"Um, your shirt. It's going to get all wrinkled," she said, not that she cared with him pressed against her. She could feel the hard ridge of his cock nudging her butt cheeks, and her pussy reacted with a flow of damp heat.

"Later for that," he mumbled. "First there's this." He cupped her pussy through her panties, and Catherine's legs went as weak as wet noodles.

Oh, God, yes, she thought. "Will we be late?" she asked, as she felt his mouth against the pulse in her neck.

Dean froze, then cursed a few times. "Probably."

Catherine gathered enough strength to pull out of his arms and turn around. She went up on her tiptoes and kissed him. "Hold that thought for later, then," she said against his lips. "When we have more than a few minutes to spare."

He closed his eyes tight and fisted his hands at his sides.

"Go, woman, cover up that hot body before I forget I have employees waiting on me and I take you against the damn wall."

Catherine's blood heated at the guttural words. Without another teasing remark, she sped from the room.

Catherine was suitably impressed with Dean's business. It was bigger than she'd imagined. He was quite successful. He'd shown her the lumberyard and she'd met his foreman, a kind man with gray hair and a strong workingman's build. A few men had whistled at her, but when Dean glared at them they'd quickly gone back to work. Now he was seated at his desk going over a bid he'd worked up for an office building. She walked around the room and smiled when she spied a picture of his family. She picked it up and realized it must have been taken at a family get-together. He had his arm around Deanna, and she was smiling. Jonas stood to Deanna's right. Wade and Gracie were on opposite sides of Mrs. Harrison. Not for the first time, Catherine wondered what it would've been like to grow up in a family like that. Love and laughter, sibling rivalry. Her parents had been wonderful, but they were old school. Homework and chores after school, then dinner and bedtime. If it'd hadn't been for Mary's friendship her life would've been horribly boring and lonely.

She turned toward Dean and held the picture in the air. "You have a beautiful family, Dean. You're very lucky."

Dean looked up, then crooked a finger at her. "Come here."

She put the picture back the way she found it and crossed the room. "Yes?"

He stood and caged her in with both arms on either side of the desk. "I see something more beautiful," he murmured.

Catherine knew he was referring to her, but she couldn't wrap her mind around it. When he touched his mouth to hers and stroked his tongue over her bottom lip, her body thrummed to life. One arm came around her lower back and pulled her toward him. He moved backward, and before she knew it she was in his lap.

Scandalized by the fact they were in his office and anyone could walk in at any moment, Catherine pushed against his chest, breaking the kiss. "Dean, we shouldn't. Not here."

"Yes, here," he said in a tone that left no room for argument. She hesitated, torn between what she wanted and propriety. Dean immediately took advantage of her indecision by coaxing her lips apart and slipping his tongue inside. His taste, now so familiar, was better than cheesecake and chocolate put together. He explored the inside of her mouth and slid his palm lower to cup her bottom. Catherine wound her arms around his neck and sank into his seductive touch.

Since arriving at his office, he'd been rather distant. As if he didn't want anyone to know they were more than merely friends. It made her want to throttle him. Now that she had him close, she wasn't going to waste any time. She drifted her hands down his nape to his shoulders, then his pecs and ripped abs. He was so hard and muscular all over it nearly melted her every time she touched him. He was a powerful, arrogant, handsome god. Feeling wild and impetuous, Catherine coasted her palm over the bulge in his faded jeans, cupping his rigid length. He was as turned on as she, Catherine was pleased to notice.

As he continued to eat at her mouth, Catherine played. Soon, his free hand moved up her calf, beneath the back of the knee-length skirt she'd worn. He caressed his way up her thigh and cupped her mound. Catherine lurched at the feel of him there. It was in the middle of the workday and they were at his office. What were they thinking?

With the little willpower she still had left, Catherine forced her mouth off his and moved her hand away from his crotch. "Stop, Dean," she said in a hushed whisper. "We could be seen."

Dean chuckled. "We won't be seen, sweetheart. I locked the door when you were nosing around earlier. Now, be still and let me have some fun."

Catherine wanted to protest the nosy comment, but his mouth moved to her neck and he began to nibble and lick. She'd protest later, she decided. "God, I love when you do that."

Dean moved to her ear and whispered, "I've only just begun." He sat back in the chair. "Straddle me so I can play."

Catherine cringed as she became aware that she had all her weight on him. "I'm not too heavy?"

He frowned, clearly confused. "Heavy?"

She plucked at her skirt. "I'm larger than average, that's all."

In a flash, Dean gripped her around the waist and lifted her. "Straddle me," he demanded. When she obeyed, he plopped her back down on top of his thighs. Her skirt was hiked up to midthigh and her satin-covered pussy was now pressed against his fly. "Do not put yourself down. You aren't heavy. You're perfect. Every inch of you."

Her face heated. "I wasn't putting myself down." His black look called her a liar. "I have a mirror, Dean."

He grasped a handful of her hair in a possessive hold. "Every man here leered at you the minute you walked onto the property. I can't keep my damn hands off you for five minutes, and you think you're heavy?" He shook his head as if exasperated with her. Catherine started to protest his ridiculous claim, but Dean plowed right over her. "Make no mistake, sweetheart, you are in my mind day and night. I think of you when I go to bed. Your touch, your sweet, sweet curves, and this pretty mouth. I can't get enough."

Her eyes welled up, but she refused to let the tears spill over. "I think of you too. I've never wanted a man more than I want you."

His smile was possessive and proud. "Good, let's keep it that way, shall we?"

Her heart seemed to stop beating for a second. What was he saying? Catherine wanted him to clarify. Was she more than a sex partner to him? As he went back to kissing her, Catherine knew that discussion time was over. In true Dean style, he chose to prove his point by showing, rather than telling.

His talented mouth pressed against hers, and Catherine's mind fogged over. There was only Dean. All her questions fell away. She opened her mouth and danced her tongue over his lips. At his rumble of approval, Dean took over and their tongues mated. Catherine's hands clutched onto Dean's biceps, anxious and aching. Her body was on fire. She wanted him, inside of her, around her, drinking her in and filling her up. He was a craving in her blood, one she could no more deny than she could her next breath.

Catherine's fingers trailed over his muscular arms, and she drew in a breath when they came around her waist and pulled her in tight. A moan escaped. He was so strong, so virile. She was safe and secure with Dean. As the thought flitted through her mind, Catherine went still. Fear shot through her as she realized the truth. She was in love with him. Her body already belonged to him, only now her soul seemed tethered to him as well.

"I want this pussy. It's mine," Dean quietly declared. "Say you want me. Deep. Here and now."

"Yes, right here. I can't wait a second more."

He slipped his hands beneath her skirt and pushed her panties aside. "Unzip me," he whispered.

Catherine's fingers fumbled over the buttons in his jeans as she tried to obey. When she had his fly open, she peeked at his navy blue boxer-briefs and her desire increased tenfold. She licked her lips and gently drew him out. The head of his cock tempted her to taste, but in their position there was no way she

148 / Anne Rainey

would be able to get him into her mouth, not unless she moved to her knees on the floor.

Dean stroked her hair and murmured, "Later, we'll take our time," he said, as if reading her thoughts. "For now I need to feel your tight little pussy holding my dick."

It was the same for her. "Yes."

"Guide me in," he instructed. "Show me how much you want it. Take us both there, sweetheart."

His erotic words had her heart pounding harder and her body quaking with need. "My pussy is dripping for you," she said, giving him the carnal words she knew he wanted to hear. "It's been too long, Dean."

He chuckled. "It was only this morning."

"Like I said, too long," she whispered. Then she took his heavy cock in her hand and slid him inside. Her body closed around him, tight and hot. She shuddered, flung her head back, and rode him.

"That's my girl. Fuck it good," Dean urged as he clutched her hair in his fist and tugged until her back was resting against his arm. He lowered over her and sipped on her breasts right through the plum-colored blouse she'd put on earlier. The heat of his mouth seeped through the thin material, sucking the breath out of her and driving her into another world. When his fingers found their way over her nub, expertly flicking it the way she liked, Catherine's nerve endings sizzled to life. Her muscles clenched as she rode him faster, harder, their bodies wrapped around each other, melding until there was no separating them.

Soon Catherine was there, spiraling out of control. Her hot pussy bathing him in her juices as she climaxed. Dean sank his mouth over hers and captured her shouts of satisfaction. As the desire began to ebb, Dean clutched her hips and pushed into her once, twice, then he arched his neck and moaned her name as he emptied himself deep.

Catherine's breath came in short pants, her body sweating from exertion, the skirt clinging to her overheated skin. Her legs shook as she collapsed against Dean's heaving chest. "I'm so not moving. Ever again."

Dean's arms came around her shoulders, holding her tight against him. "Works for me." She wiggled, gaining his attention. As his gaze snared hers, Catherine saw raw hunger in their passionate depths. If Dean hadn't just spent himself inside her, she would have thought he was ready to go all over again.

"I think I'm going to be a bit sticky," she teased, trying to inject some casualness into the intensity that seemed to surround them all of a sudden.

"I could make love to you twenty-four hours a day, seven days a week, and it still wouldn't be enough."

She had no words for such a bald statement. Good thing he didn't seem to expect any. Dean sighed and slipped his cock free, then grabbed a tissue from a box on the corner of his desk and tenderly wiped her pussy clean. He tossed it in a trashcan beneath the desk, before he readjusted her panties. When his heavy length was once again confined, he slid a palm up her thigh and cupped her mound in a possessively hold. "You never cease to amaze me. You can be so bold and incredibly shy all at the same time. So much of you still mystifies me." He leaned in and kissed her lightly on the forehead, then wrapped his strong hands around her middle and placed her back on the floor in front of him. "So, do you want to look around some more?" he asked.

She laughed. "Uh, I think I've seen enough for one day. I feel like a bath. A long one."

He nodded. "Let me finish up and we can head out." He looked at the computer and rubbed his chin. "What time did you say you're meeting Gracie?"

Crud, Catherine had forgotten all about the concert. "Six o'clock. What time is it?"

"It's only two," he said, a slow sexy smile spreading across his face. "We have time."

She knew that look. He was making plans. Naughty plans. "Time for what exactly?"

He wagged his eyebrows. "For me to play your bath buddy."

Intrigued at the idea of spending more time in the Jacuzzi-style tub with Dean, Catherine said, "Only if I get to be in charge of the soap this time."

Dean reached up and gave a playful tug on her hair. "You should know by now that I'm always the one in charge. At least when it comes to playtime."

Frustrated, Catherine crossed her arms over her chest. "But last time I didn't get a chance to wash you. Not fair."

He winked. "Fine, you can go first, how's that?"

Catherine grinned as she thought of all the wicked things she would do to him. She rubbed her hands together. "Oh, this is going to be fun."

Dean grunted and started to shove some papers into a drawer. "Hell, I might not survive it."

Catherine's mind went back over all they'd just done, and her mind glommed on to one thing. "Dean?"

Without looking up from his desk, he said, "Hmm?"

"Earlier you called me . . . your girl. Did you mean that?" She hadn't meant to sound so vulnerable, but she needed to know where she stood with him.

Dean stopped what he was doing and looked over at her. He never took his gaze from hers when he said, "I meant every word." He stood and closed the distance between them. They were only a breath apart when he asked, "Do you have a problem being mine, sweetheart? If so, you should tell me now."

Her stomach flip-flopped. She felt utterly desirable around Dean. His words and caresses made her come alive. "I don't have a problem with it. And you should know that I consider you mine now too."

He reached out and stroked a single finger down her cheek. "Suits me just fine."

"This could prove interesting though, considering I live in Georgia and you still don't trust me."

His eyes turned hard. "I don't want to think of you leaving."

Catherine noticed he didn't address the trust issue. She knew at some point they'd have to. It was the white elephant in the room whenever they were together. She took the last remaining step and wrapped her arms around his waist, cuddling close. She didn't know what was going to happen to their fragile relationship, but for now she planned to make the most of every second. "Let's go play in the tub."

His lips brushed the top of her head in a gentle caress. "I love the way you think, sweets."

19

Dean looked at the time on his alarm clock next to his bed. Christ, he'd only been away from Catherine for a few hours and he couldn't stop thinking about her. What was wrong with him? Normally he was relieved when the woman he was dating didn't smother him twenty-four hours a day. He hated the clingy types. Catherine definitely wasn't clingy. In fact, right now she was off listening to some orchestra perform and probably having a great time. He shook his head and put the graphite pencil back in the cup. As he stood back, he surveyed the sketch. Damn, it was the best thing he'd ever drawn. He wondered if Catherine would like it. When he heard the doorbell, Dean's stomach knotted. It couldn't be her. The performance wouldn't be over until nine, Catherine had said. She'd told him that she'd call when she made it back to the hotel. Still, a guy could hope. The doorbell chimed again, and Dean strode from the room. By the time he reached the front door, he was frowning. He yanked it open, ready to blast his visitor when he was brought up short by the sight of his mom and sister.

"Took you long enough to answer the door," Deanna said, rubbing her hands together to ward off the chill.

"Was it really necessary to ring the bell twice?" he asked as he stepped aside to let them in.

"Sorry," Deanna said, sounding anything but. "What were you doing?"

"I was working, Little Miss Busybody," he answered as he tweaked her nose.

"This late?" his mom asked.

"Here," Dean said as he helped her with her coat. Not that she needed it. At sixty-two years old, his mom still got around just fine. She had fair skin that barely showed her age and dark brown hair sprinkled with gray. Dean knew she'd joined a yoga class and that she took good care of herself. He still worried about her though. Since his dad's death from a brain aneurism a few years ago, his mother had been left alone in the large house he'd been raised in. It bothered Wade, Deanna, and him that their mother refused to sell and find a small apartment.

"Nothing strenuous, I swear," he answered her. "Just working on a bid." He hated to lie to his family, but he hadn't shared his love of art with them. He hadn't shared it with anyone, until Catherine. It made him feel exposed whenever he thought of showing his sketches to his mom and sister.

She looked at him with the astuteness only a mother seemed to possess. "Are we interrupting?"

"Of course not, Mom. You're always welcome at my house." He leaned down and hugged her, before saying, "Sorry if I was rude."

"Well, in that case, you wouldn't happen to have some coffee made, would you?" she asked as she shivered. "Some really hot coffee?"

"Coming right up," he said as he led the way to the kitchen. "For you too, Dee?" he called over his shoulder.

"I'd love some," she answered as she followed close behind. "I thought you were dog sitting. Where's Duke?"

"Back at home. His owner came home early from his trip." As the women sat, Dean asked, "So, is there a particular reason for the visit? Or is it that you missed my pretty face?"

His mom laughed. "I always enjoy seeing the pretty faces of my children."

"Yeah, but I'm the prettiest, right?" Deanna chimed in.

Dean snorted as he poured water into the well on the back of the brewer. "I'm the good-looking twin, remember?"

"That's not what Jonas says," Deanna shot right back.

Dean rolled his eyes. "His vote doesn't count," he said, scooping coffee grounds into the basket. "He's biased."

"Stop it, you two," his mom said. "I swear, sometimes your bickering could drive me to drink."

Deanna laughed. "But you love us anyway."

Dean grabbed three mugs from the cupboard and sat them in the center of the table. He pulled out a chair, turned it around, and straddled it. He wasted no time getting to the point. "I can see you have something on your collective minds." He looked at his mom, then his sister. "Might as well spit it out."

"We came because we're concerned about you, Dean," his mother replied, her tone softening a measure. "You and Catherine both."

Dean glared at his twin. "Big mouth." At least Deanna had the good grace to blush. It was something, he supposed.

His mom reached over and patted the back of his hand. "Don't be upset with your sister. She's worried, that's all."

"About me? What the hell for?"

His mother frowned. "Watch your language."

"Sorry," he muttered. "But seriously, why are you two worried? I'm fine."

"Not from what I can see, you aren't," his sister interrupted, unwilling to back off. Stubborn woman.

When the coffeemaker dinged, indicating it was finished, Dean stood to get it, welcoming the distraction. "Well, you don't see everything, Dee," he told her as he poured them each a cup.

"Have you decided to believe Catherine's story?" she asked with a knowing look. Dean refused to answer. "That's what I thought. So, you aren't fine."

He put the carafe back on the warming plate and leaned against the counter, leaving his mug on the table, untouched. "That topic is off-limits. Let it go."

"Dean," his mom said. "Have you considered that a good deal of your distrust of Catherine might stem from what happened between you and Linda? Not to mention the two losers before her who broke your heart."

Of course he'd thought of it, but he didn't want to get into that ugly can of worms with his mother, of all people. "Mom, that was all years ago. I'm over it."

"You're over them, that's true, but are you over what those women did to you?"

"Yes," he bit out, knowing it was the biggest lie of all. In his mind, Dean would always see that moment when he'd walked into the bedroom all prepared to propose marriage only to find Linda with another man.

His mom shook her head. "You care for Catherine, don't you?"

He shrugged, not willing to discuss his feelings for Catherine with anyone but Catherine. Hell, he wasn't even sure what they were. "I don't know what I feel yet." At least that was partly true.

"The truth, Dean."

He'd forgotten how determined his mother could be. He felt like a little kid all over again. "Yes," he admitted. "I'm beginning to care. The thought of her going back to Georgia has me in knots. Happy?"

His mother stood and walked toward him. She placed a hand on his shoulder. "I won't be happy until you're happy. I want all my kids happy. And holding on to this hate, Dean, keeping that wound fresh, isn't healthy."

Dean started to put two and two together. "Is this like an intervention or something?"

"Don't get an attitude," she said, chastising him as if he weren't an adult. "We love you, and that's the only reason we're here."

He held up both hands in surrender. What was a guy supposed to do when he went up against two strong-minded women? "I love you too," he said, meaning it. "And I get the message, loud and clear. But I'm a big kid and I need to deal with this in my way. Okay?"

Deanna moved up beside him, adding her own weight to their mother. "Talk to Catherine," she demanded. "Tell her how you feel. If you don't you could lose her, Dean."

Put like that, Dean knew the pair of meddlers were right. As Jonas had put it, he needed to get his head out of his ass. He leaned down and placed a gentle kiss on both their cheeks. "Thank you for being so nosy."

Deanna beamed. "Anytime."

After the performance, Gracie and Wade dropped Catherine off at her hotel. She'd had a great time, but she'd been so tired that she'd yawned, more than once. Gracie had noticed and asked her about it. Catherine had caved and told her sister about Dean showing up at her hotel, and about what happened afterward. She'd thought Gracie would be happy, but if anything she appeared more worried than ever. Catherine didn't understand it.

She kicked off her black high heels and stripped out of her

clothes, then slipped into an old nightshirt. She looked at her cell phone, wondering if Dean was still awake. She glanced at the clock by the bed—ten in the evening. He would probably need to be up early for work. She should let him sleep. She was exhausted anyway.

"I can make it through one night without hearing his voice," she told herself.

Besides, she was about to fall over from lack of sleep, thanks to Dean and his insatiable appetite. Not that she was complaining, she thought with a grin. Catherine crossed the room and pulled back the covers. That was as far as she got before her cell started to buzz. She froze and stared at it, willing it to ring. Could it be? When the perky little tone sounded again, Catherine fairly leaped across the bed to grab it.

"Hello?"

"I was wondering when I was going to hear your pretty voice."

Her heart did a few cartwheels when Dean's deep baritone came over the line. "I just got back. I thought about calling, but I was afraid to wake you."

"I'm a night owl. Call me anytime."

Catherine liked the 'anytime' part. It made her think of their relationship as long term. "I'll make a note of that." She scooted backward on the mattress and got under the covers. Once she was comfortable she said, "I missed you tonight." She thought of how that might sound to a man like Dean who seemed to covet his independence, and thought to add, "Not that it's a big deal, considering it hasn't been that long since we saw each other."

"I missed you too." He went quiet a moment, and Catherine was afraid the call had been dropped. "I have a surprise for you," he said in a quieter voice.

Equal amounts of shock and excitement zipped through her. "You do?"

"Yep," he said. "I hope you like it."

Intrigued, Catherine asked, "What is it?"

She heard him chuckle, and the deep, sexy sound sent shivers up and down her spine. "It's a surprise," he replied. "You'll have to wait and see."

She scooted up higher on her pillow. "When will you show it to me?"

"Are you busy tomorrow night?"

"No. Yes. Well, sort of. I'm going over to Wade and Gracie's tomorrow for lunch and to hang out, but my evening is free."

"Good, I'll show it to you then. Want to come over around seven? Or I could swing by and get you, if you want."

Her heart began to beat faster at the thought of seeing Dean. "I'll drive, but thanks."

"Now that that's settled, what are you doing right now?"

She picked at a stray thread on the blanket and said, "I'm in bed."

"Mmm," he murmured, "nice visual."

All the blood in Catherine's body seemed to rush south at Dean's sensual tone. "What are you doing?" she asked, curious if he was in bed as well. An image of him naked and all sprawled out in his big bed sprang to mind. Yum.

"I'm on the couch," he replied, kicking her visual to the curb. "I was waiting for you to call me, but the phone never rang."

She winced, hating that he'd waited in vain. "I'm sorry. I was afraid to wake you."

"Tell me what you're wearing and maybe I'll forgive you," he said with a hint of mischief.

Catherine laughed. "A snowsuit and cowboy boots."

His chuckle seemed to go straight to her pussy. "Very funny." He paused a second before saying, "Maybe you need a spanking. What do you think?"

Catherine pictured herself bent over Dean's knee as he delivered several swats to her rear. Her pussy throbbed at the erotic visual. "Maybe I do."

"Has a man ever done that to you before, sweetheart?"

Her face flamed, and she was only too glad Dean couldn't see her. "No," she said with total honesty. "Remember, I'm the unadventurous one here."

She heard him shuffling around. "You just need the right teacher."

The phone wobbled in her suddenly unsteady hand. "Are you the right teacher for me, Dean?"

"Would you like me to be?"

Her breath caught in her throat, and she had to tell herself to exhale. "Yes," she said, going for broke.

"I have some ideas for us, Catherine, but I'm not sure you're ready yet."

Oh, curiouser and curiouser. "That depends on the ideas. What do you have in mind?"

"I'd much rather tell you in person," he murmured huskily. "Tomorrow night, when I have you all turned on and anxious, I'll tell you all the ways I plan to dirty you up."

That stunning comment had Catherine's jaw going slack for a moment. "You're a very a bad influence on me," she whispered.

"Probably," he said, sounding far too serious. There was a pause and then, "Now, tell me what you're really wearing. Give me something to think about tonight while I'm in bed."

She looked down at herself and cringed. "Well, to be honest, I'm wearing an old green nightshirt. Nothing special or fancy. Sorry."

"Don't apologize," he chastised. "I like you dressed up or down. Either gets me going, believe me."

She fell a little harder for him in that moment. "Thank you," she replied.

"You're welcome. Now, tell me about your panties. Are you wearing any?"

"Yes," she murmured as her breathing increased. "What are you wearing?"

"Pajama pants."

The way he said it made her think of his gorgeous, kissable bare chest. "That's all?"

"Yep," he answered. "Now, what color are those panties? Describe them to me."

Catherine hesitated. Not sure how far she wanted to go. "Is this anything like a dirty phone call?"

"No, because I don't want you coming," he boldly stated. "Not unless I'm there to lick you clean."

She grinned and decided to tweak him a little. "I could just take matters into my own hands after we hang up. You'd never know."

"But you won't because you know it'll be ten times better when it's my mouth bringing you to climax."

Oh yeah, he had her there. "I'm wearing black satin panties," she said, describing them like he'd wanted. "They have lace trim around the top."

"Ah, now that's hot," he growled. "Damn, Catherine, I want to be there so badly."

"I wish you were," she breathed out. "My bed feels cold without you." She turned her face to the side and inhaled. "But I can still smell your scent on my pillow. It's turning me on." A fresh wave of heat swept over her as she imagined Dean striding in right at that moment. He would rip the covers off her and take her, hard and fast. Good Lord, it was going to be a long night if she kept this up.

"You're all over my bedroom, woman," he bit out, as if frustrated by the idea. "On my pillow and blankets both. It's half the reason I'm in the living room. Sitting in there was making me horny as fuck."

The image of his cock, all thick and hard, made Catherine's mouth water. "Hmm, if I have to wait, then so do you."

He snorted. "My hand would be a damn poor substitute anyway."

Catherine imagined being bold enough to get in her rental and drive over to his house. She could show up in her coat and nothing else. But she wasn't that bold, she thought miserably. Never had been. Dang it.

"You still there?"

"Sorry, yea." She yawned as her body started to succumb to lack of sleep. "I'm getting tired though." She smiled. "Someone kept me up last night."

"You'd better get a good night's sleep tonight, then, because you'll be up tomorrow night too," he confirmed, his voice low and filled with dark promise.

She yawned again and knew she was about done for. "I'm glad you called."

"Me too," he murmured. "Sleep tight, sweetheart."

"You too, Dean."

When they hung up, Catherine thought of what Dean had said. He had a surprise for her. She couldn't even begin to guess what it might be, but it thrilled her that he'd thought of her. Tomorrow was Thursday, though, and she'd be going home in a few days. Home, which meant miles away from Dean. What was she going to do then?

The thought had her tossing and turning until the wee hours of the morning.

20

The next day, Catherine arrived at Wade and Gracie's in time to watch Gracie pull out a large pan from the oven. "What is that?" she asked as she laid her coat over a chair. "It smells delicious."

"Wade made lasagna." She pointed to a stool by the counter. "Pull up a seat. You're going to love this."

Catherine's stomach rumbled as she took the seat nearest the stove. "Mmm, I can't wait. You snagged yourself a pretty handy guy there, you know? He cooks *and* takes down bad guys. Is there anything he can't do?"

Gracie laughed as she placed the potholders aside and picked up a large knife. "I happen to think he can do anything, but I'm somewhat biased."

Catherine looked around. "Where is the man of the hour anyway?"

"He and Jonas are working a case. An embezzler or something." Gracie threw her hands in the air. "I can't keep track."

The dangerous nature of Wade's private investigating job prompted Catherine to ask, "Does it worry you when he's away?"

"Definitely, but I know he takes precautions. I can't ask for more than that."

She admired Gracie for her strength, and for the faith she obviously had in her fiancé. "Has he ever considered a different line of work?"

Gracie started to cut the lasagna into large squares. "Nah, he loves his job. He'd be miserable doing something else."

A knock on the door interrupted them. Catherine frowned. "Are you expecting someone?"

Gracie put the knife down and wiped her hands on a dish-towel. "I almost forgot that I asked Wade's mom and sister to come over." She bit her lip. "Do you mind?"

"Of course not." Catherine laughed. "I wondered who was going to eat all that lasagna."

Gracie headed for the door and let the two women in. "You have great timing. The lasagna just came out of the oven."

"Oh, man, that brother of mine is an amazing cook," Deanna said as she tossed her coat on top of Catherine's. "I think that gene skipped me or something."

Catherine watched as Dean's mother took off her own coat. The older woman looked her way and smiled. "I hope you don't mind us horning in on your visit with Gracie."

Catherine waved a hand in the air. "Not at all. I was just say-ing that I was glad I wasn't going to have to eat all that lasagna by myself."

Deanna pulled out a stool and sat next to her. "No worries. Food never goes to waste when I'm around."

Catherine laughed. "But you're so thin. What's your se-cret?"

"Her metabolism is turbocharged," Dean's mom answered. "It's the only explanation."

When Gracie took plates out of the cupboards, Catherine thought to ask, "Is there anything I can do?"

Gracie looked over her shoulder at her. "Would you mind

getting out the glasses? And there's a pitcher of iced tea in the fridge."

"No problem." Catherine got off her stool and moved around to the other side of the counter, then stared at the many cupboards. "Uh, which one are the glasses in?"

Gracie pointed toward the refrigerator. "The one on the left there," she said.

"Is there anything we can do, dear?" Mrs. Harrison asked as she went to the sink and washed her hands.

"There's a salad in the fridge. If you can get that out it'd be great." She looked over at Deanna. "Deanna, would you mind getting out the silverware?"

"Sure thing," she said, as she hopped off the stool and got to work.

Together they had lunch set out and were digging into the food within minutes. It was the best lasagna Catherine had ever eaten. She was amazed when Deanna went back for a second helping, considering how large the slices were. The woman really did have an amazing metabolism. She wished it'd rub off on her. As the thought entered her mind, she remembered Dean telling her he loved her curves and had to bite back a smile.

After lunch, Gracie brewed a pot of coffee and they moved into the living room. Catherine sat on the couch next to Gracie, while Deanna and her mom took the chairs opposite them.

"So," the older woman said, "Deanna tells me that you and Dean are seeing each other."

Catherine could feel her cheeks heating up as she thought of how Deanna had come by that particular kernel of information. "We've gone out a few times," Catherine answered, keeping it vague. It was a lame reply, she knew, but she couldn't very well tell the woman that they'd spent most of their time together in bed.

"Do you like him?" she asked, a friendly smile on her face.

"He's a wonderful guy," Catherine told her with total honesty. "I've enjoyed our dates." Definitely the understatement of the year there. She looked over at Deanna and saw her attempting to hide a grin.

"He is a wonderful guy, but he can be stubborn and difficult." When Catherine started to protest, Mrs. Harrison held up a hand. "No, it's okay. He's my son and I love him, but he's a lot like his father, impulsive and demanding."

Catherine sighed. "He doesn't trust me," she admitted. "He thinks I'm hiding something. Like I'm going to try something underhanded with Gracie." Catherine got angry all over again as she thought about his total lack of faith in her. "I can't figure it out."

"Do you care about him?" Mrs. Harrison asked.

Catherine looked at the three women. All of them seemed to be holding their breath for her answer. "Yes," she replied, her voice trembling a little. "The idea of going back to Georgia isn't at all appealing. I'm going to miss Gracie terribly, and my relationship with Dean is so fragile."

"You're worried he'll forget about you once you're gone," Deanna surmised.

Catherine nodded and looked down at the floor. "I get the feeling he's holding a part of himself back and I don't know why." She ran a hand through her hair. "How can I fix it if he won't open up to me?"

The room went quiet, and Catherine looked up to see Deanna and her mom exchanging a telling look. The pair clearly knew something. Deanna spoke up first. "Dean hasn't had the best of luck in the dating arena, but I know that he cares about you."

Afraid Deanna was only saying that to make her feel better, she asked, "How can you possibly tell?"

Gracie laughed. "Um, it's pretty much all over his face whenever someone mentions your name or you two are in the same room together."

"And he's done a good job of monopolizing your time whenever you aren't busy with Gracie. My brother doesn't spend that much time with a woman unless he really cares about her."

Catherine shrugged, not quite convinced. "That's lust, which is *so* not the same thing." She realized what she'd said and who she'd said it in front of, and promptly wanted to swallow her own tongue. "Sorry," she mumbled, feeling like a complete idiot. "That was totally inappropriate."

All three women laughed. "It's fine, trust me," Mrs. Harrison said. "Dean's father had a rather healthy sex drive too."

"Mom!" Deanna exclaimed. "Way too much information!"

Soon they were all cracking up. After they settled down and the room was silent once more, Catherine asked, "So, do you ladies have any tips for me? I'm desperate here."

Dean's mom leaned over and patted her on the arm. "Don't give up on him, sweetie. He's crazy about you, I know it. He needs a swift kick in the pants, but he's one of the good guys, trust me."

Deanna nodded. "Mom's right. He's annoying and obstinate at times, but he's worth an extra headache or two."

Catherine's hopes lifted a few notches. "I can be plenty stubborn too. Especially when I see something I want."

Gracie laughed. "Another thing we have in common." She stood and placed her hands on her hips. "Now, who is in the mood for chocolate cake?"

There wasn't a single "no" among them. Catherine decided on an extra-large slice. She figured she'd need the energy for later. Lord knows, Dean was bound to keep her up until dawn. She couldn't wait.

"So," Gracie said a few minutes later around a mouthful of cake. "I have some news to share."

"What?" they all said at once.

"Wade and I set a date for the wedding."

"Finally!" Deanna said. "I wondered when you two would get around to that."

"When is it?" Mrs. Harrison asked, her face beaming with happiness.

"We're thinking late September," Gracie answered. "When the weather is beginning to change and it's cooler out. What do you think?"

Catherine imagined watching her sister walk down the aisle in a gorgeous white gown and tears sprang to her eyes. "I never thought I'd be attending my sister's wedding," she said in a quiet, shaky voice. "I'm so happy for you, Gracie. This is the best news in the world."

"I agree with Catherine," Deanna said. "This is the best news ever."

"And, Catherine," Gracie added as she stared at her, "I want you to be my maid of honor. Are you up for it?"

Catherine clapped her hands together. "Oh, I'd love to!"

"I think a September wedding sounds lovely, Gracie. And I'm thrilled that my son had the good sense to pick you for his wife."

Gracie grinned. "Thank you. I feel pretty lucky to have him too."

Mrs. Harrison tapped her chin as if in thought. "So, do you want a small affair?"

"Yes," she replied. "Wade and I want to keep it simple, if that's okay with you?"

She waved a hand in the air. "Of course it is, but can I ask one thing?"

"Sure," Gracie said. "What is it?"

"May I bring a date?"

All three of them stopped and stared at Deanna's mother. None of them seemed capable of speech. As far as Catherine knew, Deanna's mom hadn't dated since the death of her husband. At least that's what Gracie had told her. Judging by

Deanna's frown she was none too pleased about the news that her mom had met someone.

"A date?" Deanna asked. "Where on earth did you meet a man?"

Her mother blushed. "He's a counselor at the women's shelter I work at. His name is Mac Cantrell, and he's a really sweet man."

"Mac," Deanna said, as if in shock. "From the shelter."

Mrs. Harrison rolled her eyes. "It's not a big deal, Deanna. He's simply a friend. We started talking one day and found out we have a lot in common. He has grown children, like me, and his wife passed away from breast cancer about three years ago."

Deanna quirked a brow. "And you want to bring Mac to the wedding with you," she stated as if the concept was total foreign to her.

"Yes," her mom bit out. "Is there a problem?"

Deanna appeared to give the question some thought before saying, "I guess not. I mean, it'll be a little weird to see you with another man, that's all." When Deanna looked down at the floor, Catherine felt as if she were intruding on something private.

Deanna's mom left the chair and moved to sit next to her daughter. She wrapped an arm around her shoulders and said, "If it's too hard for you because of your dad, I'll understand, sweetie."

Deanna looked at her mom and smiled. "No," she replied in a softer voice, "you should bring Mac to the wedding. It's been long enough, Mom. It's time to move on."

Mrs. Harrison shrugged. "I don't know about moving on. To be honest, I feel a little guilty for even talking to Mac. Like I'm betraying your father."

Deanna vehemently shook her head. "No, Mom, really. Dad would want you to be happy. He wouldn't expect you to be alone the rest of your life." She took her mom's hand in hers and said, "You have my support all the way."

"Thank you, dear, that means so much," she said, as both women shared a tearful hug. When they pulled apart, Deanna's mom let out a long sigh. "Now, to tell your brothers, that's not going to be fun."

All four of them groaned. Gracie was the first to speak. "Expect Wade to run a background check on him," she bit out, clearly recalling the way he'd done that with Catherine. "And he's absolutely going to want to have a heart-to-heart with Mac, too, I bet. He's very protective that way."

Deanna laughed. "Oh, man, I can't wait to see their faces when you tell them, Mom."

Catherine snorted. "You have a mischievous streak a mile wide."

"Hey, Dean and Wade still have it coming, considering the hassle they gave Jonas and me when we started to see each other."

That surprised her. "But you two are made for each other!"

"Yeah, but I'm the little sister, so no guy is ever quite good enough." Deanna rolled her eyes. "Ridiculous nonsense, if you ask me."

"They've accepted him now though," Gracie said. "And speaking of Jonas, he'll probably be an usher. Dean will be best man." She pointed to Deanna and said, "You'll be a bridesmaid."

The rest of the afternoon was spent discussing wedding preparations. Catherine felt so comfortable with Gracie and Dean's family that she forgot for a minute that she would be going home soon.

The thought was more depressing than ever.

21

When she arrived on Dean's doorstep at seven sharp, Dean answered the door after the first knock. Catherine's entire body went on high alert when she caught sight of him. He was dressed in a pair of black jeans and a plain white T-shirt. His hair was a wet, tousled mess as if he'd recently showered. And he was barefoot. Staring at the man could easily become a new favorite hobby of hers.

"Hi," Dean said as he reached for her hand. In a lust-induced daze, Catherine stared at it a second before finally placing her hand in his. He intertwined their fingers and pulled her into the house, then kicked the door shut. Catherine started to ask him about his wet hair, but Dean quickly dragged her into his arms and proceeded to kiss her senseless. Catherine's mind went blank and she melted against him as every fiber in her being raged to life.

When he pulled back, they were both breathing heavy and the animalistic look in his eyes sent butterflies to flight inside Catherine's stomach. "Damn, I needed that," he gritted out.

"Me too," she confessed, wishing he hadn't stopped so soon.

Dean helped her with her coat. He looked her over and Catherine could almost feel the stroke of his gaze as he stopped for a few fiery moments on her breasts. "Beautiful," he murmured. "Then again, your curves could make a burlap sack look downright indecent."

Catherine smoothed her hands down her sides. "I still think I need to lose a few pounds, but thank you."

"Don't even think about going on a diet." He paused, then said, "Speaking of that, I made some more hot chocolate. Want a cup?"

She rubbed her hands together to ward off the chill. "Oh, it sounds wonderful, thank you."

Once in the kitchen, he turned toward her. "I hear you visited with my mom and sister today."

Catherine sat at the table and crossed her legs. For some reason she was nervous. She wasn't sure why, but she suspected it had something to do with the fact that she'd discovered she loved Dean and wasn't too confident the feeling would ever be reciprocated. Yeah, that could have a girl on edge.

"Catherine?"

She snapped back to reality, embarrassed that she'd forgotten his question. "Sorry, I got sidetracked. What did you say?"

Dean grabbed a potholder and took a steaming pan off the stove. "I was saying that I heard you visited with my mom and sister today. How'd that go?"

"Oh, yeah, they came to Gracie's and had lunch with us," she explained. "I enjoyed talked with them. Your family is pretty great."

He nodded, then turned back to the counter to pour their drinks. Catherine took a moment to admire the view. Her gaze traveled over his strong shoulders and back, all the way down to his butt, where she got stuck for a few seconds. When she recalled how good that particular body part felt beneath her fingers, immediate meltdown occurred.

After Dean finished making the sweet chocolaty delight, he came back to the table and sat in the chair next to her. She took her drink and blew on it to cool it off. Catherine noticed the little marshmallows floating on the surface, and joy swept through her. The fact that he'd remembered made her feel special. She carefully plucked one out and popped it into her mouth.

Dean groaned. "I love watching you with hot chocolate. It's sexy as hell."

Catherine nearly choked. "No way is hot chocolate sexy, Dean."

"I beg to differ, sweetheart," he murmured as he reached over and picked out a chocolate-soaked marshmallow from her cup and held it to her lips. "Open up," he gently ordered. Catherine obeyed, and he placed the sweet treat onto her tongue. She closed her lips around it and swallowed, while Dean watched on. A low rumble of sound came from deep in his throat. "Mmm-hmm, definitely sexy." He sat back and took a drink of his own chocolate before asking, "So, did my family warn you away from me? Did they tell you I'm a troublemaker?"

She laughed. "Of course they didn't. Their love for you came through loud and clear." She hesitated to tell them what all they'd discussed, but in the end opted for total honesty, and prayed it was the right choice. "There were some questions."

He quirked a brow. "An interrogation, you mean?"

"Oh, no, not at all. They're merely curious about us." She looked down at her mug. "So am I, to tell the truth."

Dean's hand covered hers. "You're curious, huh?"

Catherine dipped a finger into the now-warm liquid and swirled. "I leave in a few days, Dean. I don't know what's going to happen—with us."

She felt a finger beneath her chin, and Catherine lifted her head. Dean gave her such a scorchingly hot look that she could've sworn her blood caught fire. "I think it's time for your surprise, sweetheart."

At the reminder that he had a present for her, Catherine's mood lifted. "You really have a surprise for me?"

He stood and held out a hand. "Come with me and you'll see."

"Okay," she said as she put her hand in his and let him steer her out of the kitchen and into the bedroom.

He released her and pointed to the bed. "Have a seat while I get it."

Catherine grinned from ear to ear as she did as he instructed. She couldn't imagine what he might have for her. When he went to a set of doors and slid one open, her curiosity piqued. Catherine watched on as Dean picked up something large and covered in a cream-colored cloth. She couldn't tell what lay beneath.

When Dean reached the side of the bed, his gaze on her, he said, "I hope you like it."

Catherine caught a hint of uncertainty in his voice and she wanted to reassure him, but when he yanked off the heavy covering, she literally felt as if all the air had been sucked out of the room. Her mouth dropped open as she took in the treasure before her.

"Oh, my God," she whispered. Catherine's surprise was a sketch of herself, sleeping. Dean had drawn her as she lay curled up in bed, her hair all around her, the blankets draped over her with one leg uncovered. She leaned closer and realized it was her hotel room. The morning after he'd spent the night? He'd drawn her from memory? He'd even framed it in a gorgeous cherrywood frame. Tears sprang to her eyes at the thoughtfulness of his gift to her.

Dean crouched in front of her and cupped her face in his palms. "Are you crying? Ah, hell, you hate it, don't you?"

"No, Dean," she rushed to correct him, "not at all. It's . . .

it's simply stunning." She didn't know how to put into words what his present meant to her. "It's absolutely the most beautiful thing I've ever seen."

His smile was one of pride. "I had a gorgeous model."

She wanted to cry. "It must have taken you quite some time to complete though. There's so much detail. The crinkled bedding, my sleep-tousled hair." She looked at him and asked, "When did you draw this?"

"While you were at the performance with Gracie. I . . . had some free time on my hands."

"But you framed it, even." Catherine was still dumbfounded that he'd managed to complete something so beautiful in such a short amount of time. "How'd you get it done so quickly?"

He shrugged. "I had the wood for the frame on hand."

In that moment, Catherine saw a vulnerable side to Dean. He'd seemed so confident and in control. Watching him now, she knew she wasn't the only one with their emotions in overdrive. It went a long way to soothing her ravaged nerves.

After one last lingering look, Dean recovered the sketch and took it to the other side of the room. He sat it against the wall and came back to her, his strides long and purposeful. His powerful body had her fairly tingling with need.

"It's time we talked about my trust issues," he stated in a firm voice. As he sat on the bed next to her, Catherine noticed that their thighs were close but not touching. He needed distance for whatever he was about to tell her? A sense of dread filled her. Still, even without knowing what he was going to say, Catherine knew this discussion was way overdue.

She took a deep breath and let it out, then said, "I'm all ears."

Dean placed his arms on his thighs and stared down at the floor, as if attempting to figure out how to begin. "Her name was Linda," he finally said with a bitterness that spoke of real pain.

Catherine hated the woman already and wanted to say as much, but instead she stayed silent, waiting for him to continue.

Dean swiped a hand over his face before he straightened and caught her gaze. "And I was in love with her."

Catherine paled, suddenly afraid for him to say more. Afraid she wouldn't be able to withstand what he was about to tell her. She remembered Deanna saying that Dean hadn't had much luck in the dating arena and knew this must have been what she'd been talking about.

She reached over and placed her hand on his thigh. "What happened?" she asked.

"She cheated on me," he bit out. "The day I was going to propose to her, I walked in on her with another man." He grimaced, as if reliving the moment. "She was my whole world, Catherine, and she betrayed me."

Catherine wanted to do some serious bodily harm to Linda. It was one of the few times in her life, Catherine actually used the B word.

Dean's head shot backward. "Ouch," he said with a playful half smile curving his lips.

Catherine shrugged. "All I know is that if she tossed a man like you to the side, then she must've been off her rocker."

"Yeah, well, the point is it's hard for me to trust because of her. Because of what she did to me. He paused a moment then added, "Sadly, she wasn't the only girlfriend to walk all over me either."

"I understand" Catherine said. "It would be difficult for anyone to trust after that."

"Yes," he gritted out.

"Is that why you've had it in your head that I was lying about my adoption? That I was up to no good?"

"Yeah," he answered as he reached over and took possession of her hand. Enthralled, Catherine watched as he brought it to his mouth and pressed his lips against her palm. "I'm sorry for being a complete shit," he said. "I'm sorry for not having faith in you. I know I don't deserve it, but if you'll let me I promise to make it up to you."

God, her heart was breaking for him. For a man as passionate and loyal as Dean, a betrayal like the one he'd just described would be worse than if the woman had stabbed him in the back with a butcher knife. "It's okay. I'm sorry you had to go through that."

He shook his head. "Don't be. It was a long time ago. It's in the past." His gaze caught hers as he said, "The point is, I treated you badly and it wasn't fair, sweetheart."

"Yes, you did, but I know why now," she said, her heart softening for the strong man sitting next to her, baring his soul. "Linda left quite an impression on you, and it's hard to get over something like that."

"Yeah, and it's frustrating as hell." He frowned, a muscle in his jaw jumping erratically. "I'm no good for you, Catherine."

"How about I be the judge of that?" She stroked his cheek with her free hand and murmured, "Besides, I only have so much time left in Ohio, and I want to make the absolute most of every minute."

Dean wrapped his hand around the nape of her neck and drew her close. "Mmm, not a bad idea," he growled as he kissed her. It was so brief and soft, Catherine barely had time to take in his taste before he pulled away. "This evening is for you, sweetheart."

She had no idea what he meant by that, but when he released her and pushed her backward until she was sprawled atop the cool blankets, Catherine gave up on attempting to think clearly. Her worries about their relationship flew out the window as erotic images of her gorgeous lover filled her head.

Dean, in all his tanned, dark-haired glory, stood and stripped out of his clothes before sprawling out on the bed next to her. His well-muscled body and the intensity in his dreamy hazel eyes were enough to have any woman drooling. The heavy length between his legs made Catherine's face burn. He was hard and ready and he was all hers.

Catherine tore her gaze away from his erection and searched his face for answers. He didn't wear his heart on his sleeve the way she did, but she felt loved in that moment. Was she deluding herself?

Dean wrapped his arm around her shoulders and pulled her stiff body in tight. She was as rigid as a wooden plank, every muscle strung tight with nerves and fears.

"Relax. Leave all the big questions for later. For now, just feel my body against yours," Dean softly commanded, his voice, so rich and smooth, sliding over her skin, relaxing and firing up her libido at the same time.

"This feels ... different somehow," she confessed as she buried her nose into his side.

"What's different, sweetheart? Talk to me," Dean asked, his voice a smooth caress.

"I don't know," she said, as she attempted to put into words what she felt. "Up until this very moment you didn't trust me. You made it clear that what was between us was only physical. It doesn't feel that way now. At least not to me."

Dean shook his head. "Sweetheart, it hasn't been purely physical for me since the moment you so bravely came to my front door offering a truce." He grinned. "You have this soft, giving nature that people respond to, including me. I love that you're stubborn and shy and funny. Every part of you intrigues me."

"So it's not just my red hair you like, huh?"

He chuckled. "No, it's not just the hair." He smoothed a hand over her belly, setting off little fires everywhere he touched.

"Now, relax," he growled as he began removing her clothes. "Leave everything for later. Think only of pleasure, Catherine, nothing more."

Soon Catherine was totally nude, Dean's strong, rough hands caressing her body and bringing her higher. "Touch me," he whispered against her ear. She reached out with her right hand and smoothed it over his pectorals, running her fingers through the sprinkling of hair that littered his chest. She inched her leg up and over his, letting her sex slide along the side of his muscular thigh. Dean groaned his approval, and Catherine continued, encouraged by the deep sounds coming from him.

She teased her fingers down the front of him, giving herself free rein. In some dark part of her soul, Catherine wanted Dean at her mercy. She wanted him begging for her. Out of control.

"Jesus, you're soft, Catherine," Dean complimented. "Soft and lush and mine." His hands skated over her overheated skin, toying with her belly button ring a few seconds before moving lower. "More," he said. One second Catherine was lying next to him, and the next she was spread out on top of his huge body. He smiled at her surprise and kissed her tenderly. His lips, so warm and eager, tasted her as if he wanted to spend a good long time pleasuring each and every part of her with his mouth. Lips parted and tongues met in a wild mating dance, and all the while his hands massaged and caressed. When his fingers came within an inch of her clitoris, Catherine broke the kiss and opened her eyes. "Touch me, Dean," she quietly urged.

"Always," he murmured as he stroked her nether lips. Catherine's body vibrated at the bare touch.

Catherine's heart soared to the clouds and beyond at his one-word reply. She lay atop the wild and rugged Dean Harrison, his hands all over her, stroking and touching and driving her crazy with need. Hot damn.

22

___

Catherine's body began to climb higher and higher. She moaned his name. Dean cursed and went still. "What—"

"Shhh," he said, his voice rough. "First things first."

Unhappy with that ridiculous answer, Catherine slapped his chest. "I had hoped that would be first," she replied, feeling woefully neglected.

He winked and asked, "Do you still want to be adventurous?"

With only a few days left to spend with the man, the answer came easily to Catherine. "Yes."

In another heartbeat, she found herself flat on her back as Dean stood up and walked away from the bed. She waited, unsure what he would do next. He went to the closet again and retrieved a small wooden box. Intrigued, Catherine asked, "What is that?"

"Something for your pleasure."

"I thought that's what *you* were for," she shot back, feeling naughty as she lay in wait for Dean to work his magic.

He grinned down at her. "Mmm, you're in a mood, aren't you?"

She couldn't deny it. It'd been too long since she'd had him inside of her body. She was desperate for the connection. "Yes, so hurry."

"Impatient little thing," he crooned as he moved to sit on the bed beside her. She rolled to her side and propped her head on her hand to watch as he opened the box. She let out a startled squeek when he raised the lid. Enfolded in red velvet lay a dildo and a tube of lubricant.

"Uh, why do you have a dildo?"

He chuckled. "It's for you, smart-ass. Have you ever imagined being with two men?"

Her face flamed at the carnal image, and she couldn't bring herself to answer.

He leaned down and kissed her. "That's what I thought. I can't give you that though. I think you know me well enough by now to understand that I do not share well with others."

She nodded, understanding completely, because she felt the same way about him. "Ditto."

"So, since there is no chance in hell of you fulfilling that little fantasy, maybe this will suffice."

When he lifted the flesh-toned toy from its bed of velvet and brought it between her legs, she stiffened. With tender care, Dean stroked her clit with it. Catherine was amazed to note its warmth. She'd thought it'd feel cold, but it didn't. Of course, it wasn't as if she'd never seen or felt a dildo before. After all, what single woman wasn't familiar with one of those babies? Still, it was the first time she'd ever had a man use one on her during sex.

"Get up on all fours for me," he murmured, his voice lowering an octave. "I'll make it good, sweetheart, trust me."

It was the *trust me* that did it. Despite what Dean had been through with his past girlfriends, he'd still been able to overcome it. He believed in her now. She could do no less for him.

Catherine obeyed, her blood racing, her body wild with anticipation. As she turned her head, Dean moved up behind her, then took out the lube and squirted a portion of it all the way down his hard cock. Catherine forced her gaze away as fear welled up inside her. She was worried she'd somehow disappoint him and scared she wouldn't be able to go through with it.

Now on his knees, Dean stroked the seam between her buttocks with a single lubricated finger. A moan erupted from deep within as Catherine felt it drift back and forth over her puckered opening. Did she want him there? Could she possibly handle him and the toy both?

Dean covered her body with his and kissed the back of her neck. "I want to fuck your pretty ass, Catherine. Do you want that? My dick in that tight little hole?"

"God, Dean," she whispered. "I don't know." She paused. "Yes, maybe . . . I'm not sure."

"I'll fuck it real slow and easy, while the dildo fills your hot pussy. Do you think you can handle both at the same time, sweets?"

"Dean, please . . . I-I'm not sure."

"Yes, you are," Dean urged, then he let his finger penetrate her, little by little, until he was buried deep inside her ass. She shuddered and pushed against him. "Oh, that feels . . . it feels so good," she breathed out.

"Son of a bitch, Catherine," he gritted out. His finger moved in and out, fucking her slow like he'd promised.

As Catherine started to think she could take no more of his teasing, one of Dean's big, warm hands picked up the dildo and caressed her clit with it. She writhed and moved in time to his strokes. When she squeezed her bottom, Dean growled. "Such sweet torture you are, Catherine."

Catherine couldn't concentrate on Dean's words. A second finger joined the first, penetrating deep, while the dildo slid back and forth over her nubbin. She felt every heated touch and stroke. Dean kept it slow at first, then faster, and soon a third finger entered her ass, stretching and preparing her for the thick invasion of his cock. Inhibitions dropped away as need rushed in and took command. She gyrated against Dean while he tormented her with the toy. When he leaned down and bit her hip, she lost it.

Her climax came from somewhere deep inside as Catherine screamed hard and loud, her back arching as her body flew apart. Everything she thought she knew about sexual pleasure seemed to pale in the wake of what she'd just experienced. Dean's rough voice barely broke through the quagmire of her mind.

"I want this ass, Catherine," Dean hissed, then he moved his fingers out of her and cupped her dripping mound. "Look at me, sweetheart."

She turned her head, already limp and sweating from her orgasm, but when she saw the intensity, the insane yearning etched into his not-so-perfect features, her body went from sated to hungry all over again.

"You're mine. From this moment forward, you belong to me."

No words sprang to mind over such a bold claim, so she stayed silent. When the heavy weight of Dean's cock entered her bottom and the thick toy nudged into her dripping pussy, inner muscles clenched up and she automatically attempted to close her legs, panicked and scared. It was too much, too soon.

"No, Dean," she cried out, her body tensing further.

Dean pulled out instantly. "Shhh, sweets. We're going to take it easy. There's no rush, okay?"

Catherine relaxed a measure, relieved by Dean's words. He slowly slid the toy deep inside her vagina and held it there, then leaned down and kissed her shoulder. She rocked against him, and when his tongue flicked over the sensitive spot behind her ear, the panic that had been riding her disappeared as her body hummed back to life.

"You will enjoy this," he whispered into her ear, "you only need to have a little faith in me."

"I do," she said, unwilling for him to think any differently.

"No, you think I'm going to hurt you."

She wanted to deny his claim, but he didn't wait for a reply, only began stroking her hair and smoothing a palm down her arm and over her hip where he cupped her bottom and kneaded the plump flesh. She melted, giving them both what they needed. Her total surrender. Dean seemed to sense it, and he began to slowly glide his cock into her ass, even as the dildo filled her pussy.

"Fuck," he growled as he pushed in an inch at a time, slow the way he promised, until soon he filled her completely.

Inner muscles stretched to accommodate his overwhelming size. Catherine felt utterly surrounded by Dean. Tethered to him in a way that had tears stinging her eyes. It was like nothing she'd ever experienced. The silky inner walls of her vagina were caressed with gentle thrusts from the toy as her ass gripped Dean's cock. The taboo nature of what they were doing sent a rush of rapture through her.

"Reach between your legs and take hold of the dildo," he said, his voice hoarse with passion. "I want you to fuck that tight pussy with it, Catherine."

Catherine couldn't speak as she took possession of the toy, and with each inward stroke of Dean's dick, Catherine pulled the dildo outward, then thrust it back in again. Her inner muscles held them both snug.

"Christ, yeah," Dean groaned as he thrust in and out, his moves becoming more frantic.

"I'm going to come," Catherine moaned as she sped out of control.

"Now, sweets," Dean growled, as he pushed into her again and again.

All at once, Catherine spiraled out of control as her orgasm slammed through her, sending her into oblivion shouting his name.

Dean thrust once more, deeper than before, filling her ass with hot jets of his come. Catherine could feel every spasm as his cock emptied inside of her. She knew the moment would be forever branded onto her heart and soul.

They were both breathing as if they'd sprinted up a mountain. A few deep breaths later and Dean carefully pulled the toy free and tossed it aside. They both collapsed onto the bed, Dean's heavy body pinning her to the mattress. Catherine never wanted to move again. He brushed her damp hair from her face and kissed her cheek. "Mine," he whispered against her overheated skin.

Catherine ached to respond in kind, but she simply didn't have enough energy. She'd been sexed to death. Not a bad way to die, really.

23

The light filtering in through the window across the room dragged Dean back to the land of the living. He opened his eyes and caught Catherine awake and staring at him, a sweet smile on her face. "Morning," he mumbled.

"Morning," she said, her voice husky. Probably from all the screaming she'd done, Dean thought with a grin.

He kissed her forehead. "I would do better than that, but I have morning breath."

She slapped a hand over her mouth and muttered something unintelligible. Dean pried it and away. "Huh?"

She turned her head in the other direction. "I said, I probably do too."

As he stared at her, Dean thought about what all they'd done the night before. "Are you sore, sweets?"

She blushed and shook her head. "You made sure of that last night when you bathed me."

Dean's morning erection hardened further when he recalled how she'd quietly lay against him in his tub while he'd delicately washed her. "I—" Dean started to say, but his cell phone rang, interrupting him. He reached over and grabbed it on the second ring. "Hello?"

"Well, you asked for it," Jonas said on the other end.

He sounded pissed, and Dean knew immediately what he was referring to. Catherine watched him with interest, and Dean was forced to keep his response vague. "You have something for me?"

"Yeah," Jonas shot back, "and you aren't going to like it."

Dean went still. What could he possibly have found on Catherine? The bigger question was, did he really want to know now that their relationship had moved to the next level? He'd just poured his heart out to her the night before. She'd been so understanding, and Dean had felt like the luckiest bastard alive, considering she hadn't blasted him for practically punishing her for another woman's sins.

"You still there?"

Jonas's voice in his ear pulled him out of his bleak thoughts. "I'll meet you at the office in half an hour," he said, hoping it wasn't the biggest mistake of his life.

"Yeah, see you there."

Dean hit END and tossed his phone back on the table. "I need to go in to work." He turned toward her and saw the sadness in her eyes. "I'm sorry, sweetheart," he murmured as he pulled her into his side. "I had hoped to spend the day with you."

"It's okay," she replied, snuggling up close. "I didn't really expect you to take the day off work. Besides, Gracie and I were going to do some girl stuff today."

Dean played with the length of her hair. Jesus, he loved her hair. It was the stuff of fantasies. "Girl stuff?" he asked.

"Manicures, pedicures, waxing, that sort of thing." She danced her fingers over his chest and said, "Should be fun."

"Waxing?" Dean reached between them and cupped her

mound in his palm. "Not here, I hope. I like these fiery-red curls."

"God, no." She shuddered. "I'm a total wuss when it comes to pain. Waxing that area is not my idea of a good time. No, I'm going to get my eyebrows waxed."

"Good," he growled as he became distracted with the feel of her beneath his hand. She hadn't bothered to put her panties back on after they'd made love. "I could get used to waking up to this every morning, sweets," he whispered against the top of her head as he teased her clit with his thumb.

"Me too," she said in a barely-there voice.

Dean felt a trickle of moisture and knew she was turned on. "How about I give you something to think about while you're out with Gracie today?"

"I-I would like that," she murmured as she reached down and pressed his hand more firmly against her pussy. "God, you have the most talented fingers."

Dean yanked off the covers and whispered, "My fingers thank you." As he sat up and moved between her smooth, supple thighs, he looked his fill. Catherine's red curls glistened with her juices. He took her swollen clitoris between his forefinger and thumb and gently squeezed. She moaned and grabbed at the bed on either side of her body. "Oh, yes, like that," she whimpered.

"I need a taste of your sweet cream. Something to keep me from craving you every second of the day." Her plump nether lips were totally exposed to his view, and Dean spread her legs wide, then lowered his head, licking her clit and her soft, puffy pussy lips. Her legs moved to rest on his shoulders, and Dean hummed his approval. He held her firmly in place and tasted her tangy flavor on his tongue.

"I've never sampled anything as sweet as you," he whispered.

Dean inhaled her womanly scent and sucked her clit in between his teeth, nibbling on her. Catherine's hands flew to his head, clutching and grasping handfuls of his hair in stinging desperation for more. When his tongue thrust between her folds, she seemed to lose it completely, pushing against his face and undulating as he tongue-fucked her. A few more licks to her clit and Catherine burst wide, screaming and straining against the unyielding hold his hands had on her soft thighs.

He stayed still and stared up at her as she became lost in the delirious aftermath of her orgasm. Dean kept his mouth against her wet mound while she gained control. When Catherine collapsed back, the muscles in her thighs going slack as they fell open, her hands dropping back to the bed, Dean kissed her clit and lifted up. His gaze took in everything. Her satisfied smile, the perspiration on her forehead. She made the most tempting picture. She looked nearly asleep, but when Dean dipped his finger into her slippery opening, her eyes flew open. "Ah, there you are," he said as he pulled it back out and brought it to her lips. He rubbed her lube all over her mouth, then leaned down and kissed her clean. Catherine moaned and wrapped her arms around his neck, pulling him down on top of her. Just as her breasts came into contact with his chest, he caught himself and stopped.

Dean raised his head, regret filling him as he said, "I need to go, sweetheart."

Catherine went still. "Wow, I already forgot." She swatted him on the arm. "See what happens to my brain when you're around?"

He chuckled. "I have a pretty redhead naked in my bed. Do you think my brain isn't total mush right now?"

A wicked gleam lit her eyes. "Maybe I should try and make you forget about work."

That easily, Dean had an image of her mouth wrapped tight around his cock, and it nearly blocked out all rational thought. "I really want to take you up on that right now, *really*, but it's going to have to wait until later. There will be a later, right? I want to see you."

She nodded. "I was hoping you'd say that. Want to call my cell when you're finished? We can plan a time to meet."

"Sounds good to me." Dean leaned down and kissed her once more. He let his tongue drift out and tease her lower lip and they both groaned. "I'm going to be late," he muttered. "I should give a damn about that, but I don't."

She pushed at his chest and smiled. "Go, you can't keep your employees waiting."

Guilt washed over him, knowing he wasn't going to his office to work but to meet Jonas instead, and they'd be discussing her.

Dean got off the bed and started getting out clothes. "Tonight, you and I are going to do something a little different," he said, as he tossed a pair of jeans onto the bed. "Are you up for it?"

She sat up and pulled her legs into her body and wrapped her arms around them, hindering his view of her lovely tits. "That depends on what it is," she replied, tilting her head to the side. "I draw the line at standing on my head, running down Main Street naked, and orgies." She shrugged. "Other than that, I'm good."

He reached over and tweaked her nose. "Nothing quite that crazy, but do you remember when we talked about handcuffs, spankings, and role-playing?"

All signs of teasing vanished, and her green eyes were once again filled with desire. "Uh, I couldn't very well forget a discussion like that, Dean."

He grabbed a gray T-shirt from the bottom drawer of his dresser and slipped it over his head. "Well, that's sort of what I have in mind."

He yanked his jeans up his legs and turned toward her. She was watching him. He took his time zipping and buttoning his fly. When Catherine licked her lips, Dean had to bite back a smile. "Catherine?"

"Hmm?"

"Did you hear me?"

"What?"

"Role-playing, spankings," he reiterated.

"Oh, uh, yeah. I'm not sure about that, Dean."

"That's what you thought about the dildo, but it turned out okay, right?"

She rested her chin on her knees and said, "It turned out better than okay. Still, I'm just not sure I want to be as adventurous as what you're implying."

"I understand. You do have to be able to leave your inhibitions at the door. And you would need to trust me, completely." He paused, then added, "How about if you think about it?"

She frowned and pulled the covers over her. "I suppose I could do that."

Dean sat down on the bed next to her. "Think on it today while you're out with Gracie. For me."

She smiled. "Only for you."

Dean's possessive side loved those three little words. He reached out and toyed with her hair. "There's something I want you to read."

He got off the bed and crossed the room, then grabbed a book from a shelf along the far wall. He took it back to her and handed it over. "Here, read this. Chapters twenty-eight through thirty-two, to be specific. I think you'll find them . . . informative."

"*The Adventures of Mira,*" she said, reading the title aloud. "What is it about?"

"A man and woman who like to play sexual games. The master and slave type."

Her face flamed, and she dropped the book onto the bed as if it were a snake. "Oh," she mumbled. "That's . . . nice."

Dean reached out and cupped her cheek. "Read the chapters, Catherine. If you hate it, then we'll forget I ever brought it up."

She bit her lip and looked down at her lap. "Will you be disappointed if I don't like it?" She peeked up at him. "I mean, I'm not sure I could play those types of games."

Dean winked. "Sweetheart, there are about a million other sexual things I can think of where you're concerned. I have a very vivid imagination. If you don't feel comfortable with this one, then we'll scrap the idea and go to idea number one hundred and ten. My pleasure comes from your pleasure. It's as simple as that."

She laughed, but Dean could tell she was worried. "You're sure?"

"I'm positive," he said, hoping to alleviate her concerns. "Just read the chapters and we'll talk. No pressure, no expectations. Got it?"

She nodded.

Dean wrapped an arm around her middle and drew her close, then covered her mouth with his. He forced her lips apart and swept inside, needing a bigger taste of her on his tongue before he left her to meet with Jonas. Their tongues teased and Dean's dick went hard all over again. With the last shred of willpower he had left, Dean released her. "God Almighty, your mouth would tempt a saint."

"Right back at ya," she whispered.

He stood up and pointed to the bed. "Stay as long as you want. Use the shower, raid the fridge, whatever."

"And read the book," she helpfully supplied.

He wagged his eyebrows. "Definitely read the book," he said, then he left, lest he be tempted to skip the meeting and spend the day in bed with the seductive woman. It wasn't until he was in his truck and down the road that it dawned on him what he'd done. He'd left a woman in his house alone. He hadn't done that since he'd been living with Linda.

"Damned if she hasn't sneaked right under my radar," he said to himself, a stupid grin on his face. But when he thought about where he was headed and why, the grin swiftly vanished. He'd pried into her life like a dog with a bone. What the hell had he been thinking? If a woman had done that to him, he'd be livid. If he screwed up with Catherine, Dean knew he'd be doomed to a life alone, because no way in hell could any woman ever hold a candle to her.

24

When Dean arrived at his office, Jonas was already there, pacing back and forth. "How'd you get in here?" Dean asked, frowning down at the doorknob. "I thought I locked up yesterday."

"You did." Jonas shrugged, completely unrepentant. "It's not my fault you need better locks."

"You picked my lock?" Dean shook his head as he moved around the desk to sit down. "Why am I even surprised by that?"

"Beats me," he said as he took the chair across from him. "The file is there"—he pointed to a manila folder—"and it's not pretty."

Dean looked down at the innocent-looking file, a feeling of dread filling him. He should throw it in the trash and forget about the whole damn thing. He trusted Catherine. He knew he'd always trusted her. It'd been Linda's betrayal that had clouded his judgment, but he was seeing things clear now. Catherine wasn't Linda. She wasn't anything like the other women who'd hurt him either. Dean had been a damn fool to even think of comparing her to anyone else.

"Well?" Jonas said, obviously annoyed. "Are you going to open it or stare at it all day?"

Dean picked up the folder, but for the first time in his life he wasn't sure what to do. Opening it seemed like a betrayal to Catherine. If he trusted her then he shouldn't look in the folder. Right?

Jonas cursed and reached across the desk. He snatched the folder right out of his hand and opened it, then said, "You're making me nuts." He yanked out a few papers and tossed them at him. "There, read it."

Dean looked at the top sheet. It was a legal court document. It took reading it twice before the full meaning hit him. "What the fuck," he muttered.

"My sentiments exactly," Jonas bit out.

Dean read it again, unwilling to believe his own eyes. "According to this, Catherine's biological mom was raped?"

"Gracie and Catherine's biological mother, you mean. Don't forget that."

"Jesus H." Dean pushed his fingers through his hair. His hand shook as he stared at the text. "How did you find this?"

"It took some doing, but I managed." Jonas curled his lip in distaste. "I felt like I needed a shower after I read what that bastard did to Gracie and Catherine's mom."

Dean went still when he read the date the incident was reported to the police. "This occurred the same year Catherine was born." He looked across the desk at Jonas. "Don't fucking tell me that means Catherine was conceived as a result of—"

Jonas held up a hand. "Don't even say it. It makes me sick to think what that asshole did." Jonas shook his head. "I don't think I have to tell you that Catherine and Gracie would both be devastated if they found out about this. They don't need to know what their mother endured."

In complete agreement, Dean nodded. As he stared down at the information Jonas had uncovered, another bit of data popped out at him. "According to this, they didn't convict the guy." He cursed. "Not enough evidence."

The grin that came across Jonas's face sent a chill down Dean's spine. "They didn't convict on the rape charge, but he ended up busted later on down the line for killing a store clerk during a robbery."

Dean nodded, glad that the animal was off the streets. "So he's in prison, good."

"Well, not exactly."

Dean quirked a brow. "What's that supposed to mean?"

"He's dead. The loser ended up falling on a knife while showering. Imagine that?" Jonas crossed his arms over his chest and sat back in the chair. "Good riddance, if you ask me.

"I agree." Dean imagined how devastated Catherine would be if she ever found out. "What the hell am I supposed to do with this information?"

"Destroy it?" Jonas said, offering up the most sane answer. "It's what I'd do. Don't let that piece of shit cause any more pain, Dean."

Dean knew Jonas was right, but it felt wrong to know who Catherine's biological father was and not tell her. Of course he didn't know for sure, but considering the date the rape was reported and the date Catherine was born, any moron could do the math. It made more sense now why the woman had given Catherine up. A woman would have a difficult time raising a child knowing how that child had been conceived. His gut clenched in pain for Catherine.

"Why the hell did I ask you to go digging?" He threw the paper down. "Fuck!"

"Because you're a paranoid dick?" Jonas said obligingly.

"Thanks," Dean growled. "I feel so much better now."

"Look, it's up to you what you do with that paper, because

by all appearances Catherine belongs to you, but if she were mine I'd want to protect her."

"Great idea, but there's one problem. What if she goes looking for her biological father on her own and finds this herself? It could be even worse for her. Wouldn't it be better if I told her?"

Jonas stood and leaned across the desk. "Damn it, she's happy now that she's found Gracie. Ever since Catherine found those letters, they've both made peace with the woman that brought them into this world," he said, his voice rising along with his temper. "Leave it the hell alone, Dean, or you'll end up hurting them both."

Dean's anger boiled over and he shot out of his chair. It fell backward and hit the floor. "Don't you think I know that?" He scrubbed a hand over his face and started pacing. "The last thing I want is to hurt either of them, but now that I know all this it feels wrong not to tell Catherine." He stopped and turned to Jonas. "That's exactly the sort of shit her adoptive parents did to her, Jonas, and look where that ended up. Gracie and Catherine missed out on so much, and all because of secrets. The secrets need to stop."

"Fine, do what you think is right," he said, throwing his hands in the air. "But you'd better tell Wade first. He's going to be livid if this news reaches Gracie before he gets a chance to break it to her gently."

Dean nodded. "I'll talk to him. We'll decide what to do together." He looked up and their gazes locked. "I'm sorry for pulling you into all this. Sorry as hell."

Jonas cursed. "I just hope you know what you're doing."

"Me too," he muttered as Jonas left.

Dean picked the paper up and folded in, then stuck it in his coat pocket. It seemed to burn a hole clear through to his skin. He took off the heavy Carhartt and tossed it over a chair. God,

NAKED GAMES / 197

how was he going to tell her? The idea of causing Catherine even an ounce of pain nearly had him doubling over. But damn it, enough people had screwed with her life as it was, and he wasn't about to do that to her too. She had a right to know the truth, all of it. He only prayed it was the right decision and wouldn't end up blowing up in his face.

That's when it hit him. He loved Catherine. He wasn't entirely sure how the hell it had happened, and it didn't really matter. She was smart and quirky and kind, and the sexiest woman he'd ever laid eyes on. Dean knew deep down that she was too good for him, but he was just selfish enough not to care. He aimed to keep her.

On impulse, he grabbed his cell phone and sent Catherine a quick text.

DID YOU READ THE CHAPTERS?

When only a few seconds went by before he heard a small tinkling sound to indicate he had a message, Dean's heart sped up. As he read the text on the screen, he grinned.

YES. I'M WILLING.

The three words were enough to have his dick harder than a damn railroad spike. Still, he wanted her to be 100 percent. Role-playing the way he wanted to wasn't for the innocent, and in a lot of ways Catherine was very innocent. Would she truly be able to call him master?

ARE YOU SURE? he sent back.

A minute, then two. Three minutes went by, and Dean had to pick his chair up off the floor and sit down. He suspected that maybe she was going to back out. His phone sounded again, and Dean about came in his jeans at her neatly typed reply.

YES . . . MASTER.

DAMN, I MISS YOU! he sent back, wishing he were with her, where he could show her just how much with his lips and tongue. He wanted to tell her he loved her. He wanted her to know before she left and went back home. And God, he desperately wanted to hear the words back.

LOL, DITTO. She texted back.

He grinned and sent a text back. MEET ME AT MY HOUSE. SEVEN?

THAT WORKS.

SEE YOU THEN, SWEETS.

K, DON'T WORK TOO HARD.

Dean tossed his phone onto his desk when he read her final text. He looked over at his coat. Maybe Jonas was right, maybe some things should stay buried. What purpose would it serve for Catherine to know that her mom had been raped and that her biological father was the scum of the earth? None.

Still, he picked up his cell and hit his brother's number. Wade would want to know, even if they both decided to bury the information. Together they would decide what to do.

"Are you having fun?" Catherine said from the chair beside Gracie. They'd already gotten their eyebrows waxed and their fingers painted. Now they sat beside each other as a salon tech did their toes. Catherine had decided on a mauve shade of polish, while Gracie went for fire engine red.

"Definitely!" Gracie said. "I love learning all the little similarities and differences between us."

Catherine laughed. "Me too. Like the fact we're both ticklish."

"Exactly," Gracie replied.

Catherine noticed Gracie squirming, and the technician gave Gracie a dirty look. Catherine had an urge to apologize for making both women's jobs that much more difficult, but her phone buzzed, distracting her. She looked down at her purse sitting in her lap, wondering if it was Dean calling. She took it out and hit the text messaging icon. The first name to pop up was Dean's. Catherine smiled when she read the short text. He wanted to know if she'd read the chapters. *Uh-huh,* Catherine thought. What Dean really wanted to know, the part left unsaid, was had she liked what she read and would she be willing to try it with him. Before she lost her nerve, Catherine sent a quick confirmation back to him, then waited.

"Is that Dean?"

Catherine turned her head to see her sister watching her with a gentle smile.

"Yeah."

"I thought so, considering the way you were staring at the phone all gooey-eyed." Gracie paused then asked, "What did he want?" She winced. "Sorry, that's rude."

Catherine shook her head. "No, we're sisters. It's okay to ask those types of questions, right?" She wondered if she should talk to Gracie about Dean's penchant toward the kinkier side of sex, but she wasn't sure she should. Would Dean see it as a breach of trust? Then again, girl talk was girl talk, no men allowed.

Catherine leaned close, hoping the nail techs were too busy to pay them any mind, and asked, "Can I ask you something?"

"Sure," Gracie replied, "you can ask me anything."

In a quieter voice, Catherine asked, "Does Wade ever want to do anything . . . kinky in bed?"

Gracie laughed, but Catherine noticed she also turned beet red. "Uh, yeah. Quite often actually." She tilted her head to the side and asked in a hushed whisper, "Why? Is Dean into kink?"

Catherine knew by the way her entire face and neck suddenly felt like she'd stepped into a volcano that she was blushing now too. "He wants me to try role-playing." Catherine's phone buzzed again. She quickly grabbed it and read the message on the screen. Dean wanted to know if she was sure. Was she?

Gracie's brows scrunched together. "Er, I'm not certain I'm following you."

"He wants me to call him master," Catherine blurted out. She heard one of the nail techs cough, but Catherine didn't have the nerve to look and see which one.

"Oooh, I see," Gracie whispered back. "So, it's like a dominant and submissive thing?"

"Yes, that's it exactly. Has Wade ever . . . ?"

Gracie covered her mouth to stifle a laugh. "Let's just say Wade and Dean have a lot in common."

Somehow that made Catherine feel ten times better. "I told him I'd give it a try," she confided. "Do you think that was a mistake?"

"No, definitely not." Gracie shrugged. "I mean, with some men I suppose it could be weird or scary, but if Dean is anything like his brother, then he'll make sure you're enjoying it or he'll stop."

Catherine thought that over then said, "He did say that his pleasure comes from mine."

"That's pretty much the way Wade feels too. I mean, I don't think it would be a turn-on for them if we weren't into it too."

"I guess when I think of it that way, what do I have to lose?" Catherine went for broke and sent another text. A few messages later, she tossed her phone back into her purse. "Done," Catherine said, as excitement skittered through her.

When Gracie didn't say anything, Catherine looked over at her and noticed the way she stared at the tile floor, as if working over a problem in her head.

"Gracie?" Catherine asked, curious what her sister was thinking about.

"You're in love with him," Gracie said as she turned her attention to her once more.

She hadn't stated it as a question, but Catherine answered all the same. "Yes, and I have no idea how I'm going to be able to leave him." It would break her heart if she never saw Dean again. He'd somehow very quickly become an extremely important part of her life. He'd stolen her heart, and Catherine was loath to take it back.

Gracie looked over at her, sympathy causing her bright green eyes to dim a little. "I think this is where I come up with some sort of wise advice for you, since you're my little sister and all. Truth is, I'm not real experienced with these things. Matters of the heart always boggled me until Wade pushed his way into my life."

"It's okay. I guess if it's meant to be then we'll figure out something."

"Does he feel the same way about you?"

Ah, the million dollar question. "He hasn't said the words, but I know he cares. I know he doesn't want me to go back to Georgia. And he trusts me now. Completely."

"Finally!" Gracie said. "He's over the whole 'she must be a con artist' thing then?"

"Oh, he's definitely over it, just in time for me to head back home." She snorted. "Thing is, I don't want to go. I don't want to leave either of you."

Gracie's face fell. "I'm not looking forward to you leaving either. I wish you lived here."

Catherine reached over and took hold of Gracie's hand. "Yeah, I'm beginning to wish that too, sis," she said, her voice not quite steady any longer.

Gracie squeezed her hand and smiled over at her. "We're going to figure something out, you'll see. I'm not going to let you go, not now that we've finally found each other."

Unable to speak, Catherine nodded. The rest of their salon visit was spent in quiet. Tomorrow she'd be going home. The thought made her feel hollow inside.

25

When Catherine arrived at Dean's she knew immediately that something was different. The man in front of her seemed to be a total stranger. Gone was the sweet and gentle Dean, in his place was a man bent on possessing her in the most basic way possible. He stared at her the way she imagined a dom might stare at his sub, as if he owned her, body and soul.

Dean took her hand and brought her over to the couch. Once they were both seated next to each other, he said, "In your message you said you're willing to submit to me. Does that still hold true?"

"I haven't changed my mind," she said, all at once anxious. "But I'm not terribly sure what is expected of me."

Dean reached out and caressed her cheek. "You're going to do as Mira did in the book," he murmured. "I'll be in control of how much pleasure you receive, as well as when and how you receive it. You'll do as I say without question. Understood?"

Catherine's libido woke right up at Dean's explanation, but she still had concerns. "What if I can't? I can be rather independent, Dean. And the whole calling you master thing is a bit much to expect of an independent woman."

"Then we'll stop." He shrugged as if it didn't matter one way or the other to him. "I don't want you uncomfortable, Catherine. The only thing I expect is for you to trust me to make you feel good."

She tapped him on the nose. "And you expect me to call you master while you do it," she reminded him.

He wagged his eyebrows. "The idea isn't abhorrent to me, that's for damn sure."

Catherine grinned, but as she looked into his eyes, she sobered instantly. This was the moment. It was now or never. If she chose not to go through with it, would she regret it? That answer was obvious.

"I'll try," she said, her cheeks burning as the words came out of her mouth.

Dean leaned forward and kissed her gently. "Good girl," he growled. "There's one other thing I wanted to tell you before we go any further."

"Oh?"

"I love you," he blurted out as he pressed another kiss to her mouth. "I think I've loved you from the moment I saw your photo."

Tears sprang to Catherine's eyes. "I was so afraid," she whispered, her throat suddenly feeling strangled.

Dean quirked a brow. "Afraid?"

"That I'd be the only one saying those three little words," she admitted as she stared at him wondering if this was truly happening. If it was a dream, then it'd be cruel to wake her.

One corner of Dean's lips curved upward. "Uh, you haven't actually said them yet."

She took his face in her hands and said, "I love you too. I

don't know how it happened and I have no clue how we're going to make this work, but I love you."

"We will make it work though," he said, his voice brooking no argument, "because I'm not giving you up. No matter what happens, Catherine, you belong to me." He looked far too serious when he added, "Remember that later."

Catherine was confused, but when Dean stood and brought her with him, she forgot about everything else. All that mattered was that she was with Dean. It was their last night together, and she wanted it to be perfect.

"In the bedroom," he ordered as he stood back and waited for her to precede him.

Catherine took a deep breath and headed toward the other end of the house. She could feel Dean's gaze on her, and it fueled the inferno burning inside her. When Catherine reached his room, she turned and awaited Dean's orders. Or rather, her master's orders, she thought as the tension in the room seemed to grow.

Without saying a word, Dean stripped out of his clothes. His movements weren't meant to be sexy, but Catherine took in the yummy show all the same. His strong chest, ripped abs, and the heavy weight between his muscular thighs. Every inch of him was superb, and Catherine practically drooled as she stared. When he slipped on a black silk robe, Catherine wanted to protest at not having full access to his scrumptious body.

The soft material should have made him seem less forbidding, but it didn't. The hard body was still plenty lickable, just as the look in Dean's brown eyes was as frightening as it was stimulating. His imposing manner made Catherine feel utterly insignificant in comparison. The wicked-looking leather riding crop he picked up off the bed and held loosely at his side seemed to emphasize his wild masculinity, and sent her nerves rioting.

She was the submissive and he the master; that was the game

they were to play. She'd read the chapters of the book he'd in-
dicated, and they'd turned her on. She knew the idea. Leave
Catherine Michaels, website designer and good Southern girl,
at the door. In here, she was required to experience pleasure,
the kind that only Dean, as her master, could bring about.

Catherine wished she'd had more time to prepare herself,
but she knew that if she had, she would've lost her nerve. Given
time to think, she never would've said yes to the game. When
she thought of it, Catherine was grateful she hadn't let her
brain talk her out of something she knew deep down she was
going to enjoy.

Amazing, Catherine thought. It hadn't been that long ago
that she'd been sitting in her parents' safe and cozy house,
going through mail and wondering when some handsome
rogue was going to ride in and take her away from it all. Well,
he had, more or less, and Catherine had fallen head over heels
for him. So much so that she was ready to be his sex slave for a
night.

"Take off your clothes."

Dean's quiet demand brought her back to the present and
soothed her frazzled nerves a measure.

"I don't think so, bud," she said, as she recalled the way the
scene had played out in the book he'd given her. "What makes
you think I'm willing to undress for you?"

For a second, Catherine could see the surprise in Dean's
dark eyes. He quickly recovered and said, "I never repeat the
commands."

His voice didn't rise above a hoarse whisper. It was clear he
felt in total control, of his body and hers, Catherine realized.

"That's too bad, because I have no intention of taking off my
clothes." She crossed her arms over her chest and stuck her
nose in the air, getting into the game a little more now.

Dean stepped forward, and instinctively Catherine stepped
back. He smiled as he saw her retreat, but he never wavered.

Too quickly, he stood close enough that her breasts touched his chest. The contact caused a shiver to run through her. In fear or anticipation? Suddenly she didn't know. Maybe both. Who knew Catherine Michaels had a penchant for the kinkier side of sex?

Still, as she took in the fact she was alone with a man much more experienced at bedroom games, Catherine wondered if maybe she'd bitten off more than she could chew. Maybe she should've told him no when he'd asked her to read the book. But if she had, then she would never know if she would like being at his mercy. Knowing beat not knowing every time.

The dark, rough stubble on Dean's chin looked sexy as hell. His hair, a rich shade of espresso, swirled over his brow and just barely reached the collar of the black robe. His nose was a little crooked, she noticed, as if it'd been broken at some point, but somehow it only added to his appeal. His eyes . . . oh, wow. His eyes were devastatingly dark, and they were devouring her at the moment. No, Dean's face and body wouldn't win any *GQ* awards, he was too hard and rough for that, but she would bet her bottom dollar that women flocked to him in droves. He could have his pick. The predatory sort of alpha male no woman would ever want to tie herself to permanently but wouldn't mind tumbling around with in the heat of the night. At least once. Had he played these games with them? Catherine swiftly scrubbed the thought from her mind, unwilling to go down that murky road.

His touch to her cheek stopped the crazy train of her thoughts, and she widened her gaze. Would he hurt her? Of course not. She felt bad for even thinking it. *This is Dean, the man you've fallen in love with in five days flat.*

"You're beautiful, you know," he murmured. She wasn't given a chance to respond as he took his large, callused hand on a journey down the length of her neck. He popped the first button on her blouse free, and Catherine's body all but purred.

She let him pop another before she remembered her role and promptly smacked his hand away. He merely stared at her, with those too intense eyes of his, and seemed to enjoy watching her squirm, if the wicked smile that quickly crossed his face was any clue.

"If you don't do it, I will," he growled. "And it can be gentle or . . . not so gentle. The choice is yours, always."

He seemed to be attempting to tell her something in that moment, but Catherine couldn't be sure. Without a second thought, she cursed at him, using a few words she'd never said before. Catherine felt her cheeks heat, and she covered her mouth when she realized what she'd said. Had she crossed a line?

His face hardened and his mouth thinned. Before she could blink, Dean grabbed her around the waist and tossed her over his shoulder.

"Dean!" she yelled, forgetting the game a moment.

"No, you're to call me master, remember?" He strode to the side of the bed, then put her back on her feet.

"What are you—" Catherine didn't get a chance to finish the question as Dean turned her around to face the mattress. He bent her over, then moved to stand behind her. "I guess you want the not-so-gentle approach, huh?"

She didn't know quite what he meant, until she felt her skirt being lifted. When Dean tore at her blue silk panties, Catherine froze. "No."

Dean lowered over her and whispered into her ear, "Is that truly what you want? We'll stop now and we'll never have to open this door again. Your choice, Catherine. It's always your choice."

Did she want to stop before they'd even had a chance to start? Dean wouldn't hurt her, not really. He wanted to bring her pleasure, he'd said. And she trusted him to keep his word. "No," she decided. "I don't want to stop."

"Mmm, that's my girl," he said as he lifted off her. She heard Dean groan when he ripped the rest of her panties and they fell away from her body, revealing her bottom and the damp curls covering her mound. She felt his large hand again, only instead of caressing her face, it stroked her intimate flesh. As if he had the right. As if he owned her.

He smoothed his fingers up and then down, all the while holding her in place with his other hand. Not that she was struggling to break free. Wild horses couldn't get her to move away from Dean's caresses.

"I'm not going to fuck you," he said, "not until you desire it. Not until you ask me nicely."

Despite his promise, Catherine knew she was helpless to him. She'd never felt so powerless. "I won't beg," she said, unsure if she spoke the truth.

He tsked. "You need to learn obedience, little slave."

It wasn't what she had expected from him, but then his hand moved away and she stiffened. She didn't have to wait long to feel the first sting of the riding crop. Catherine yelped, more out of shock than actual pain. Her head dropped to the bed as tears stung her eyes.

"Will you take your clothes off on your own, or do you require more encouragement?"

"No," Catherine growled. Crap, why had she said that? She didn't really want him to spank her . . . did she?

There was another smack from the soft leather against her bottom, this one not quite as hard as the first. She groaned and bit down hard onto her lower lip. Catherine had taken her clothes off for Dean more than once already, but for some insane reason she'd wanted to feel that delicious sting against her flesh.

"Will you do as you're told?"

Catherine nodded, giving in for the first time since they'd began the naughty game.

Dean cursed, then tossed the riding crop to the other side of the room. It hit the blinds and fell to the floor.

All sane thought fled as Catherine felt his hard cock against her upturned bottom. It was such a brief touch that she thought maybe she'd imagined it. Slowly, he stepped away and let her stand up.

"The clothes," he softly demanded.

Catherine looked down her body and started undoing the pearl buttons littering the front of her blouse. After she released the last one and the material hung open, Dean pushed it off her shoulders. It pooled into a silk heap on the floor, and she dared to look up at him. The feral look in his eyes was something to behold. He was severely aroused and staring at her white, lace-covered breasts as if she were a feast.

"Perfect," he murmured. "You may go into the bathroom and change. When you're finished, come into the kitchen."

Catherine couldn't believe Dean was going to let her walk off and change clothes. She'd been all prepared to be ravished. She had envisioned stripping out of the rest of her clothes, then Dean would take her down onto the bed and they'd make love. When she remembered the chapters she'd read, Catherine recalled how Mira's master had instructed her to dress in a specific outfit. To wear her hair a certain way. It'd turned Catherine on something fierce when she'd read how excited Mira had gotten when her master had seen her and known she'd followed his instructions to the letter. Mira had received a very special reward for such good behavior. Catherine knew that if she were going to follow the game, then she would need to go all the way. No half measures.

As she started across the room, Catherine looked back at Dean. His eyes were fixated on her bottom, which probably bore red marks from the crop. The heat in his gaze scorched Catherine to her marrow.

Inside the bathroom, Catherine slowly took off her bra. She

took her time and shored up her nerve, but when she felt moisture trickling down her thighs, she knew the truth. Dean could ask her nearly anything and she'd most likely say yes. She was that far gone over the man. Oh, she might've been somewhat scandalized when Dean had swatted her, but deep down in some secret part of her, Catherine had felt electrified at the first strike from the leather. Heck, it nearly made her come just thinking about it.

Catherine couldn't afford to lose her composure though. She needed to remember the game. He was the master and she was the submissive. In the story, Mira had had almost more control over the game than her master, simply because if she weren't so wiling, then the game would come to an end. Simple as that. Knowing that helped Catherine take off her skirt. When she recalled the feel of Dean's hand as he'd touched her bottom, her clit swelled. Dean had been hugely aroused and ready to take her, she was sure of it.

Catherine forced erotic images of Dean's rugged body out of her head and looked around the room. She saw a long, black nightgown hanging over the shower rod. She picked it up and looked it over. It was made of a stretchy mesh material, and it had clever patches of lace across the bosom and crotch area. She slipped it off the hanger and shimmied into it. The rich material slid over her body like a second skin. She looked into the freestanding cherrywood mirror in one corner of the room and was shocked by the sensual picture she presented.

"I cannot believe I'm going through with this," she said to her reflection. She sighed and walked to the door. "Here goes nothing."

When she entered the kitchen, Catherine immediately saw Dean seated at the table. His black robe had drifted open in the front, and she could see the curls littering his powerful chest, but the table hindered her view of the rest of him. God, she wanted him. A part of her ached to scrap the game in favor of making love. But as she looked into his eyes, she could see the gentle understanding in his gaze. He was all but waiting for her to back out. That single thought had her crossing the room.

She waited next to the chair, knowing he would need to give her permission before she took her seat. It pricked her feminine pride, and Dean's grin told her he knew it. He took his time, looked her over, slowly, as if committing every curve and valley to memory, then smiled. "I had a feeling you'd look beautiful in that nightgown."

She plucked at the expensive material and asked, "When did you have time to go shopping?"

"Today."

"It must have been expensive though," Catherine said, feeling a little giddy that he'd gone shopping for her.

He pointed to the chair across from him and said, "Have a seat, sweetheart."

Catherine crossed her arms over her chest and stayed rooted to the spot. "I'm not real hungry, thanks."

He smiled for the briefest of moments, but he swiftly schooled his expression. "Don't force me to come over there and get you. The riding crop is only a few feet away."

Catherine wasn't going to think of him using that thing on her, because when she did her body responded with excitement. Instead, she stayed where she was and quirked a brow at him, egging him on the way a very naughty sub might.

"You need food, Catherine," he said in a softer tone. "If you pass out on me, it'll put a real cramp in the evening's fun, don't you think?"

Forgetting the role she was supposed to be playing, Catherine said, "I'm going to need my energy, is that it?"

"Definitely," he growled. "Lots and lots of energy."

Catherine dropped her arms and sat in the chair. She tucked her gown around her legs, hoping to maintain at least a modicum of modesty. Dean picked up his napkin, placed it across his lap, and began to eat what appeared to be some sort of stew. Catherine inhaled the rich aroma and her stomach growled obscenely. She blushed.

One corner of his mouth tilted up, indicating he'd heard her body's plea for food. "Eat. You'll feel better."

She didn't much care for the way he told her what to do. One half of her got annoyed at being ordered about, while the other half seemed aroused by it.

Catherine picked up her spoon and took a small bite, but when the steaming hot liquid burned her tongue, she dropped it back into the bowl. "It's too hot," she mumbled as she frowned at him.

Dean's heated gaze held her in place as he stared at her mouth. He leaned forward and picked up her spoon, then scooped up some of the stew. She watched, helplessly mesmerized as he blew on it, all the while his gaze never leaving her face. When he was satisfied, he held it to her lips and ordered, "Open up, Catherine."

She did.

It was odd to have a man feed her. Somehow, the act seemed more intimate than having sex. Catherine chewed the bits of meat and vegetables and swallowed, surprised when he leaned forward and wiped at a drop of beef broth from her lips. He brought the droplet to his own mouth and sucked it off. Her body thrummed to life.

They finished the rest of their meal in silence. Catherine suspected he was giving her time to prepare for what was yet to come. She was just glad to have food in her belly. It was strange how hungry she'd been. She'd eaten lunch with Gracie, but she'd been too nervous about the evening to come to eat more than a few bites of grilled chicken and a side salad. Now the food and the silence had the affect of calming her nerves. When Catherine dared to glance at him, watching as he bit off a piece of French bread, she knew she was in big trouble. Becoming woefully attracted to a man she was going to have to leave tomorrow wasn't the smartest thing she'd ever done.

Suddenly, Dean swiped the napkin across his mouth and shoved back his chair. Towering over her, he reached out a hand to her and asked, "Ready?"

Catherine gulped back a bit of stew. "Ready for what, exactly?"

"To be my little submissive," he murmured.

Oh, God, why did that make her pussy throb with pleasure? "You're awfully familiar with this sort of thing," she said, hoping to get her mind off her raging hormones. "Why is that, I wonder?"

"You ask a lot of questions," he said around a grin. "Let me ask you one this time. Did you enjoy the riding crop?"

Catherine stayed silent. No way was she giving him that kind of information.

"I think you did," he murmured as he stepped closer to her. She could feel his breath against her cheek, and she shivered. "Actually, I think you were frustrated that I stopped so suddenly. Isn't that the truth, sweetheart?"

"Maybe," she said, neither confirming nor denying.

"Mmm," he whispered as his lips barely grazed the skin of her left cheek.

The small contact had Catherine ready to explode. Dean lifted away, and she could see that the touch affected him just as much. It helped to know that she wasn't the only one insane with need.

"You can keep your little secret for now," he said. "We'll get to the riding crop soon enough."

When he turned and left the room, leaving her to either stay seated or follow, Catherine froze. Following would be daring and not at all levelheaded, but wasn't that at least half the reason she was here? Dean made every single one of her senses stand up and take notice. Quite possibly, he would be her ultimate adventure.

When she started to get up to follow, Dean reappeared. "You have a terrible time obeying, don't you?" Before she could reply, he leaned down and plucked her out of the chair, then slung her over his shoulder.

"Dean!" Catherine yelled as she swatted his back. It was no use, though, because that part of his body was like the rest of him, hard as a rock. He was too big, too strong, and the arm holding her in place didn't budge an inch. "You really need to stop carting me around. Seriously!"

"Master," he murmured. "You keep forgetting that part, sweetheart."

When he set her back on her feet, Catherine was once again in Dean's bedroom. His gaze scorched a path over her body. "Master," she said, using the word more as an insult than a sign of respect.

He chuckled. "Call me what you want. It doesn't matter."

Her eyes widened at that morsel of news. "It doesn't?"

He shook his head. "All that matters is you and me," he whispered. "I want you. Hell, I think I've wanted you forever. And you want me too, or you wouldn't still be here playing this game."

Her gaze darted away from his. She couldn't bear for him to see how much she truly did want him. How much she loved him. She trembled as Dean stroked a finger down between her cleavage and said, "So sweet and soft. I'm on fire for you, Catherine. Only you."

Her pulse quickened at the candid statement. He placed a clenched fist under her chin and forced her to look at him. It seemed he refused to let her hide from him. "Say it," he murmured.

"Yes, only you," she said, using the same words he'd used for her.

Dean groaned, then his lips pressed against hers. He didn't caress her with tender touches. Instead he was rough and eager as he drank her in. It still wasn't enough for Catherine. His tongue demanded entrance inside the hot cavern of her mouth, and Catherine gladly let him in. There was never any other choice. Desire warred with common sense, and desire came out the victor.

"You taste feminine, like the most delicate flower, especially when you surrender so beautifully for me," he whispered against her mouth.

His romantic words had her heart doing backflips. Catherine wound her arms around his neck and whimpered when he pulled her body in tight against his. His hard cock pushed against her belly and passion sizzled in her veins.

Dean left her mouth and traveled kisses over her chin, then her neck, where he took his time nibbling and sucking. Catherine felt his heavy erection harden even more and she couldn't catch her breath. "Don't make me wait another minute, Dean," she shamelessly begged. "Please."

"Screw the game," he muttered as he covered her mouth once more.

Hallelujah, Catherine thought with a satisfied smile.

26

Catherine dragged herself out of the pleasurable haze Dean so effortlessly wove around her and peered up at him. He looked edgy and wild. It was scary and exciting, and she wanted to feel all that untamed strength between her thighs. She shouldn't give in to him so easily. She knew that, but she had no defenses where Dean was concerned. She hadn't from the beginning.

"More," she whispered against his voracious mouth.

He pulled back, and she witnessed the surprise in his eyes, and something else she couldn't quite put a finger on. He quickly masked it and kissed her again. The second meeting of lips was every bit as urgent as the first.

Bending low, Dean picked her up and placed her on the bed. "You won't regret a second you spend with me," he said as he straightened. "I'm going to make you feel so damn good tonight."

She hid her face in his chest in her hands and mumbled, "I think I already regret it."

She felt strong fingers prying her hands away. When Catherine opened her eyes, Dean was staring down at her with a frown marring his darkly handsome features. "What did you say?"

"I figure I must need my head examined, Dean," she said, as her frustration over their situation mounted. "I'm leaving to-morrow. What are we doing? How is this going to work? How could *we* possibly work? It makes no sense at all." It mattered little to her libido, but her head and heart were beginning to thing she was certifiable.

He lay down next to her and propped his head on his hand, then touched her cheek with his index finger. "Catherine, I love you. You love me. What we're doing right now is the only thing that does make sense. No matter where you go, my feel-ings for you won't change."

There wasn't a chance for Catherine to reply or even give his statement the consideration it deserved. Too quickly he stood up and untied the belt holding his robe closed. He pushed it off his shoulders and let it fall to the floor in a black heap.

"God, I love looking at you," she admitted as Dean's tall, broad-shouldered body was bared to her. Every inch of him was powerful and masculine. He was stunningly naked, and his cock jutted out, swollen and pulsing.

"Touch me," he bit out.

Ah, he was back in command mode, Catherine realized. It was in the harsh tone of his voice and his compelling, watchful gaze. Still as a statue, hands at his sides, Dean waited for her to obey. It was her move. The only sign of agitation was the clenching of his fists at his sides.

Every fiber in her being sat up and took notice. All of a sud-den, she ached to surrender to him. She wanted to prove to him that she trusted him, unconditionally.

Catherine reached a hand out and touched his stomach, anx-ious to feel his ripped abdominal muscles against her fingertips. Her palm flattened out and massaged over his bulging muscles and wide rib cage. His chest received equal attention. Her fingers sifted through the sprinkling of curls she discovered there. She flicked his left nipple, and he jolted. Catherine's pussy grew damp at the knowledge that she had the power to make such a strong man jump at the barest of touches.

Dean grabbed her wrist, his warm brown gaze capturing hers while he pushed her hand down his body. "You know what I want," he gritted out. "Hold my dick in that silky-soft palm, Catherine."

Catherine had a sudden flash back to the book, when Mira had pushed her master to the breaking point. Should she push Dean? It might be the dumbest thing she'd ever done, but Catherine didn't want to make it easy, not for either of them. Not tonight. She wanted Dean to capture her, to take her rough and wild, the way Mira's master had done in the story. It was their last night together, Catherine thought. It only made sense to make every attempt to drive the man crazy.

With that single thought in Catherine's mind, she asked, "What if I don't?"

His eyes narrowed and a muscle jumped in his rigid jaw. "What?"

She cocked her head to the side. "Maybe I don't feel like touching your cock."

One side of his mouth kicked up. "I bet I could make you want to," he whispered as he released her hand and took a step back, putting a measure of distance between them. "Move off the bed and get on all fours in front of me," he softly demanded.

Oops, maybe she'd pushed too far. After all, they both knew that sex games were way out of her range of expertise. She was a simple Southern girl. How was she supposed to give a man like Dean the erotic night he craved?

"Do you need another taste of the riding crop?"

His scandalous words fluttered around in her brain, and Catherine took a second too long to obey. When she got off the bed and started to get down on her hands and knees as Dean instructed, she was surprised to see him walking off. He went to the far corner of the room, and Catherine saw him pick up the leather whip. Her pussy throbbed knowing what would happen next. Dean came back to her and held it at his side, his nostrils flaring as he looked her over from head to toe. Catherine's body came to life everywhere his gaze roamed.

"Will you take my cock in your hand, sweetheart?"

"No," Catherine said, knowing full well he would punish her. "I don't think I will."

For an instant, Dean's implacable mask slipped. "I'd never cause you pain, Catherine," he said, his voice hoarse with emotion. "Only a little sting, nothing more."

Catherine's heart melted. Even when he was wildly turned on, Dean still sought to reassure her, to comfort her. Her mouth went dry and her throat felt tight when she thought of how much she loved him in that moment. Nervous and even a little scared, Catherine turned her head and murmured, "I know." A naughty grin crossed her face for a moment before she contained it.

Dean licked his lips and growled, "God, you're amazing."

Catherine didn't reply. She simply turned her head away and waited. She began to lose her nerve when she felt the first strike of the leather. She jerked and her bottom stung. On the heels of that one came another and another. Dean spanked her four more times before he stopped and said, "Mmm, your ass is all pink now, Catherine." He ran his palm over each cheek, massaging away the sting. "So pink and so damn fuckable."

An inferno raged inside of Catherine. She was desperate to feel Dean's cock stretching and filling her. "P-please, I need you."

"Turn around and face me," he gently ordered.

Catherine was too turned on to disobey. As she turned around she was faced with a rough and dominating side of Dean. He was ready to take her to new heights of carnal pleasures, and she was more than ready to be taken. He gripped the riding crop in his right hand and stroked her cheek with it. Catherine froze as the leather slid down over her shoulder to her arm. When Dean used the whip to caress her breasts, Catherine moaned.

"Ah, that's so damn pretty," he groaned. "Now, touch yourself for me."

Catherine's pussy was sopping wet, and she was more than happy to do as she was told. She reached between her legs and smoothed her fingers over her clit, her gaze riveted to his heavy erection the entire time. Dean's cock was thick and hard.

"Fuck, yeah, you look so damn good like that," he gritted out.

She bent her head backward to see his face, mesmerized by the feral savagery she witnessed. He looked ready to explode. As she moved her hand over her swollen mound and started to smooth two fingers into her tight opening, Dean gripped a handful of her hair and tugged her head forward, forcing her to look at him. "No more playing, sweets." She kept her fingers where they were, and Dean growled, "Enough."

Catherine pulled her hand away and frowned. "Why?"

"Because I want your mouth," he explained. "Suck my dick, sweetheart."

Catherine desperately wanted her tongue on him—she loved the taste of Dean's cock—but she was annoyed that he wasn't allowing her a few more minutes to play. Besides, how much fun would it be if he didn't have to work a little for the prize?

With the single thought of making Dean as hungry for her as she was for him, Catherine got to her feet and quickly sidestepped him. When he called her name, Catherine smiled and kept walking.

Dean couldn't believe Catherine had the nerve to stand up and walk out. He could drive a nail with the rigid length of his dick, for Christ's sake. "Where the hell do you think you're going?" he asked as he went after her.

She shrugged. "I'm thirsty."

Dean smiled as realization dawned. She wanted him to chase her, the way Mira had forced her master to go after her. "It's going to be such a pleasure punishing you."

He heard her laugh. In a few long strides, Dean caught up to her just as she reached the fridge. He swung her around. "As I see it, the only way to make sure you stay put is if I tie your sexy ass to my bed."

Catherine's emerald gaze widened. "Uh, Dean, I don't know about this."

"I do," Dean whispered as he lifted her into his arms and brought her back into his bedroom. After he dropped her onto his bed, Dean held her down with one hand and got on top of her, straddling her waist. He wasn't about to give her a chance to escape him again.

He leaned down and murmured, "Now, where were we?" His gaze took in the swollen temptation of her lips. "Oh, yeah, your pretty mouth," he said as he dipped his head and kissed her, tasting her sweetness. Dean felt his self-control going up in smoke. Catherine lit his body on fire with her addicting flavor.

He licked her bottom lip and sucked it into his mouth, nibbling at it. She arched up and moaned, as if ready to plead for him to fuck her. Dean wanted to. Hard. Slow. Both. She would give it to him; he knew it in his bones. Instead, he looked around for something to tie her down with and spotted the belt from his robe hanging off the edge of the bed. He picked it up and wrapped the silk securely over her wrists before tying it to the headboard.

"Dean," she said with a hint of fear in her voice, and her big green eyes were eating him up.

"You've been a bad girl, Catherine," he said with a smile. "I gave you a specific order, and you chose to ignore it."

With Catherine's arms tied above her head and her body all sprawled out and naked for him, Dean knew he'd never seen anything hotter in his life.

She wiggled her hands, testing the knot, and pouted. "I can't touch you like this. Release me."

"Not quite yet. I sort of like you at my mercy, sweetheart."

"Well, I don't like this game anymore," she muttered.

"You love my games," he whispered. "Give it a chance."

She turned her head away, refusing to speak.

He took hold of her chin and forced her to look at him. "Catherine, I'll release you if it's really want you want," he reassured her. "Is it?"

She appeared to mull that over before tentatively replying, "I'm willing to try, I suppose. But I don't like that I can't touch you."

He stroked his thumb over her lower lip. "You're so stubborn and incredibly sexy and you're all mine, every part of you. Trust me to make you feel good."

"Dean," she moaned, "I can't think with you on top of me."

His body hummed to life at her words. "Mmm, I love feeling your soft curves under me. You make me so fucking hard, Catherine. I want to be buried inside your tight pussy right now." Dean spread himself out over her, covering her body with his and pinning her to the mattress. "You're the only woman I've ever wanted to be with like this," he told her. "The only woman I've ever made hot chocolate for. And the only woman I've ever sketched. No other could ever compare to you, Catherine."

"Oh, Dean," she whispered, "when you say things like that I fall in love all over again."

He smoothed his fingers over the swell of her left breast and then moved to her rib cage. A finger dipped into her belly button, and he took a moment to play with the ring he found there.

"I need to buy you some jewelry so you can have a different one for every day of the year."

Catherine arched upward. "I can barely stand it, Dean. I feel like I'm burning up inside."

"I've dreamed of having you like this."

"Then take me, Dean. Make love to me," she begged.

Dean watched her as he anchored one arm beside her head and smoothed her hair away from her face with the other. He kissed her and watched as tears sprang to her eyes.

"Why the tears, sweets?"

"Because I don't want this to end. Ever."

"Then let's make it last a lifetime," he murmured as he moved down her body and kissed her pussy. Catherine tasted like the juiciest fruit, tangy and sweet. Dean wanted to eat her up. Catherine held still as he pulled her legs over his shoulders on either side of his head and began lapping at her throbbing clit. His mouth suckled her hard bud into his mouth and flicked it back and forth with his voracious tongue. She moaned his name and mashed her lower body against his face. When he slipped his tongue into her tight passage, the rhythm akin to what he wanted his dick to do, she cried out and arched upward. His hands toyed with her breasts, kneading and pinching the pretty tips. Too quickly, Catherine screamed his name as she burst all around him in a magnificent climax.

Seconds passed before she opened her eyes. At the knowledge that he'd so thoroughly satisfied her, a sense of predatory satisfaction took him. "No way am I going to live without you," he bit out. "One way or the other, Catherine, you belong to me."

"I'll always be yours," she said, but Dean could see the uncertainty in her eyes. She didn't think they could make it work. Dean would simply have to prove her wrong on that score.

He gently placed her legs back down onto the bed and rose

above her. They held each other's gaze as Dean carefully positioned himself against her entrance. "Now, sweetheart."

Catherine took hold of the headboard and smiled her acceptance. Her gentleness sucked the air out of him. She was so beautiful and willing, and Dean wanted to hold the image of her like this in his head forever.

He began pushing inside her heat, and tears sprang to Catherine's eyes. Dean paused. "Catherine?"

"I love you," Catherine whispered.

Her words made Dean want to howl at the moon. He covered her mouth with his in a claiming kiss as he thrust his cock deep. He swallowed her moans as he began making slow, sweet love to the woman of his heart. Soon, Catherine was pleading for more. Dean gave up any hope of maintaining his control and fucked her faster, harder. She matched his rhythm stroke for stroke. All at once, Dean lost control.

He threw his head back and let out a low, rumbling growl. The untamed sounds coming from Catherine had him nearly careening over the cliff. His hips gyrated against hers, forcing her body into the mattress as he fucked her with feral abandon.

Dean watched as Catherine appeared to climb higher and higher, the sensitive bud of her clitoris rubbing against his body with each thrust. His thoughts splintered as his climax began to pull him under. Dean flexed his hips and shoved deep once more, then he poured his come inside her, filling her up.

Catherine moaned and clutched the headboard in a tight grip as she shouted, her orgasm pouring over her. To Dean, watching Catherine come was the single most beautiful thing he'd ever witnessed. Once she'd settled back to earth, Dean untied her hands and began massaging her wrists. Once she lay limp, Dean pulled out of her. Her eyes opened, and they stared at each other, no words passing between them. Tomorrow she would be going back to Georgia, and Dean would have to watch her go. He didn't know how the hell he would survive it.

He lay down beside her and pulled her into his body, holding her close. His name came out as a breathless whisper, and it was the sweetest sound Dean had ever heard. He ached to hear it night after night, but how? The thought kept him awake until after dawn.

27

Dean woke instantly alert. Something was off, he could feel it. He reached out and found Catherine's side of the bed cold. When he opened his eyes and looked around the room, only to find it empty, he frowned. He shoved out of bed and pulled his jeans on. When he heard a noise in the kitchen he thought maybe she'd decided to make breakfast, but as he entered the room, Dean found her sitting at the table, papers spread out in front of her. Oh, God, no. It can't be. Catherine looked up. Tears were streaming down her cheeks only to fall to the table unchecked.

"When were you planning to tell me about this?" She grabbed one of the papers in a tight fist and waved it in the air. "When were you going to tell me that my father was a rapist!"

Dean saw the devastation on Catherine's face, and it tore him up inside. "I just got the information yesterday," he said in a quiet voice. "I was going to tell you about it today."

She threw the paper down and shoved out of the chair. "You had me investigated, didn't you? You never truly trusted me at all."

Dean shook his head and crossed the room. He took hold of her shoulders and shook her. "Stop it, Catherine. You know that's not true. I do trust you. Hell, I'm in love with you." He pointed to the papers and bit out, "I did ask Jonas to do some digging, but that was before, sweetheart."

"Before we had sex the first time, Dean?" He winced. "Yeah, that's what I thought."

She tore out of his arms and headed to the bedroom. Dean followed, his stomach in knots. "Just give me a chance to explain."

"Explain that you had me investigated? Explain that you had these papers last night and didn't say a word about them?"

Dean stood helplessly by while Catherine went about getting dressed. "I didn't trust you at first—you knew that, damn it. I did have you investigated, but when I told you I trusted you, I meant it. When I told you I loved you, I meant it."

She snorted. "Yeah, right. Did you get a kick out of finding that information, Dean? You were right all along. As it turns out there were more secrets. You must be so freaking thrilled!"

"Damn it, Catherine, that's not the way it happened!"

She slumped. "God, I'm such a colossal fool, but then again I'm the product of a rape, so maybe it's in my DNA to be a complete loser."

Dean's anger boiled over. He closed the distance between them and took hold of her upper arms and shook her. "Don't ever say that to me again," he bit out. "That son of a bitch has nothing to do with you, Catherine. Nothing, do you hear me?"

Catherine yanked away and turned around. "It doesn't matter. It's over. I'm going home."

"Don't go, not like this. Please, sweetheart, talk to me."

"The worst part of it is, I actually thought you cared."

Dean felt as if someone were ripping his heart out with their bare hands. He needed her to know how much she meant to him. How much he loved her. He'd screwed up royally and he had no way to fix it.

"Catherine, I do care," he said, urging her to hear him. "I love you. Please, if you believe nothing else, then at least believe that."

She turned back to him. "The games are over. We've had our fun, but it's time for me to go home," Catherine stated in a voice so devoid of emotion that Dean barely recognized it as the same woman who'd not so many hours ago declared her love for him.

He stepped into the doorway to block her exit, unwilling to let it end this way. "Give me a chance," he said, holding his hands up in surrender. "That's all I ask."

"You hurt me, Dean," she replied as she looked down at the floor. "You promised you wouldn't, but you did." He started to speak, but Catherine looked back up and their gazes caught. "I know your reasons," she said, her voice softening a fraction. "Linda's betrayal tore you up, and I get that. I even understand your need to have me investigated. I was practically a stranger when I came here, and you were protecting your family." She swiped at the tears on her face and muttered, "But none of that explains why you didn't share that information with me the minute you received it."

He shoved his hands in his pockets to keep from reaching for her. The pain in her eyes was killing him. "I wanted the night with you," he said in a gentle tone. "It was selfish, I know, but I wanted our last night together to be perfect. I swear, I planned to tell you everything."

Catherine frowned. "I need time to think. Please, don't stop me, Dean. I feel like I'm shattering here," she said, her voice trembling. "Please."

Dean had the sinking feeling that if Catherine left now, she'd be leaving for good. But he couldn't stand to see her in pain either. Besides, it didn't matter where she went, he would find her. She was his heart, and he would do anything to keep her.

Dean stepped out of the way and watched as she gathered her coat and purse, then walked out his front door. For what seemed like hours, Dean stood there, staring, willing her to come back. It didn't happen. She was gone. He didn't know if she would forgive him, but he was willing to give her a little time. And if she didn't come back to him, then he would go to her, because there was no way he could live without her.

When Catherine got in her rental car her hands were shaking and she felt like she was about to break into a million pieces. She started the car and took off down the road, not really caring where she went. Dean had investigated her behind her back? And the information he'd discovered; Catherine still couldn't comprehend it. She wanted to throw up when she thought of what her mother had endured. Her and Gracie's mother, she reminded herself. Did Gracie know about this? She didn't think so.

God, no wonder her mother had given her away. What woman would want the constant reminder of such a horrific event? The knowledge that she was the product of something so cruel sent a wave of nausea through her. She frowned, wondering if her adoptive parents had known how she'd been conceived. It would explain why they hadn't wanted to tell her she was adopted. They had to suspect that she would one day be curious enough to seek out her biological parents. She supposed she had Dean to thank for saving her the trouble, she thought bitterly.

Catherine turned a corner and realized she was heading straight for Gracie's house. When their place came into view she slowed and parked along the curb directly in front. She turned off the engine and got out. Gracie met her at the door, her eyes filled with tears and her face ashen. Catherine knew in an instant that Gracie knew everything.

When she walked up the front walk, Gracie pulled her into her arms for a hug. Catherine lost it. She cried herself dry. Several minutes later she found herself on the couch, Wade on one side, Gracie on the other. "I'm sorry," she mumbled as she blew her nose. "I don't usually cry like that."

"You had good reason," Wade said. "I just talked to Dean. He was worried about you."

Catherine frowned at the knowledge that he'd called looking for her. God, she loved him, but knowing that he'd dug into her life behind her back still made her feel betrayed. "He needn't be. I'm fine."

Gracie patted her on the hand. "Do you want to talk about it?"

"I'm not even sure where to start. I-I just can't take it all in."

"Me either. I feel awful for thinking such rotten thoughts about our mother all these years." Gracie shook her head. "What she went through, it must have been horrible."

"And to top it all off, she ended up pregnant as a result." Catherine felt sick. "My father was a—"

"Stop beating yourself up," Wade said, his tone firm. "Both of you. This whole thing took place years ago. Neither of you are responsible."

"I know, but knowing I have his DNA . . ." Catherine couldn't finish the sentence; it was too disgusting to say aloud.

"You are Jean and Russ Michaels's child, Catherine," Gracie said, her voice stronger now. "They're the people that raised you. They're the ones that matter."

Catherine looked into her sister's eyes and said, "I wish I could go back in time. I wish I'd never found those papers in Dean's kitchen."

"How did you find them anyway?" Wade asked. "Dean didn't say."

"I'd gotten up early to make us something to eat." She smiled. "I was going to surprise him with breakfast in bed." She had to swallow back the pain when she said, "His coat was tossed over the table, and when I went to hang it on the chair the papers fell out of his pocket."

"Damn, I'm sorry as hell you had to find out that way."

"Me too," Catherine said, getting angry all over again.

"I don't know if it helps, but Dean planned to tell you. I know that for a fact. And when I talked to him just now he sounded . . . pretty beat-up."

She didn't want to get into whether Dean had intended to tell her. As far as she was concerned, when he went to Jonas to get information on her would've been the time to tell her. Still, the thought of Dean suffering made her heart ache. "He told me he loved me, and God help me, but I believed him."

"He went about this all wrong, Catherine, and I'm not going to sit here and defend his actions," Wade said. "Still, Dean doesn't say those words to a woman unless he feels them deep down in his soul. If nothing else you can be certain of that much."

"What does it matter?" She shrugged. "I'm leaving today. I'll be in Georgia, and Dean's life is here. The honeymoon is over."

"Don't bet on it," Wade bit out. "If I know my brother, he'll give you some breathing room, but don't make the mistake of thinking he's just going to let you walk out of his life."

"The Harrisons are stubborn that way," Gracie said with a smile that lit up her entire face.

Catherine's hopes lifted a measure. Would Dean forget her after she left or would he come for her? And what would she do if he did?

Unwilling to ponder that frustrating quandary, Catherine stood. "Well, I probably should head back to the hotel. I need to get packed and get to the airport."

"I wish you'd let us see you off," Wade said as he hugged her close.

"No, those types of big good-byes just make me cry. I've cried enough for one day." She smiled and took Gracie into her arms next. "Thank you, for everything."

Gracie sniffed. "I'm going to miss you."

"I'll be back for the wedding though," Catherine said, feeling a fresh bout of tears coming on. "And you and Wade are more than welcome to visit me anytime you want."

Gracie pulled back and asked, "Are you sure you're okay?"

Catherine pasted on a smile. "I'll be fine, really."

After they said their good-byes, Catherine got back into her car and drove away, tears welling up in her eyes. "The flight home is going to be damned miserable," Catherine groused.

28

Catherine had been depressed for days. Her website design business, which she usually loved, seemed tedious now. She couldn't stop thinking about Dean. He was on her mind 24/7. At random moments throughout the day, she would get bombarded with thoughts of him. He was everywhere. She couldn't even bring herself to sleep in her own bed because it felt empty and cold without Dean holding her close. Since arriving back home two weeks ago, Catherine had been sleeping on her parents' couch.

Mary had called her several times, but she'd avoided her. Catherine didn't want to have to put on a false front. She didn't feel like pretending she was fine. That she wasn't hurting and missing Dean like crazy.

It was Thursday night, and she found herself sprawled out on the couch, sucking down a beer. She didn't even like beer all that much, but wine made her think of Dean so she avoided the stuff like the plague. Her hair looked like crap, her clothes were wrinkled, and she couldn't even bring herself to deal with the rest of her parents' things.

Catherine was angry at herself for falling for Dean. Angry that he'd called her every single day since she'd arrived back home. Angry that he'd sent her flowers—three times. "Men are trouble," she grumbled.

When the doorbell rang her heart stuttered. She knew it couldn't possibly be Dean, but she couldn't help hoping he'd come for her, ready to profess his undying love. When she heard her friend Mary call out to her, Catherine rolled her eyes. "Go away!"

"Open up or I'll pick the lock."

Catherine frowned, but deep down she was glad to have her friend's company. Leaving the couch behind, Catherine went to the door and unlatched it. "You know how to pick locks?" Catherine asked as she opened the door.

Mary merely pushed her way inside and said, "Yes, now what the hell is going on with you?" She looked around at the mess and screwed up her nose. "Uh, it looks like shit in here. What have you been doing for the last two weeks?"

"Working, what else?" Catherine growled as she headed back to the couch. When she picked up her beer to take a drink, Mary arched her brow and plucked it right out of her hand.

"Enough already. Get your butt in the shower before I have to drag you there myself. You look horrible."

Catherine didn't take long to think over Mary's threat. She knew her too well. Mary was always as good as her word. Besides, she was right, she did look like hell.

"I'll be back."

"Take your time," Mary said as she looked her over. "Seriously."

Catherine rolled her eyes and left the room. She tried not to think about Dean when her gaze strayed to her bed. God, how she wished he were there. She felt her stomach quiver in response as she imagined him sprawled out on top of her blankets, a delicious grin on his gorgeous face as he held a hand out to her. Damn, there went the tears again. Evidently, she wasn't quite through. Yippie.

After she finished her shower, Catherine slipped into a clean pair of heather-gray cotton shorts and a white tank. She tucked her hair under a towel and went to find Mary. She was surprised to see the living room all spick-and-span. When she went into the kitchen, Catherine found Mary doing the dishes. "Might as well get a pot of coffee going," Mary said when she looked over at her. "I think we're going to need it."

"I don't want to talk about Dean," she mumbled as she took the coffee can out of the freezer.

"Too bad," Mary said as she rinsed the last dish and set in the drainer to dry. "You're going to anyway."

Catherine slammed a couple of mugs on the counter, surprised when they didn't break, and asked, "Geez, since when did you get so bossy?"

Mary chuckled. "All part of my charm, hon."

For the first time since leaving Ohio, Catherine laughed. The sound was foreign to her ears, but it was a start. Catherine looked over at her friend and said, "Thanks for coming over."

Mary pointed to a kitchen chair and said, "Sit, while I get the coffee."

Catherine did as she was told and sat down. She watched Mary pour the coffee and felt like a heel for being such a jerk. "I'm sorry for being a grump," she said. "I'm lucky to have a friend like you."

"We're lucky to have each other," Mary said as she sat across from her. "Now that we're all lovey-dovey, what are you planning to do about the hottie who has your panties all in a twist?"

"I don't know," Catherine said, as she stared down at her coffee."

"Do you love him?"

"Yes," she muttered. "I feel like my insides are being torn apart."

Mary threw her hands in the air. "Then what's the problem?"

"He lied to me," Catherine gritted out. "He pried into my background and didn't bother telling me about it."

Mary winced. "Wow, you told me he didn't trust you, but I didn't think he'd go that far. What'd he discover?"

Catherine took a sip of her coffee. The hot liquid reminded her of the way Dean had made her the yummy hot chocolate. The coffee tasted like dirt in comparison. "He found out information about my real father," she told Mary.

Her eyes widened. "Your biological father? Seriously?"

Catherine nodded as she related the story to her. "I'm the product of that monster, Mary." She recoiled thinking about it. "I can't wrap my head around it."

"That's crap and you know it," Mary said, her lips thinning in anger. "You aren't the product of anything except your mama and daddy. We both know that."

She pushed her coffee away, no longer wanting it. "It makes sense why they didn't tell me I was adopted, at least."

"Yeah. They were trying to spare you the pain." Mary paused, then asked, "So, Dean was a total bullheaded ass. What do you plan to do about it?"

"What do you mean?"

"I mean, if it were my man acting like that, I'd want to smack him upside the head. I'd want to make him grovel a little, but I wouldn't give up on him. Not if it's the real deal."

"It is the real deal, but—"

"But nothing!" Mary shouted. "I saw the flowers he sent. I read the cards. He loves you and he wants you back. Don't you think you owe it to both of you to at least talk to him?"

Catherine frowned down at the table, considering Mary's words. "I don't know," she admitted.

Mary reached a hand across the wood surface and laid it on

top of Catherine's. "Look, I don't know him, but it doesn't appear to me that he sees you as some passing fancy."

Catherine remembered the stricken look on his face when she'd left. He'd looked as if she'd kicked his puppy. She didn't want to think of him hurting. "I know he cares about me, but I can't stop thinking about the way he went behind my back to dig up dirt on me. If he'd only told me."

"No doubt about it, he screwed up, but do you want to risk losing him for good over it?"

As Mary's words sank in, Catherine felt sicker and sicker. "Oh, God, you're right. I'm miserable without him."

Mary smiled and sipped her coffee. "If you ask me you're both a couple of stubborn mules. Heck, you sort of deserve each other."

"Great, but there's a catch," she muttered. "He lives in Ohio, not exactly a quick trip back and forth."

"If you love him, then you'll figure something out. And I'll bet my last dollar that he's kicking himself in the ass for letting you walk away." Mary winked and said, "Maybe you should invite him here. I wouldn't mind meeting him."

Could she be so bold as to call him and invite him to Atlanta? It'd been two weeks and she hadn't returned a single one of his phone calls. Would he even want to see her after all that time?

Still, Mary was right. She loved him. She was miserable without him. It was time to stop moping and do something about it.

The next morning, Catherine stood in her bathroom, staring at the little plastic stick in her hand, willing it to change. It didn't. The little plus sign wasn't going away. It was the second test she'd taken.

She was pregnant. Dean Harrison was going to be a father.

The first thing she needed to do was call him. This was so not the way she'd hoped their meeting would go.

"How is it possible that the first chance I let myself have some fun I end up pregnant?"

She wanted to shout to the heavens at the unfairness of it. Fat lot of good that would do. Wishing it away wouldn't help the situation. She'd tried to wish her parents back alive, and it hadn't worked. She'd tried to wish her biological father wasn't a rapist, and that hadn't worked either. Catherine stomped on the miserable thoughts and concentrated on her current situation.

"A baby," she said as she covered her stomach with her hand. What sort of mother would she be? Sadness welled up as she thought of how happy her mama would be if she were alive. She could almost hear her soft voice making plans for a nursery. No doubt about it, her parents would've spoiled her baby something fierce.

She looked up at the ceiling and whispered, "I miss you, Mama."

When the phone rang, Catherine jumped. Could it be Dean? This time she wasn't going to send him to her answering machine. She ran out of the bathroom and bounded across her bed, answering it on the third ring. "Hello?"

"Catherine?" Gracie said on the other end. "Is that you? You sound winded."

Her sister, and one of the few people who would understand her predicament. "Oh, yeah, I'm fine. What's up? Is Wade treating you right?"

Gracie and Wade were moving right along on their wedding preparations. The last time she'd talked to Gracie, she and Wade were having issues about the flowers. Gracie felt they were too expensive, but Wade had insisted she go all out, considering it'd be the only time she ever walked down the aisle. Catherine thought Wade was perfect for her sister.

"I threatened to drag Wade off to the nearest judge if he doesn't stop insisting on having the best of the best of everything. This wedding is going to cost a bloody fortune."

Catherine laughed. "That man is so stupid in love with you, Gracie. I'm so happy for you."

"Thanks, sis." There was a beat of silence, then Gracie said, "Uh, there's something else I wanted to share with you. A bit of news. I wanted you to be the first to know."

Boy, do I have news for you. "Spill it, the suspense is killing me."

"Um, well, I'm pregnant."

Was it even possible? She went back to the bathroom, holding the phone to her ear, and stared at her own two tests.

"Catherine? Did you hear me?"

"Oh, yeah. I'm here." Then she realized she hadn't congratulated her. "Oh, Gracie, this is fantastic news!" Something else occurred to her and she grinned. "I'm going to be an aunt!"

Gracie laughed, and Catherine heard Wade say something in the background. "Wade says it's the potent Harrison DNA. He's outrageous," she said, love and happiness in her voice.

Catherine nearly choked. Potent Harrison DNA? Yeah, Gracie didn't know the half of it. "So," Catherine said as she went back to the bedroom, "let me get this straight. You're getting married to the most wonderful man in the world, and you're going to have his baby. Now that's what I call a happily ever after ending."

She heard Gracie sigh. "I know, it's too much sometimes. I have to pinch myself to make sure it's not all a dream."

"Of course it's real. No one deserves it more than you, hon."

"Thanks, Catherine," Gracie said in a shaky voice. "I love you so much."

"Don't get all wishy-washy or I'll start crying, and then we'll each be an emotional mess."

"I've been like that a lot lately. I wonder if it's the hormones," she said.

"Probably," Catherine replied, since she was feeling pretty darn weepy too.

"Well, I need to go," Gracie said. "Wade is pestering me to get in touch with the flower shop. He says he needs to keep wielding the whip so things stay on schedule. He's quite the taskmaster."

They said their good-byes and Catherine placed the phone back on the cradle. She looked down at the two test sticks in her hand and sighed. She'd ached to tell Gracie, but she hadn't wanted to dampen her sister's happiness in any way. Besides, she needed to tell Dean first. She frowned as she considered Dean's reaction and that of his family. What would they all say once she told them? Either way, it wasn't going to be a fun conversation.

Would Dean want her after he learned he was about to be a father? Would he want his child? She didn't know the answers to those questions and that scared her. Before she lost her nerve, Catherine slipped the little pregnancy sticks in the dresser drawer and picked up the phone. She called the airlines and booked the earliest flight to Ohio. Her hands were shaking as she got off the phone. The extra trip would cut into her savings, but she had to have a little faith. She loved Dean and he'd said he loved her too. It was time to put those declarations to the test.

29

It'd been two friggin' weeks. Two weeks of dreaming of Catherine's perfect freckled skin and sexy green eyes. He missed her smiles the most. Every time he walked into his bedroom he was confronted with the bed he'd shared with her, and the sketch she'd left behind. She'd done a damn good job of avoiding him, and he'd had enough. He'd tried everything to get her to open up and talk to him. He loved her, damn it. He wanted to share his life with her, but that was going to be damn hard to do if she wouldn't even answer her phone.

Dean remembered the way she'd looked tied to his bed. He kept seeing her face as she'd exploded all around his cock. And just like that, his dick swelled and hardened. He had to shift around in his chair so his cock didn't feel strangled in his jeans.

"Damn it," he muttered as he stared at the screwed-up bid he'd been working on for the last hour. He wadded up the paper and tossed it in the trash before starting to figure it up all over again.

A sound outside his office drew his attention away from his

thoughts. It was a woman's voice. And not just any woman. He'd know that sexy tone anywhere.

Dean shot out of his chair and headed out to the front. She'd come back to him? His heart sped up when he spotted her. For whatever reason, she had come to him, and this time he wouldn't be letting her go. Never again. He wouldn't survive it.

"I'm sure he is busy," Catherine said, "but I want to talk to him."

Dean watched from across the room as Catherine frowned at his new receptionist, Gloria. The girl was young, but she was smart and he thought she'd been doing a good job so far. But he didn't much care for her attitude toward Catherine.

While the women were distracted, Dean took a moment to drink Catherine in. God, she looked good. Her hair was up in a ponytail, and she wore a white T-shirt and jeans. Dean had never seen anything more beautiful.

He heard Gloria deny Catherine's plea, and Dean frowned. Hell, when he'd told his receptionist that he didn't want to be disturbed, he hadn't expected Catherine to pop up out of nowhere.

"Look, miss, he's busy. Come back tomorrow, or better yet, call and make an appointment with him."

"I don't need an appointment and I'm not coming back," Catherine said, clearly frustrated. "I want to see him now."

Dean figured Catherine had had enough. He cleared his throat, drawing the women's attention immediately. Gloria rolled her eyes and said, "She said she knows you, but I told her you're busy."

Catherine looked up and their gazes locked. Even from across the room, Dean could see how nervous she was. "I'm sorry to just burst in here like this, Dean, but we need to talk."

Dean crossed his arms over his chest and leaned against the doorjamb to keep from striding across the room and taking her into his arms. "Thanks, Gloria, I'll take it from here."

Gloria gave him a grateful look. "Good luck," she muttered.

Yeah, he'd need all the luck he could get, but he didn't much care for the way Gloria acted toward Catherine.

"Let's make something clear," he said to the young woman. "Catherine doesn't need an appointment and she is never to be kept waiting. Remember that in the future, okay?"

Gloria visibly paled. "Of course, Mr. Harrison."

Dean sighed. "I told you to call me Dean," he muttered. He looked over at Catherine and held out a hand. "Come on, we can talk in my office." It didn't escape Dean's notice when Catherine didn't take his hand as they headed to the back.

After they entered the small room he closed the door. He moved around the desk and sat, then waited as Catherine sat in the chair across from him. Her back was ramrod straight and she clutched her purse in her lap. God, it was killing him to keep his distance, but until he knew what she was up to he couldn't very well come at her like a bull in a China shop.

With her mass of red hair tied back in a ponytail and no makeup on, she looked all of eighteen. He had to grip onto the arms of the chair just to keep from leaping across the desk. "Gracie didn't tell me you were coming," he said, hoping to get them around the awkward silence.

Catherine's eyes lit with humor. "She doesn't know I'm here. I haven't told her. I plan to surprise her later."

Damn, she was so pretty when she smiled. It'd been way too long since he'd seen here. He felt it like a punch to the gut. He'd been a miserable bastard since she'd left. Everyone had been steering a wide path around him, but one smile from Catherine and his world was right again.

Christ, he was so fucking in love with her. He knew now that what he'd felt for Linda paled in comparison. Catherine was the real deal and he would do anything in his power to prove they belonged together.

"You wouldn't take my calls."

She looked down at her lap. "I know, and I'm sorry."

"Don't apologize. I hurt you and I'm sorry, sweetheart," he said, his voice hoarse with emotion. "More sorry than you can ever know."

Catherine started to fidget, as if trying to figure out how to tell him something. For the life of him he couldn't imagine what. "The direct approach is always best," he said, his voice softening.

She looked across the desk and blurted out, "I'm pregnant."

Dean blinked, unsure he'd heard her correctly. "Say again?"

Catherine covered her belly with the palm of her hand and said, "I'm pregnant, Dean."

Dean's gaze zeroed in on her still-flat stomach. "Wow."

She shot from the chair and paced around the room. "I thought you should hear it in person. You're going to be a father."

Dean came out of his shocked stupor and said, "Are you certain?" He shook his head. "I mean, I thought you were on the pill."

She stopped and turned. "I'm certain. And I was on the pill, but in all the . . . excitement I got off schedule, I guess." She turned red and looked at the far wall, as if finding the dull tan paint fascinating.

He stood and went to her. Dean quickly noted her pale face and trembling body. Was she about to cry? He took her into his arms and held her tight. God, she felt good there. She felt right.

"Shhh, calm yourself, sweetheart," he murmured. "You took me by surprise, but we can deal with this together. It's going to be okay." She nodded and buried her head into his T-shirt. "Jesus, Catherine, I missed you something awful."

Dean could feel her relaxing against him, and his hopes soared. "I missed you too," she admitted in a quiet voice.

He began massaging her back and whispered, "Can you ever forgive me for what I did?"

Her head came up, and once more her expressive eyes were holding him captive. She seemed to be debating whether to bolt or stay. Finally, she said, "I came back because . . . because I love you, Dean."

The words had Dean wanting to howl at the moon. His hands shook as he cupped her face in his palms and whispered, "I love you too. So much I've been going slowly crazy without you."

Dean lifted her into his arms and carried her to his chair. He sat with her in his lap and said, "The way I see it there's only one way to handle this."

Catherine went rigid in his arms. She lifted up and glared at him. "If you're suggesting we get rid of the baby, forget it. It's not an option, Dean."

Dean flinched, his jaw going rigid with anger. "There is no way on earth I would kill my own child. Don't ever insult me like that again."

Catherine blinked rapidly and bit her lip. "God, I'm sorry." She clenched her eyes closed tight. "Of course you would never suggest that. I'm so sorry."

Dean forced himself to remain calm. She was on edge and jumpy. She'd come back to him, and he knew how much courage that had taken for her. Even with all he'd put her through, she'd come back to him.

"I've been screwing things up from the beginning, Catherine," he admitted. "But when you left it broke me. I gave you time to think because I didn't want to rush you. But you should know that I booked a flight out to Atlanta. I was going to be leaving tomorrow morning. I was determined to make you listen. One way or the other."

"You should've told me about the investigation from the moment you went to Jonas."

He winced at the reminder. "I know, I fucked up. Never again, Catherine." When she sat silently in his lap, waiting for him to continue, Dean poured out the rest of it. "When Linda cheated on me I thought nothing could feel worse. I'd bought the woman a ring and the whole time she had another man on the side." Her gaze softened, but before she could say anything, Dean took her face in his palms and said, "When you went back to Georgia I knew the truth. You're the woman my heart belongs to. You're the one I want to spend the rest of my life with, sweetheart."

Tears filled her eyes, and Dean couldn't tell if they were the good kind or not. "Are you saying you want to marry me?"

"Yes, that's exactly what I'm saying. I want to call you mine. I want the world to know you're taken and that our child is loved and cherished."

"Dean, I don't know what to say."

"Say you love me. Say yes, sweetheart," he growled. Dean kissed her forehead, her cheek, then finally their lips met. He let out a sigh of relief when she melted against him and wound her arms around his neck. Dean lifted an inch and whispered, "Only you, Catherine. It was only ever you. From the time I saw your picture you stole my heart, sweets."

"Yes, Dean. Oh, God, I love you so much and I have so much to tell you. I—"

He cut her off with a kiss, then eased her away. "You're here, that's all that matters now. I love you."

"I love you too." She shook her head. "I couldn't sleep, I couldn't work. All I could think about was you. Then I took the pregnancy tests and I was so scared."

"Scared?"

"I was afraid I'd waited too long. I was afraid you wouldn't want me." She placed her hand over her abdomen and whispered, "I was terrified you wouldn't want us."

"Ah, sweetheart, how could you ever think that? You're my world. Don't you know that?"

"It's still so convoluted though. I mean, with my parents' estate to deal with and my life in Georgia."

"As long as we're together I don't care where we live."

Catherine smiled and covered his mouth with hers. Dean had never tasted anything sweeter. "You know, I think I'd like to live closer to Gracie. And your mom and sister were very kind to me when I had the chance to visit with them the last time."

He rolled his eyes. "They both love you to pieces. They've been browbeating me for being such an ass to you."

"I think . . . I think it would be nice if our baby lived closer to her grandmom, don't you?"

Dean noticed that she'd referred to their baby as a girl, but he didn't think Catherine even realized it. He pictured a little red-haired imp, and he grinned. "Yeah, Mom will love it and we'd sure as hell never want for a babysitter." His gaze narrowed as he thought of all she'd be leaving behind in Georgia. "What about your life in Atlanta? Your friend Mary and your parents' home? Won't you miss all that?"

Catherine bit her lip and looked at his shirt. As she picked at a loose thread she said, "I would miss Mary, for sure, but my home is with you and the baby, Dean." Her gaze came back to his. "And Mary and I can still keep in touch through visits and the Internet. It's not as if I'd be living halfway across the country."

"What about your job though?" he asked, unwilling to let her make a rash decision that she might later regret.

"Dean, the baby's entire family is here in Ohio. I want her to be close to them." She shrugged. "My business is portable. That's the beauty of being a website designer."

"You need to be sure, sweetheart."

"I am," she said in a firm voice. "Besides, I was sort of thinking it'd be nice to cut back on the web work and be a mother for a while."

Dean groaned. "I love the idea of you barefoot and pregnant. Hell, careers can come later."

She laughed. "Don't go all caveman on me, Dean. I didn't say I was going to give up working all together. Just take a break."

He wagged his eyebrows at her. "Unless I keep you knocked up."

She laughed and slapped him on the chest. "Now that we've settled that, how soon can you leave here today?" She got off his lap and stood in front of him. "I want to tell Gracie the good news."

Dean got to his feet and tugged her until she was pressed up against him. He kissed the top of her head and murmured, "We'll leave now, but we're going to have to make a stop first."

She pulled back and stared up at him. "Oh, where to?"

"My house." He stopped and corrected himself. "Our house, I mean." He cupped her bottom and squeezed. "We need to seal the deal, don't you think?"

"Oh, yes, definitely," she said in a breathless voice.

As Dean stood there staring down at her, he felt like the luckiest man alive. It definitely didn't get any better than this.

Epilogue

Eight months later . . .

Dean grabbed the man by the shirt and yanked him off his feet. "She wants juice. If you have to tear apart the entire hospital, she will get juice!"

Catherine shook her head, exasperated. "Stop assaulting the poor man, Dean. I don't have to have juice. Really, it's okay."

He dropped the man, and Catherine watched as the poor orderly hurried out of the room. Dean's dark brown gaze swung back to her and her heart did a little flip. He was so handsome when he did the manly, protective thing. Would she ever get tired of looking at him? She doubted it. He was too good looking for his own good.

Catherine tried to sit up, but her back was still hurting so she gave up and lay back down. Lordy, who would have thought that having a baby could be so monumentally painful? And why did women feel the need to do it more than once? Just the thought of going through that again had her cringing. Then again, she wouldn't change a thing. Her baby was gorgeous. Perfect. She already had a head full of dark hair, just like her father. The Harrison genes had shone through loud and clear.

"Dean, we need to talk."

He strode to the bed, grasped her hand, and began to massage his thumb over the back of it. "Are you in pain? Do you want the doctor, sweetheart?"

She shook her head. "Nothing like that. But our conversation before all this happened, we need to finish it."

"Are you sure you're up to it?"

She nodded. "We need to decide on a name for our little girl."

He sat next to her on the bed and brought her hand to his lips, then proceeded to kiss each fingertip, before replying, "I thought you wanted to name her after your mom."

"I do. It's a good name, but I think we should include your mom too."

"I think that's a good idea. Audrey Jean Harrison. I like it."

She smiled. "Do you think she'll eventually shorten it to AJ?"

He shrugged. "If she does I don't see a problem with it."

She smiled. "You're going to spoil her rotten, aren't you?"

"Bet on it, sweetheart," he growled. "I love you with all my heart, Catherine, and I plan to spoil the both of you."

Her heart swelled with love. "I wish my mama could've been here to see this. She would've been so happy."

He frowned and stroked her hair away her face. "I think that she's watching you right now. I bet she's grinning from ear to ear too. And my mom will be here soon. She just got caught in traffic."

"I'm glad. I'm going to want to pick her brain about raising children." Catherine recalled that horrible moment when she'd seen the proof about her biological father. "As much as it makes me sick to know who my real father was, I'm glad I know. I'm glad there aren't any more secrets."

Dean leaned down, placing both hands beside her body, caging her in. "No more secrets, Catherine. Never again."

She nodded. "I love you so much."

His lips brushed hers, gently, sweetly, then he raised up an inch and groaned, "It's a good thing, because the feeling is mutual." His deep voice slid over her skin like velvet. "You belong to me, sweetheart. The baby and I are your present and future."

"Yes," she agreed breathlessly.

Dean pressed his lips to hers and kissed her with predatory heat. He was hard and demanding. She gave him access to her mouth and he swooped in, scouring and drinking in her moans of pleasure. When he lifted, they were both panting and out of breath.

"Without you I felt lost, Catherine. I'm so sorry for not trusting you. I'm sorry for not believing in you."

"I know, and it's in the past," she rushed to reassure him. "Besides, we both made mistakes, Dean."

Dean nodded, then stood back up. "Shall I go find out if our daughter is ready to be fed?"

Because their baby was a preemie, she had to stay in an incubator for a few days for observation, though the nurses had all said she was a healthy girl and had the lungs to prove it. "Yes, my breasts are beginning to ache."

His gaze shot to her swollen chest. "You are beautiful when you feed my daughter, Catherine."

She felt like a great big whale, but Dean's praise always made her feel beautiful. "Go, before you start something you can't possibly finish."

"Oh, I can finish all right," he huskily whispered. "We'd just have to be a little creative since I can't penetrate you for the next six weeks."

She frowned. "How do you know how long?"

"I asked the doctor about it." He grinned, totally unrepentant. "He said you need to wait until your six-week checkup. He needs to be sure you are healed properly."

Her cheeks heated as she imagined that intimate conversation. "I can't believe you asked him about that."

"I look forward to inventing interesting things for us to do until then, sweetheart," he murmured just before he turned and left the room.

She couldn't help the giggle that bubbled over. The man was insatiable. As the door closed behind him, the phone rang. Catherine smiled, wondering if it was Mary. "Hello?"

"Uh, guess where I am."

"Gracie? What's going on?"

Her sister laughed. "I'm in the hospital, not too far down the hall from you actually."

"Oh no, is everything okay?"

"Everything is fine, but the baby is insisting on being born."

Catherine nearly dropped the phone. "You're kidding me!"

Gracie laughed, but Catherine could tell it was strained. "Nope. The contractions started about an hour ago. It seems our babies were determined to have the same birthday. Is that something or what?"

Catherine grinned, happier than she'd ever thought possible. "I'm so glad, sis. I love you."

"I love you too, but I need to go before I scream in your ear." There was some rustling and then, "Hey, Wade wants to talk to Dean. Is he there?"

Dean came back into the room then, carrying a tiny bundle in his powerful arms, his face awash with pleasure. Catherine felt tears of happiness spring to her eyes. When he saw her, he frowned. "Is everything okay?"

"Better than okay," she whispered, then she handed the phone to him. "Your brother has some news for you."

Dean gave her the baby, then sat on the edge of the bed, watching her every move. Catherine pulled the flap of her gown down and began nursing their very hungry little girl. Dean's eyes darkened and his free hand came up to cup her other breast in his hand, as if needing to take part in the experience. She knew the instant Wade delivered the happy news. Dean's lips curved.

Catherine couldn't imagine how she ever could've considered living without Dean. He was the best sort of man. Strong, yet gentle. Kind and loyal and every bit as devoted to her and the baby as she was to him.

She knew her life with the hardheaded man wouldn't always be an easy road, but even their arguments were fraught with heat and passion. It was more than she'd ever dreamed of having.

Apparently taking a walk on the wild side all those months ago hadn't been such a bad decision after all.

Dean stood tall and proud under the rose-covered arbor, love welling inside his chest as he watched his sweet Catherine walk toward him. Her pale yellow dress set off her straight red hair beautifully. He was a lucky man.

Audrey, their baby, clutched tightly to her very proud grandmom. Hell, between Deanna, Gracie, and his mom, the little squirt couldn't make a peep without someone running to her aid. He was the worst of the lot, he admitted to himself with a proud grin.

Catherine had long since sold her parents' home, and they'd been married going on six months. Still, his mother hadn't been thrilled about the quickie wedding and had eventually talked them into a small summer ceremony in the backyard of the home he'd grown up in.

Dean was glad he'd held firm about having a small outside affair, at least, as it was only their close family in attendance. Gracie sat with her squirmy baby boy, Jacob, held protectively in her arms, with Wade close by her side. Deanna and Jonas sat next to his mom and her friend, Mac. Dean and Wade hadn't been crazy about the man at first, but he treated his mom well and that was all that mattered to them. He looked at them all with pride as they watched on, pleased grins on their faces.

Yes, he'd definitely made the right decision when he'd insisted on a small gathering. It would make it so much easier for him to sneak off with Catherine later.

His wife fairly bloomed beneath the summer sun. Her hips swayed as she walked toward him, driving him wild with thoughts of what he'd be able to do to her once he had her alone.

As she reached him, Dean held out his hands and a jolt of possessiveness shot through him when she placed her own delicate hands in his with trust and love shining in her eyes.

"I love you," he whispered, never tiring of saying those three little words.

"I love you," she said, tears of joy shining in her eyes.

No doubt, Dean had made many mistakes in his life, but marrying Catherine was definitely one of the smartest moves he'd ever made. And he intended to spend the rest of his life proving to her that she'd been right to accept his proposal.

Their life had only just begun.

Turn the page
for a sizzling preview
of Kate Pearce's

SIMPLY VORACIOUS

An Aphrodisia trade paperback
on sale now!

1

1826, London, England

"Are you all right, ma'am? May I help you?"

Lady Lucinda Haymore flinched as the tall soldier came toward her, his hand outstretched and his voice full of concern. She clutched the torn muslin of her bodice against her bosom, and wondered desperately how much he could see of her in the dark shadows of the garden.

"I'm fine, sir, please . . ." She struggled to force any more words out and stared blindly at the elaborate gold buttons of his dress uniform. "I'm afraid I slipped and fell on the steps and have ripped my gown."

He paused, and she realized that he had positioned his body to shield her from the bright lights of the house and the other guests at the ball.

"If you do not require my help, may I fetch someone for you, then?"

His question was softly spoken as if he feared she might flee.

"Could you find Miss Emily Ross for me?"

"Indeed I can. I have a slight acquaintance with her." He

hesitated. "But first, may I suggest you sit down? You look as if you might swoon."

Even as he spoke, the ground tilted alarmingly, and Lucinda started to sway. Before her knees gave way, the soldier caught her by the elbows and deftly maneuvered her backward to a stone bench framed by climbing roses. Even as she shrank from his direct gaze, she managed to get a fleeting impression of his face. His eyes were deep set and a very light gray, his cheekbones impossibly high, and his hair quite white, despite his apparent youth.

She could only pray he didn't recognize her. No unmarried lady should be loitering in the gardens without a chaperone. Somehow she doubted he was a gossip. He just didn't seem to be the type; all his concern was centered on her, rather than making a grand fuss and alerting others to her plight. He released her and moved back, as if he sensed his presence made her uneasy.

"I'll fetch Miss Ross for you."

"Thank you," Lucinda whispered, and he was gone, disappearing toward the lights of the ballroom and the sounds of the orchestra playing a waltz. She licked her lips and tasted her own blood, and the brutal sting of rejection. How could she have been so foolish as to believe Jeremy loved her? He'd hurt her and called her a tease. Had she encouraged him as he had claimed? Did she really deserve what he had done to her?

Panic engulfed her and she started to shiver. It became increasingly difficult to breathe and she struggled to pull in air. Suddenly the white-haired stranger was there again, crouched down in front of her. He took her clenched fist in his hand and slowly stroked her fingers. She noticed his accent was slightly foreign.

"It's all right. Miss Emily is coming. I took the liberty of hiring a hackney cab, which will be waiting for you at the bottom of the garden."

"Thank you,"

"I'm glad I was able to be of service."

With that, he moved away, and Lucinda saw Emily behind him and reached blindly for her hand.

"I told my aunt I was coming home with you, and I told your mother the opposite, so I think we are safe to leave," Emily murmured.

"Good."

Emily's grip tightened. "Lucinda, what happened?"

She shook her head. "I can't accompany you home, Emily. Where else can we go?"

Emily frowned. "I'll take you to my stepmother's. You'll be safe there. Can you walk?"

"I'll have to." Lucinda struggled to her feet.

"Oh, my goodness, Lucinda," Emily whispered. "There is blood on your gown."

"I fell. Just help me leave this place." Lucinda grabbed hold of Emily's arm and started toward the bottom of the garden. She could only hope that Jeremy had returned to the ball and would not see how low he had brought her. She would never let him see that, *never*. With Emily's help, she managed to climb into the cab and leaned heavily against the side. Her whole body hurt; especially between her legs where he had . . . She pushed that thought away and forced her eyes open.

It seemed only a moment before Emily was opening the door of the cab and calling for someone named Ambrose to help her. Lucinda gasped as an unknown man carefully picked her up and carried her into the large mansion. Emily ran ahead, issuing instructions as she led the way up the stairs to a large, well-appointed bedchamber. The man gently deposited Lucinda on the bed and went to light some of the candles and the fire.

Lucinda curled up into a tight ball and closed her eyes, shutting out Emily and everything that had happened to her. It was impossible not to remember. She started to shake again.

A cool hand touched her forehead, and she reluctantly focused on her unknown visitor.

"I'm Helene, Emily's stepmother. Everyone else has left, including Emily. Will you let me help you?"

Lucinda stared into the beautiful face of Madame Helene Delornay, one of London's most notorious women, and saw only compassion and understanding in her clear blue eyes.

Helene smiled. "I know this is difficult for you, my dear, but I need to see how badly he hurt you."

"No one hurt me. I slipped on the steps and . . ."

Helene gently placed her finger over Lucinda's mouth. "You can tell everyone else whatever tale you want, but I know what has happened to you, and I want to help you."

"How do you know?" Lucinda whispered.

"Because it happened to me." Helene sat back. "Now, let's get you out of that gown and into bed."

She talked gently to Lucinda while she helped her remove her torn gown and undergarments, brought her warm water to wash with, and ignored the flow of tears Lucinda seemed unable to stop.

When she was finally tucked in under the covers, Helene sat next to her on the bed.

"Thank you," Lucinda whispered.

Helene took her hand. "It was the least I could do." She paused. "Now, do you want to tell me what happened?"

"All I know is that I am quite ruined."

"I'm not so sure about that."

Lucinda blinked. "I'm no longer a virgin. What man would have me now?"

"A man who loves you and understands that what happened was not your fault."

"But it was my fault. I went into the gardens with him *alone,* I let him *kiss* me, I *begged* him to kiss me."

"You also asked him to force himself on you?"

"*No,* I couldn't stop him, he was stronger than me and . . ."

"Exactly, so you can hardly take the blame for what happened, can you?" Helene patted her hand. "The fault is his. I assume he imagines you will be forced to marry him now."

Lucinda stared at Helene. "I didn't think of that." She swallowed hard. "He said we needed to keep our love secret because my family would never consider him good enough."

Helene snorted. "He sounds like a dyed-in-the-wool fortune hunter to me. What is his name?"

Lucinda pulled her hand away. "I can't tell you that. I don't want to have to see him ever again."

"Well, that is unfortunate, because I suspect he'll be trying to blackmail his way into marrying you fairly shortly."

Lucinda sat up. "But I wouldn't marry him if he was the last man on earth!"

"I'm glad to hear you say that." Helene hesitated. "But it might not be as easy to avoid his trap as you think. You might be carrying his child. Does that change your opinion as to the necessity of marrying him?"

Lucinda gulped as an even more nightmarish vision of her future unrolled before her. "Surely not?"

"I'm sorry, my dear, but sometimes it takes only a second for a man to impregnate a woman," Helene continued carefully.

"I will *not* marry him."

"Then let us pray that you have not conceived. The consequences for a woman who bears an illegitimate child are harsh." Helene's smile was forced. "I know from Emily that you are much loved by your parents. I'm sure they would do their best to conceal your condition and reintroduce you into society after the event."

Lucinda wrapped her arms around her knees and buried her face in the covers. Her despair was now edged with anger. If she refused to marry her seducer, she alone would bear the disgust of society, while Jeremy wouldn't suffer at all. It simply wasn't fair.

Eventually she looked up at Madame Helene, who waited quietly beside her.

"Thank you for everything."

Helene shrugged. "I have done very little. I wish I could do more. If you would just tell me the name of this vile man, I could have him banned from good society in a trice."

"That is very kind of you, Madame, but I'd rather not add to the scandal. I doubt he would relinquish his position easily, and my name and my family's reputation would be damaged forever."

"And, as your father is now the Duke of Ashmolton, I understand you all too well, my dear." Helene stood up. "But, if you change your mind, please let me know. I have more influence than you might imagine."

"I'd prefer to deal with this myself." Lucinda took a deep, steadying breath. "I need to think about what I want to do."

Helene hesitated by the door. "Are you sure there isn't another nice young man who might marry you instead?"

Lucinda felt close to tears again. "How could I marry anyone without telling him the truth? And what kind of man would agree to take me on those terms?"

"A man who loves you," Helene said gently. "But you are right to take your time. Don't rush into anything unless you absolutely have no choice. In my experience, an unhappy marriage is a far more terrible prison than an illegitimate child."

Lucinda looked at Helene. "Emily told me you were a remarkable woman, and now I understand why. I'm so glad she brought me here tonight."

"Emily is a treasure," Helene replied. "I only tried to offer you what was not offered to me—a chance to realize that you were not at fault, and a place to rest before you have to make some difficult decisions. Now go to sleep. I will send Emily to you in the morning, and I promise I will not tell her anything."

Lucinda slid down between the sheets and closed her eyes. Sleep seemed impossible, but she found herself drifting off anyway. Would any of her partners have noticed that she hadn't turned up for her dances with them? Would Paul be worried about her? She swallowed down a sudden wash of panic. If anyone could understand her plight, surely it would be Paul. . . .

Paul St. Clare prowled the edge of the ballroom, avoiding the bright smiles and come-hither looks of the latest crop of debutantes. Where on earth had Lucky gone? She was supposed to be dancing the waltz with him, and then he was taking her in to supper. It was the only reason he was attending this benighted event after all.

Unfortunately, since the death of the sixth Duke of Ashmolton, speculation as to the new duke's potential successor had alighted on Paul, hence the sudden interest of the ladies of the *ton*. He'd grown up with the vague knowledge that he was in the line of succession, but hadn't paid his mother's fervent interest in the subject much heed until the other male heirs had started to die off in increasing numbers.

And now, here he was, the heir apparent to a dukedom he neither wanted nor felt fit to assume. It was always possible that the duke would produce another child, although unlikely, because of his wife's age. But Paul knew that even beloved wives died, and dukes had been known to make ridiculous second marriages in order to secure the succession. Paul's own father, the current duke's second cousin, had only produced one child before he died in penury, leaving his family dependent on the generosity of the Haymores for a home. In truth, Paul considered Lucky's parents his own, and was very grateful for the care they had given him.

Paul nodded at an army acquaintance, but didn't stop to chat. All his friends seemed to have acquired younger sisters who were just dying to meet him. In truth, he felt hunted. If he had his way, he'd escape this gossip-ridden, perfumed hell and ride up north to the clear skies and bracing company of his best friend, Gabriel Swanfield. But he couldn't even do that, could he? Gabriel belonged, heart and soul, to another.

Paul stopped at the end of the ballroom that led out on to the terrace, and wondered if Lucky had gone out into the gardens. He could do with a breath of fresh air himself. He was about to pass through the open windows when he noticed a familiar figure standing on the balcony staring out into the night.

Paul's stomach gave a peculiar flip. The sight of his commanding officer, Lieutenant Colonel Constantine Delinsky, always stirred his most visceral appetites. Of Russian descent, Delinsky was tall and silver-eyed with prematurely white hair that in no way diminished his beauty. Paul always felt like a stuttering idiot around the man.

Delinsky was looking out into the gardens of the Mallorys' house with a preoccupied frown. Paul briefly debated whether to disturb him, but the opportunity to speak to someone who wouldn't care about his newly elevated status was too appealing to resist.

"Good evening, sir."

Constantine turned and half smiled. "Good evening, Lieutenant St. Clare. I didn't realize you were here tonight. Are you enjoying yourself?"

"Not particularly," Paul said. "I find all these people crammed into one space vaguely repellant."

Again, that slight smile that made Paul want to do whatever

he was told. "I can understand why. As a soldier, I always fear an ambush myself."

"Are you waiting for someone, sir?" Paul asked.

"No, I was just contemplating the coolness of the air outside, and deciding whether I wished to stay for supper or leave before the crush." Delinsky's contemplative gaze swept over Paul. "Did you come with Swanfield?"

"Alas, no, sir. Gabriel and his wife are currently up north taking possession of his ancestral home."

Constantine raised his eyebrows. "Ah, that's right, I'd forgotten Swanfield had married."

"I'd like to forget it, but unfortunately the man is so damned content that I find I cannot begrudge him his happiness."

"Even despite your loss?"

"*My* loss?" Paul straightened and stared straight into Delinsky's all-too-knowing eyes.

Delinsky winced. "I beg your pardon, that was damned insensitive of me."

"Not insensitive at all. What do you mean?"

Delinsky lowered his voice. "I always believed you and Swanfield were connected on an intimate level."

Paul forced a smile. "There's no need for delicacy, sir. Gabriel was happy to fuck me when there was no other alternative. He soon realized the error of his ways, or more to the point, I realized the error of mine."

Delinsky continued to study him and Paul found he couldn't look away. "Perhaps you had a lucky escape, St. Clare."

"You think so?"

"Or perhaps the luck is all mine."

A slow burn of excitement grew in Paul's gut. "What exactly are you suggesting, sir?"

Constantine straightened. "Would you care to share a brandy with me at my lodgings? I find the party has grown quite tedious."

Paul wanted to groan. "Unfortunately I accompanied my family to the ball. I feel honor bound to escort them home as well."

"As you should." Constantine shrugged, his smile dying. "It is of no matter."

Paul glanced back at the ballroom and then at the man in front of him. Despite Delinsky's easy acceptance of Paul's reason for not leaving with him, Paul desperately wanted to consign his family to hell and follow this man anywhere. Gabriel was lost to him. He needed to move past that hurt and explore pastures new. And when it came down to it, he had always lusted after Constantine Delinsky.

"Perhaps you might furnish me with your address, sir, and I can join you after I've dispensed with my duties."

"It really isn't that important, St. Clare."

"Perhaps it isn't to you, but it is to me," Paul said softly. "Give me your direction."